STRANGELY FUNNY IX

Mystery & Horror LLC

Strangely Funny IX
Trade Paperback Edition
Sarah E. Glenn, Editor
Copyright © 2022 by Mystery and Horror, LLC
Published by Mystery and Horror, LLC

ISBN: 978-1-949281-20-0

Table of Contents

Carmen and the Cockateeth

By Robert Allen Lupton

"Your damn cockatoo bit me. It's got teeth. Birds aren't supposed to have teeth," complained Elizabeth. She jerked a handful of tissues from a box and wrapped her finger.

George shrugged his shoulders. "Her name is Carmen and yes, she does have teeth. So do her three brood mates. I was shocked when they hatched. I read that once upon a time all birds had teeth."

Beth ran cold water over her hand from the tap in the kitchen. "Once upon a time, my ass. This isn't a fairy tale."

"Scientists know that lizards and birds are related. Maybe momma cockatoo was fooling around with an iguana. Carmen and her sisters are double the size of a normal cockatoos and they have really big teeth."

"Cockatoos don't screw around with iguanas or any other kind of lounge lizard. Where'd you find these birds?"

"Beth, I didn't so much find them as bred them. The truth is that I injected a cockatoo hen with human DNA."

Elizabeth's face turned red. "You stupid bastard. Does the University Grant Oversight Committee know that you've gone all *Jurassic Park* with their money? You'll get us both dismissed, and I turned in my doctoral thesis last month. If I get kicked out of school, I'll feed you to your damn bird. Why in hell did you want to make birds with teeth?"

George tossed a parrot chow nugget to Carmen. "Didn't know they'd grow teeth, I just wanted them to be smart. Truth be told, I didn't even expect the eggs to hatch live young. I was bored and maybe a little drunk."

Beth threw a beaker at George. The glass vial shattered against the wall and shards splattered the room.

Carmen the cockatoo shrieked, "Christ on a motorcycle, you've gotten glass all over my feathers and I'll be hours cleaning them. If I cut myself, I'll do a flyover and crap on you when you're sleeping."

Elizabeth's eyes were wide, but her mouth was wider. The bird said, "Either speak or shut your mouth. You look like a pelican hoping a suicidal fish will jump inside."

"Sorry that I forgot to mention it," said George, "but along with teeth, the birds are smart. They can talk, but I can't say much for Carmen's language filter. She says the first thing that comes to mind."

"I get it, she's a birdbrain. We have to report this," said Beth and she reached for her cellphone. "Where are the other three birds?"

Carmen answered. "The silly twits chewed the bamboo bars off their cage and flew away. Can you believe that George locked birds with teeth in a bamboo cage? Just a little afternoon snack for the girls. They flew straight to the open window. I asked them to help me, but they left Carmen behind. Be a dear, Lizzie, and open the steel cage this idiot has me locked in."

"George, you let them get away?"

George picked up the birdcage, carried it across the room, and opened the window. "I didn't let them do anything. Who knew that cockatoos ate bamboo? Not only that, but their claws are prehensile. They can use them like hands. Carmen's penmanship is better than mine. The birds' escape shouldn't be a long-term problem. How long can they live in the wild? There were no males in the clutch and it's not like they can breed with anything out there."

"You don't know that. You aren't seriously considering releasing this bird," said Beth, and she jerked the cage away from George.

Carmen screamed and snapped at Beth's fingers with her teeth, "Shut your piehole, you silly little girl. Let Carmen go. Her sisters need her. Let her go. Let her go."

George put the cage down. "I think I'll have to release her. Isn't it like unlawful imprisonment to lock up people? You're right.

2

It'll be my ass if the university finds out, but I can't kill her. Look at her."

The cockatoo preened and flashed a toothy smile that would have done a starlet proud.

Elizabeth shook her head. "You won't go to jail for keeping a stupid bird in a cage and if you let her go, she may tell someone what you've done. Besides, I'm not really comfortable that they can't breed. You said that none of the other birds were male?"

Carmen snapped her teeth. "Who you calling stupid? I'm not the one with bloody fingers and an overbite. Who the hell would Carmen breed with, some stupid bird that can't say, 'Polly want a cracker?' I think not. Let the parrot go! Let the parrot go!"

George unlocked the cage door, but held it closed. "Beth, there's already three of them, all female, outside. One more won't hurt."

Beth put her hand on top of George's hand. "No, we have to keep this one to study. There could be unintended consequences."

Carmen's teeth flashed and she nipped George's little finger, turned her head slightly and bit Beth's thumb. The humans jerked away from her snapping teeth, the cage rolled across the floor, and Carmen pushed the cage door open with her talons. She flew to the windowsill, taking a short detour to poop in Beth's hair. "That's an intended consequence, you self-righteous witch. See you later; time for Carmen to be gone with the wind."

Three other cockatoos were waiting in nearby trees, and they joined Carmen as she streaked across the campus. Carmen squawked, "Where we going, girls?"

Adele, one of Carmen's hatch-mates, said, "Central Park. People can't hunt there and there's plenty of food. I've become fond of chips and salsa. Hot dogs aren't too bad, either. Gotta watch the pigeons; they're nothing but rats with wings. Take the food right outta your mouth."

"How about men?"

"Plenty of cockatoo males in the park. We aren't the first birds to escape captivity. The boys are big and dumb, just the way I like them."

Jana, another cockatoo, said, "One of the things I've already learned is that most males don't have anything important to say anyway."

Four years later, David Carson, a park ranger, walked into George and Elizabeth's shared office on the third floor of a hundred-and fifty-year-old sandstone building. He had a canvas bag over his shoulder. "Name's Carson. Got a dead raccoon here. I'd say that a flock of crows been at the carcass, except that the bites all got teeth marks. The boss said to bring the body to the University, and the fellas at the office said you two are the bird people, but now that I'm here, I can't say that you look like bird people."

Elizabeth almost snarled. "Sorry, I left my feathers and wings at home in the closet. Let us see the raccoon."

Elizabeth and George then shared a secretive glance. George said, "That's strange. Probably a combination of crows and feral cats, or maybe even rats. Let's have a look."

Elizabeth used a magnifying glass to inspect the corpse. She swabbed several bites. "We'll run DNA. Saliva should be present, and we can identify which animals did this."

Carson shrugged. "Take your time. I'm headed back to the park. Picnickers and illegal campers are complaining that rats or something like rats are chewing holes in their backpacks and stealing their food. Some kids are singing country music before dawn and waking everyone up. Every day's like the shambles the morning after a bachelor party in the park, and I gotta deal with it. Give the ranger station a call when you know what's up."

George said, "The DNA tests will take a few days. Mind if we stop by the park tomorrow? You could show us around."

"Sure, help yourself."

Carson closed the door behind him. "Look at the damn bites," screamed Elizabeth. "Beaks and teeth, every one. Big bites and little bites. Won't breed, my ass. We gotta get out there, find Carmen, and put a stop to this."

"Calm down."

"Don't tell me to calm down. If you weren't a beer short of a six-pack, we wouldn't be in this mess."

Carmen addressed her cackle of cockatoos in the predawn hours. "Boys and girls, today we're going to serenade everyone with

4

an old classic: 'Under Western Skies.' We'll sing up sunrise with the song."

Jana cleaned her left wing with her beak and teeth. "Remind me again, Carmen, why're we doing this? I know about singing for your supper, but what does that have to do with getting up in the damn dark and singing country music? I need my beauty sleep."

"It isn't working for you. I've been watching the television. There're these shows where folks show their best. Winners become famous and get contracts for millions of dollars. If we keep singing every day, someone'll discover us and put us on the show. After that, we'll make a fortune singing jingles; they're short songs advertising products for humans. "Snap, crackle, pop. Brusha, brusha, brusha. Away go troubles down the drain."

Jana squawked, "Why do we want to be rich?"

"Pay attention! We got teeth and we can talk and sing. We're smart. Humans will realize that we're competition for them, and they'll hunt us down and lock us up. I saw another program with singing rodents, rats, chipmunks, ground squirrels, or maybe they were prairie dogs. Could have been meerkats. Don't worry, be happy. I do like me some ground squirrels; they taste better than pigeon. Anyway, we sing better than they do. Once we're rich, we'll buy our own forest to live in. We'll hire lawyers and make the humans leave us alone."

"If you say so, Carmen. I think we could just shut the hell up and hide in plain sight."

George and Elizabeth swung their binoculars around and searched the trees for the singing cockatoos. Elizabeth finally spotted one during the end of the second chorus of "Under Western Skies."

The bird's teeth gleamed in the sunlight, and she warbled, "And I lost my true love to another under the western sky."

The humans chased the bird until nearly noon before they lost sight of it. They sat despondently against the trunk of an oak tree. George scanned the tree top and got a face full of fresh cockatoo poop. He gagged and washed his face in a nearby stream. Elizabeth was busy laughing.

George dried his face on his shirttail. A voice spoke from the tree. "Well, George, clearly you haven't heard us sing, 'Don't sit under the poop tree with anyone else but me.' Have you and Lizzie come for a little visit with Carmen? How nice! I'd offer you tea, but I'm not very good with fire, although me and the girls do a great *a cappella* version of 'There'll Be a Hot Time in the Old Town Tonight.' We all have perfect pitch, don't you know. If you've brought some of that nasty parrot chow to trap us with, you've wasted your time. Leftovers from the Tavern on the Green are more my style these days, except for their buffalo wings. Nasty stuff, tastes worse than pigeon."

Elizabeth pointed at Carmen, who was perched on a branch about ten feet above the ground. "There she is, George. Catch her."

"Catch me? Really, Elizabeth, has he learned to fly? I'd don't think so."

George said, "Carmen, can we talk? Are you doing okay?"

"Great. I practice good dental hygiene, although it would be easier if toothpaste tasted more like pigeon. Happy teeth, happy bird."

"Carmen, I hear that you and the other cockatoos are singing country songs at sunrise, and annoying everyone in the park. That's not all. We don't have the DNA results back yet, but I expect that you and your toothy kin have been stealing food from the campers and maybe even killed a raccoon."

"Raccoons, a bunch of thieving little buggers. Don't like raccoons, they wear those masks. One of my granddaughters likes toaster strudel. The raccoon tried to take one from her. What were we supposed to do?"

"Stop drawing attention to yourselves. If you keep making trouble, the park rangers will hunt you down. I'll be fired if the truth about you comes out. We need each other. Come down here and talk to me."

"I'll stay right where I am. I seem to recall you and Lizzie have an unfortunate fondness for cages. I don't plan to star in a remake of *I Know Why the Caged Bird Sings*, thank you very much. However, now that you mention it, I agree that we can help each other. You need us to not tell on you, and we want to be self-sufficient. You help us and we'll hold our silence. Not really, we won't be silent, but we'll never speak a word about where we came from. We'll be safe and so will you. If my plan works, we'll all

6

make a few dollars."

George sat down. "I can't believe I'm saying this, but I'll listen to whatever birdbrained plan you've hatched. Whatcha got in mind?"

"Me and the rest of my crackle got talent. Perfect pitch and we harmonize better than a Philadelphia street corner quartet. We dance a little, too. Jana does a mean mamba! We're better than those stiffs who appear on that *Hidden Talents* show. You and Lizzie will pretend to be our human trainers and get us on television. We'll record music, get movie deals, commercials, and even write books. We'll split the loot and all live happily ever after. Rich, rich, more rich! When we sing "I'll Fly Away," there won't be a dry eye in Dallas. You know the old saying: "A bird in the band is worth two in the bush!"

Elizabeth walked closer. "Carmen, that's not exactly right, but tell me, why on Earth do you need money?"

"Chasing pigeons to eat is wearing me out. Picnic leftovers are hit and miss. I'm not stupid. I watch television and I know how this story ends. We're smarter than you, prettier than you, and we can fly. Humans will see us as threats, oddities, or resources to be plundered. Smart talking birds with teeth are dangerous to humanity's position as top predator. Your government will want us for research, the military will want us for spies, and rich people will want us for pets. We need lawyers, guns, and money to protect ourselves. Well, maybe not guns. My sisters and I want a nice quiet forest for our own, as long as it has Internet, big screen televisions, and waffles. I like waffles, and Jana is addicted to soap operas. George started this. It's his responsibility to help us. Besides, I have a sweet tooth and think I have a couple cavities. I might need a root canal. Jana needs braces and my daughters want manicures. Truth be told, we could all use a little dental work. Hold out your arm, George."

George stood and held his right arm horizontal to the ground. Carmen spread her wings and drifted downward to him. She gripped his forearm gently in her talons. "George, we're gonna have to trust each other to make this work."

"That should be easy, I don't expect birds know how to lie."

"Don't be silly, just like humans, fledglings learn to lie

7

before they leave the nest!"

"How many of you are there?"

"The four of us, twelve sons and daughters, and thirteen grandchildren, twenty-nine, in all, not counting the males we found in the park. They can't talk, but we'll want to take them along. They have some uses."

Elizabeth asked, "Do you sing any songs that could be considered women's anthems?"

"We know all the classics, but to avoid copyright issues, we changed the words in one song a little bit to: "I am parrot, watch me soar."

"Carmen, this could be the beginning of a beautiful friendship."

Carmen and the Cockatoos won *America's Hidden Talents* the next season. They sang "I'll Fly Away, O Lord," while performing a choreographed flying ballet. George and Elizabeth signed the cockatoos to a multimillion dollar recording contract and a four-picture movie deal. Carmen had her cavities filled. She didn't need a root canal, and Jana didn't need braces. She had beak and gum disease and the dentist referred her to a parrotdonist. The dental association used Jana's face for a nationwide ad campaign. "Dental Care Isn't for the Birds."

The cockatoos decided that the term, 'cockatoo' was demeaning and staged strikes and walkouts until their contracts were modified to refer to them as 'Cockateeth.' On their websites and in the media, they aren't called 'birds;' the girls prefer the scientific term *Parrotis Dentatis*, which George immediately copyrighted.

Carmen's great granddaughter, Clarice Darrow, matriculated at Harvard and argued successfully for Cockateeth citizenship and rights before the Supreme Court. She claimed that Cockateeth rights included, among other things, life, liberty, and the pursuit of pigeons. The Chief Justice said it was a no-brainer; nobody likes pigeons.

Before she retired from acting, Carmen won two Oscars for her performance as Darkwing, the talking leader of the avian forces in a remake of *The Birds*. The humans lose in the new version. She won for 'Best Performance by a Talking Animal in a Leading Role' and 'Best Original Song,' for "When the Bird Bites," which she wrote and performed.

George and Elizabeth bought and moved to a privately owned island near Tasmania with over three hundred cockatoos, who have the run of the place. The youngest birds took to singing rap music at sunrise. George didn't like it, but Carmen insisted that "Parrot Rap" was an untapped goldmine with worldwide appeal. The first album, *Cockateeth Don't Sweat*, was released last month. The recording has flown off the shelves.

Robert Allen Lupton is retired and lives in New Mexico where he is a commercial hot air balloon pilot. Robert runs and writes every day, but not necessarily in that order. More than a hundred and seventy of his short stories have been published in several anthologies and online magazines. His novel, *Foxborn*, was published in April 2017 and the sequel, *Dragonborn*, in June 2018. His first collection, *Running into Trouble*, was published in October 2017. His next collection, *Through a Wine Glass Darkly*, was released in June 2019. His newest collection, *Strong Spirits*, was released on June 1, 2020.

His third novel, *Dejanna of the Double Star*, was published in December 2020.

His edited anthology, *Feral: It Takes a Forest to Raise a Child*, was released September 1, 2020.

Robert has been an active Edgar Rice Burroughs historian, researcher, and writer since the 1970s. His contributor page, with several of his articles, stories, and over 1200 drabbles, is on the *ERBzine* website at: https://www.erbzine.com/lupton/.

Follow Robert on Facebook and see over 1400 drabbles, his 100-word short stories based on Edgar Rice Burroughs, at: https://www.facebook.com/profile.php?id=100022680383572

Death Comes on Swift Wings

By DJ Tyrer

"Your crazy uncle escaped from the insane asylum last night," Mum said as she put down the phone and rejoined us at the breakfast table.

"They're not called that any more," said my sister, Ali. "They're care homes, or something. And people aren't crazy … they're bewildered, or …" She trailed off.

"Mentally disturbed," I said, automatically, my mind trying to process my mother's words.

"No," said Ali, "I'm pretty certain they changed it, again."

"Does it matter?" Mum asked.

It didn't. Not if you knew my uncle. A homicidal maniac who'd killed seven people we knew of, he'd vowed to exterminate our family line and, I quote, "eliminate the evil gene that infects us all."

Nice man, eh?

Learning that he was on the loose wasn't the sort of news you wanted to hear just a few days before Hallowe'en. If you've seen enough horror movies, you know that that's the date psycho killers love to strike. Why? I don't know. Maybe they hibernate the rest of the year.

We finished breakfast in silence. Mum was reading her horoscope; I glanced at it later. Apparently, she was going to have a family reunion. Apt, eh? Ali was busy on her phone, trying to learn what terminology for lunatics and their incarceration wouldn't get you cancelled. As for me, I was pondering the likelihood I wouldn't be here to see in November ...

As she collected our bowls, Mum said, "Cheer up. It's not like you'll be around to butcher. You're off on that cruise, remember?"

How could I forget? Quite easily, given her announcement. But it was true. I'd entered a radio phone-in and, contrary to my usual luck, had won two tickets to board a ship to New York. It wasn't exactly a Caribbean cruise, but then modern cruise liners are more like floating amusement parks than the ships you saw in old movies, so the time of year ought not to matter much, though the week's sightseeing in the Big Apple might not be so great ...

"Lucky ass," said Ali. She'd expected me to invite her along but, besides not wanting to share a double cabin with her, I'd been delighted to learn that Sally Wainwright, a co-worker I'd asked out a dozen times to no success and who'd threatened to slap me with a restraining order and/or a blunt object had suddenly decided that she and I were now going steady. Doubtless, she'd dump me the moment the return trip was over, but make hay, eh?

Still, in spite of all that, I answered Ali with a gloomy, "Not really. He'll stow aboard and slaughter me, I know it."

She shook her head. "Nuh-huh. You leave in an hour, and he'll want to gut me and Mum first. You'll be fine. Police will probably have caught him by the time you get back."

"I can only hope ..."

"Buck up," said Mum, "and, get ready. The taxi will be here soon."

I checked my closet and under my bed, but Uncle Norman wasn't there. Moderately relieved, I dressed as quickly as I could, wanting to be vulnerable for as short a time as possible. I didn't want to get caught with my underpants down, like Grandpa when Norman went on his first killing spree. Nobody wants that detail of their death splashed all over the papers.

Dressed, I said what I was certain was a final farewell to Mum and Ali, grabbed my case and went outside to wait, casting nervous glances up and down the street until the taxi arrived with Sally already in the back seat.

"You *have* got the tickets, haven't you?" she asked as I opened the door.

I nodded, but was busy examining the driver's side profile, trying to detect any signs of familial resemblance. Of course, I'd only seen photos of my uncle taken back before I was born, so couldn't be certain what he might look like now. But, still, was that my cousin's nose?

No, neither the bulge in his pocket nor the protuberance upon his face. Satisfied as I could be, I got in and the taxi pulled away.

Sally slipped her hand into mine.

"This going to be great."

Maybe, just maybe, it would be.

It was. With half an ocean between me and my murderous uncle, and Sally in my bed, I was having a grand old time. As I'd suspected, the ship was just like a mostly enclosed, hotel-*cum*-amusement park, which meant the chill Atlantic air didn't impede our enjoyment. It wasn't a cruise in the old-fashioned sense of deck chairs and deck quoits—there was relatively little of what I would consider deck, at all—but there was a plethora of pools, spas, dining, and entertainments.

"I could get used to this life," Sally said.

"Me, too." Unfortunately, I knew I could never provide her with it unless I managed a statistically improbable run of phone-in wins, and she wouldn't want to stick it out with me without such recompense.

Sucks, eh?

Still, I'd enjoy it while I could.

"Do you want to visit the Amenhotep exhibition?" I asked her.

Sally sighed, then said, "Fine, it is Hallowe'en."

She'd been resisting the possibility, but I guess she felt she ought to do something spooky to commemorate the date. Saunas don't really cut it.

According to one of the crew, the exhibition was in honor of the legend that the Titanic had been carrying a cursed mummy's coffin when it sank. I thought it was somewhat in bad taste, but I'm a sucker for Egyptian relics and the contents of a priest's tomb were too good to pass up.

"Come on. We'll go to the spa, after, then it's the Monster

13

Mash ball, this evening."

I grabbed her hand and dragged her to the room where the display was before she could change her mind.

It had been done up like the tomb with great chunks of stone wall, painted with hieroglyphic symbols and images of the afterlife, torn out of the very earth, and the great stone sarcophagus itself plonked down in the center, with its heavy lid laid to one side to reveal the bandaged mummy, with the various treasures in cabinets about it.

Even Sally was impressed. She might not care too much about ancient history or desiccated corpses, but she clearly found gold and jewels fascinating. She'd probably want a few replicas from the gift shop.

She leant over the sarcophagus and reached out.

"Er, I don't think we're meant to touch."

Indeed, I couldn't quite imagine anyone *wanting* to touch, but forced a strained laugh and added, "They say there's a curse: 'Death comes on swift wings.' Spooky, eh?"

Sally shook her head and continued to fiddle.

"I really wouldn't," I said. But she did.

"It's squonk," she said. "There. It's straight now."

I looked over her shoulder into the ancient stone sarcophagus. The mummified priest wore a sort of golden pendant upon his chest and a vaguely bemused expression on his bandage-wrapped face. The middle section of the medallion was loose and decorated with an image of an eye, which Sally had straightened.

"Don't touch anything else," I said. Then, I swore.

The eye had begun to glow with a green, almost-liquid, light that slowly spread across the bandaged corpse.

"What on earth ..." said Sally in a small voice.

"I told you not to touch it."

Then, the mummy sat up and groaned. Well, I guess you would, too, if you'd been dead for three millennia.

Sally screamed and ran for it. A moment later, I was chasing after her, terrified.

We only stopped when we were able to hunker down behind a large potted fern and hug each other.

"It was a man in a mask," Sally said, repeating the words

14

over and over.

"That was no man in a mask," I said. I would've loved to accept that explanation, but I'd seen the mummy and it was just too … *thin* for someone living to be hiding inside the wrappings, no matter how anorexic.

"A hologram, then," she spat, eyes wide, desperate.

I wiped my cheek, then shook my head.

"You're not telling me that was 'death on swift wings'," she said in a whiny voice. "It can't be real …"

"It was real." I paused to process what I was saying. "It—was—real. The damn mummy just came back to life."

Sally gave a slight nod of acceptance, and I resisted the urge to apportion blame.

"This is bad …"

Sally opened and shut her mouth like a deranged goldfish, but had nothing to add.

"We need to warn the captain," I said, wondering how we'd be able to convince him.

It wouldn't be that difficult, in fact.

"Careful," I told Sally, guiding her around a skeletonized crewmember.

The mummy was already busy striding about the ship, draining the life-force from anyone it caught, accompanied by scuttling swarms of carnivorous scarabs.

By the time we found him, the captain already knew exactly what was going on, even if he was still somewhat in denial. And I don't mean the river in Egypt.

"It's all my fault," Sally wailed, falling into his arms and blubbering wildly.

"What does she mean?" the captain asked when he finally managed to untangle himself from her and having failed to elicit any information other than howls or sobs.

I explained about the pendant with the eye.

"Then," said the captain, "it is clear we need to turn it."

Simple, eh?

Or not …

"And how exactly do we do that?" asked one of the crew. "Those roaches—"

"Scarabs …" I said.

"Whatever. They eat everyone in their path and, if anyone gets near that … that *thing*, it reduces them to a dried-out husk."

"Aye," said one of the others. "And the security officers went after it with guns and the bullets just went straight through it. Then, the beetles—"

"—scarabs—"

"—ate them!"

"It *is* a poser," said the captain. Then, he looked at me. "Well, son, it would seem that this is your mess, so it's up to you to deal with it.

"But … it was Sally!"

"Well, she's in no fit state. It's down to you," the captain said, as Sally collapsed sobbing once more into his arms.

Great, eh?

I looked at him. "How the hell am I supposed to stop an undead mummy? I'm a shelf-stacker, not Van Helsing."

"It's not a vampire," said the captain.

"Then, ugh, that guy from the *Mummy* films. Brendan Fraser. I'm not Brendan Fraser, okay!"

The captain shrugged. "Hard tack, it's still your problem."

Of course, that wasn't strictly true: Sooner or later, the life-draining ancient Egyptian would be all of our problem. But I was just a lowly shelf stacker and he was the captain of a cruise liner, so who was I to argue?

Instead, I decided to invest my energy in trying to stop the menace.

No phantom, it was going to be one hell of a challenge …

Okay, so the captain probably had it right: If straightening the eye had woken the horror, turning it again ought to return it to lifelessness.

Easy, eh? All I had to do was not get eaten by the scarabs and not have the life sucked out of me by the mummy and all would be well.

I was so screwed …

With a resigned sigh, I set off into the ship to locate the horror that Sally had unwittingly unleashed.

I found it in the spa, just outside one of the saunas, clutching

16

a struggling rotund man in its arms. The man collapsed in on himself, like a deflating balloon, as the mummy sucked his life-force from him with a loud slurp and an orgasmic gasp of delight.

I felt sick …

Then, I felt even more so as I looked at the mummy: It no longer appeared as thin or desiccated …

It was returning to full life!

I looked about for a weapon.

There was some sort of artwork, or perhaps a lamp, made of twisty metal poles in the corner of the room and I managed to break one free as the mummy dropped the now-shriveled man.

If I could hit the medallion just right …

I swung the pole and the mummy easily caught it in its hand and tore it free from my grasp with a mocking laugh. It said something in ancient Egyptian. I guessed it was making fun of me.

The mummy reached out for me.

I knew I was dead and wouldn't even leave a beautiful corpse behind.

Then, there was a flurry of movement and a figure leapt past me and buried an axe in the mummy's chest.

A futile gesture, of course, except …

The pendant flew away from it and hit the floor, jarring the eye out of alignment.

The mummy gave a deep and horrendous groan, then collapsed to the floor, thin and desiccated once more.

Wings clipped, eh?

The figure let go of the axe and looked down at the corpse.

"Now, who would've thought that'd work, eh?"

He turned and I knew without a doubt who it was …

"Uncle Norman!"

"The very same," he said, slapping me on the shoulder.

"But, you saved me!"

"I know, I know—I was a little surprised myself. I managed to whack your mother and sister just after you left in that taxi and only just managed to stow aboard before the ship left port. I've been stalking you for days, waiting for Hallowe'en to strike …"

I'd been right!

"Then, why help me?" I asked, then sighed. "Or was it purely

17

self-preservation?"

My uncle laughed and tapped the end of the axe handle.

"If it were nothing but self-preservation, I'd have buried this in you by now, son."

He smoothed his hair back. "No, I've been watching you. The way you managed *not* to murder that awful woman you're with impressed me. Your wife?"

"No, just a cruise companion," I said, then admitted, "You're right—Sally can be a *bit* annoying at times."

He laughed, and I told him a little about her, before adding, "She's to blame for all this, you know."

"Really? Hmm, maybe you *should've* killed her. *Still*, I'm impressed. Maybe you haven't inherited our family's evil gene or maybe you're adopted, I don't know, but you're all right. I don't think I need to kill you."

Then, he sighed. "Of course, nobody's going to believe a mummy got up and killed all these people, so they'll probably blame me. I'm going to steal a lifeboat and make my escape."

He nodded at the corpse. "I'll let you take the credit, for what it's worth. Might impress that Sally of yours into staying with you past the return voyage to Southampton."

"It might at that."

Things really were looking up: I was still alive and set to be a hero.

"Well, good luck," said my uncle. "You shan't see me again—not unless you turn to evil."

I smiled. "Then, I've got a good incentive to stay on the straight and narrow ..."

"Oh, and sorry about your mother and sister," he called as he disappeared.

"Don't worry about it," I shouted after him, "and, good luck!"

It was a shame, don't get me wrong, but I wasn't going to let anything bring me down.

Not when things were looking up ...

I took the medallion and dropped it over the side and waved a farewell to the tiny speck that I assumed was my uncle escaping in a lifeboat, then set off to find the captain and tell a suitably heroic tale.

If the liner could avoid hitting an iceberg, the cruise was going to end just perfectly.

Brilliant, eh?

DJ Tyrer dwells on the northern shore of the Thames estuary, close to the world's longest pleasure pier in the decaying seaside resort of Southend-On-Sea, and is the person behind Atlantean Publishing, and was short-listed for the 2015 Carillon 'Let's Be Absurd' Fiction Competition. Tyrer has been widely published in anthologies and magazines around the world, such as *Strangely Funny II, III, IV, V, VI & VIII* (all Mystery & Horror LLC), *Destroy All Robots* (Dynatox Ministries), *Mrs. Claus* (Worldweaver Press), *More Bizarro Than Bizarro* (Bizarro Pulp Press), and *Irrational Fears* (FTB Press), as well as on *Cease Cows*, *The Flash Fiction Press* and *The WiFiles*, and in issues of *Belmont Story Review* and *Tigershark* ezine. He also has a novella available in paperback and on Kindle, *The Yellow House* (Dunhams Manor).

DJ Tyrer's website is at https://djtyrer.blogspot.co.uk/
DJ Tyrer's Facebook page is at
https://www.facebook.com/DJTyrerwriter/
The Atlantean Publishing website is at
https://atlanteanpublishing.wordpress.com/

The Hungry Place

By Rosalind Barden

La Beach Époque's new owner ("Call me Sam!") was initially excited that a writer traveled from the States to cover his resort on 'Eua, an obscure South Pacific island ruled by the King of Tonga. Then Sam discovered my focus was not the "tropical wedding destination five star," but the rotting pier and boathouse: "You go now! Go!" But I'd paid for my stay in advance, so he was stuck with me.

It's tricky business finding fresh locales with a paranormal taint. Once I was the only game in town: Global Ghost Girl. Now, competition is brutal. The same old haunts are old hat. Fans demand new thrills. So, I research.

It was in a 1972 travel guide at the bottom of the downtown Cincinnati library's free book box that led me to 'Eua. The book, *Jet Set Guide to Pacific Islands*, described a luxury yacht in high demand for rentals because "a Peer of the Realm tumbled overboard to a watery death," but continued to haunt the yacht by throwing ghostly parties under the full moon. Well, now.

Because this was an old book, it had no email address; only a physical address in 'Eua for a resort called The Opaque, the haunted yacht's owner. While I waited for a reply, I whiled away my time making myself a nuisance at the downtown Cincinnati library, as I often did, with my odd requests to pull microfiche film from storage so I could peer at old records.

It took much peering into the microfiche projector, but I

learned: "Celebrities and aristocracy can play far from prying eyes at The Opaque," according to a newspaper article from 1971 when the resort opened for business. A minor royal Tongan Prince funded the venture, from the bungalows to the long pier "suitable for docking pleasure ships." That must be where the haunted yacht came in.

A drier academic publication explained "Opaque" was an anglicization of the place name for the resort's beach. The name may have derived from an ancient language, a relic even when the first European adventurers arrived in the 1600s. It might mean different things. One was a feast place, possibly for weddings. Though it could also mean a no-food place, or the hungry place.

Searching online, I found La Beach Époque and noticed it sounded similar to The Opaque. "In ancient times to now, this is The Wedding Place!" according to La Beach Époque's website. I compared the color website photos to the negative black and white images from the microfiche articles. The resort bungalows looked the same, as did the beach. The pier looked shorter, and the boathouse, smaller, but I could tell it was the same place.

The website didn't mention the yacht, so I emailed.

"The yacht is now a romantic sunken treasure ship, perfect for your scuba wedding photos," was my first communication with Sam. Sunken, huh? Seemed like a haunted long shot, rather like that possessed dogfood bowl in Cleveland (a complete bust). But I was desperate. I booked the trip.

On the day of my departure, I finally received a reply to my snail mail letter, which I'd frankly forgotten about. An S. Hentley wrote in shaky script: "No yacht to rent. It sunk; the resort went belly up. Good luck to the new owner. So much bad luck at that beach. But I do offer a Rare Parrot Tour. It is popular with Japanese travelers." The "bad luck" part excited me. Wasn't sure I wanted the tour, but I'd look up S. Hentley while I was in 'Eua.

At 'Eua's tiny airport, really a gravel landing strip, a silent young man in dark sunglasses picked me up in an open-top Jeep. As we bounced a little too fast along rutted roads overhung with jungle vines, I asked him what he knew about the haunted yacht.

Sunglasses sharply braked the Jeep in the middle of the road, which fortunately was deserted. He turned to look at me, though he

22

kept his sunglasses on. "You don't talk about that." He turned back to the road and roared forward.

Interesting.

The resort was smaller than I expected. I saw the bungalows, all six of them, and the "dining hall," an open-air space with tables that was topped by a thatched roof. Rustic, yes, but it seemed like a peaceful South Seas locale. Unfortunately, peaceful didn't suit my purposes, but I remained hopeful.

I spotted the pier. It was bustling with activity. A woman in a poufy wedding gown and veil stood on the pier near the boathouse. She posed with flung arms for a man on the beach clicking photos. Another man jumped about giving directions, "Yes! Wave! You are the happy bride!"

I wandered closer. The pier looked refreshed with white paint slapped over rotting boards. A pair of new kayaks rested by the boathouse. From the number of half-submerged boards sticking up from the sand, I realized the boathouse and pier must have partially collapsed at some point, explaining why they looked larger in old photos.

The director spotted me. He grabbed my arm and hauled me closer to the Bride. "The Cincinnati writer! See, perfect wedding photos are here!" This is when I met Sam in person.

While he wagged my arm and hand up and down ("Call me Sam!"), I saw the Bride start to wobble behind him. Sam spun around when he heard the soft crack of the pier's rotting boards, the bridal dress rip, her splash, and her screams: "This your fault! This place is cursed! You made me!" and so on. The object of her venom was Sam.

Sam rushed toward her. "You get back up there!" The Bride was having none of it. She tore off the soaking veil and flung it at Sam as she stormed to the dining hall. Sam turned his appeal to the photographer, "Take beach photos!" But the man eyed the pier warily and remained frozen.

Sunglasses had vanished. A grey-haired gent wearing a woven fiber tapa cloth apron over a black tunic ("Our staff wear traditional dress for your authentic wedding photo feel!") wandered over to me: "Your bag?" He picked up my one piece of luggage and walked to a bungalow.

I followed him inside the little wooden house decorated with painted tapa cloth ("Authentic art for sale!"). The man set my bag down, and stood, swaying slightly from side to side, the universal sign among hotel staff that a tip is expected.

Exploiting his vulnerability, I made my move: "I heard the Bride hollering about a curse."

He stopped mid-sway and stared wide-eyed at me.

My fingers reached inside my travel pouch slung across my shoulder. His eyes silently followed. I tugged a bill out far enough so the denomination showed, but I didn't pull it out all the way. His eyes fixed on the bill.

"Meaning to say," I continued, "what are the old stories?"

His eyes darted aside. He did not move.

I made a point of rustling as I partly pulled out a second bill. His eyes darted back to the bills.

He said nothing, then finally shifted from one foot to the other, looked at the floor, and said, "The old owner had a Folk Story Night every week to talk about that. The new owner tells the stories differently."

"I take it you did the telling before?"

He kept his eyes on the floor. "Yeah, I was Chief Storyteller."

"Got tips, huh?"

He shrugged.

"The new owner, Sam, he's taken over the story telling?"

His eyes crinkled unhappily.

I rustled again as I partly pulled out a third bill. He chewed his lip, his inner decisions at war.

"I'd love to hear the old stories."

He breathed in sharply, and it rapidly poured from him: "Long ago, a great prince was to marry a great princess from another island. For the feast on this very beach, he went fishing. He said, 'I will find a great fish to feed many people.' After looking a long time, he caught one in his great net. It was the most beautiful fish he ever saw, and big, like a whale. The fish fought him all the way when he dragged it to this very beach. He was so hungry by this time, he said, 'I will eat the heart of the fish and that will kill it right away and make it stop fighting me.' With his great spear, he cut out

24

the heart and ate it. But all at once, the fish turned into his princess. He said, 'My princess was magical and could turn into a beautiful fish, but now she is dead.' He was so heart-broken, he lay down on the sand next to her and stayed there until he died of eating nothing."

Somehow, I suspected the story was longer and he told it with more flair for the tourists when he was Chief Storyteller. But no matter. I got the gist.

"So, how does the new owner tell it?"

He sighed. "Same, except the fish never dies and keeps giving more fish to eat so the wedding feast lasts a whole year, and everyone is happily ever after."

"What story do you believe?"

"People in old days made things up." He shrugged again.

"But what about all this haunted and cursed business? People seem to believe that?"

He started swaying again, eyes hungry for the bills sticking from my pouch. "Oh, you know, long long long ago, when other kinds of people lived here, not us, no, but them—sometimes, maybe they ran out of things to eat."

Before I could ask more, his fingers snatched the bills, and he ran from the bungalow.

A start, but I needed more. I wandered outside to find Sam. He was haranguing the photographer in Tongan as the man speed away on a scooter.

Sam noticed me. His face brightened. "Ah! You would like a personal tour? We have many wedding option packages Cincinnati couples will enjoy very much."

"Actually, it's the haunting I came for."

It was at this juncture that Sam and I had our falling out ("You're messing my business!"). No matter. Perhaps it was time to find the former owner, S. Hentley.

Because S. Hentley lived in town, I needed a ride. I wandered about looking for Sunglasses. Instead, I spotted the Chief Storyteller lurking in the shadows between two bungalows. When he saw me, he said, "I'm not to talk with you!" and ran away. Fine.

I walked the sandy path to the dining hall, where the Bride stood behind a counter. She was out of the torn gown, and into traditional dress like the Chief Storyteller's. Sunglasses lounged on one of the counter stools. His tee-shirt and jeans were apparently as traditional as he was going to dress.

The Bride tried to sell me a bottle of fresh pressed squash juice. "The Japanese like it."

"What I really need," I said to her and also Sunglasses, "is a ride to town."

Sunglasses abruptly stood and walked away. Was I supposed to follow? I did, and found him already in the Jeep, engine rumbling. I'd barely taken a seat when he tore off.

Sunglasses left me at a fading yellow house abutting the small town's main street. A sign, "Rare Parrot Tours," hung over the thatched-roof porch that seemed to be the reception area. But for dusty plastic chairs and a wooden table, it was nearly empty. The front door had no door. The house inside was dark. "Hello?"

I was about to wave Sunglasses over from where he whispered with another sunglasses-wearing man at a juice stand across the street. Then I heard coughing from inside the house. A tall man, thin but for a potbelly, with faded blond hair and runny eyes emerged from the doorway. He squinted at me.

"I'm the writer. Remember, we traded letters about the sunken yacht?"

He seemed confused, but then, "Oh! Yes, please have a seat," he said in a rarified English accent that didn't match his patched shirt and khakis. "Let's have you on our Rare Parrot Tour. The Japanese love it." He settled himself at the other side of the table and quoted an exorbitant price. Perhaps noticing my eyes popping, he added, "That is for two, you and your husband."

"It's just me, and I'm writing about the haunted yacht, the cursed pier, the old stories." His eyes crinkled, so I added, "And rare parrots." I handed over half the couple's fee.

He frowned. "There is a singles supplement." Fine. This trip was plunging me into debt again, but information has its price.

Propped against the wall, I noticed a portrait of a young man dressed formally in the style of the middle of the past century. If it ever had a frame, it was long gone. Tropical mold blackened its edges and a spot in the middle. "Me," he said when he saw me looking at it. "Handsome?" he asked, smiling.

26

I had to agree, though to the past, not to this weather-beaten man who moved stiffly about his small domain.

"My father said the portrait was a waste of his money, but Mother insisted. She had her own income. Poor thing." Whether he meant his mother was the poor thing or the painting or himself, I wasn't sure.

"You are the writer!" he said, finally remembering. "Ah, you've come to talk about me, not the parrots." He smiled broadly, revealing a glimpse of the handsome young thing he used to be.

He'd gone to university with the minor Tongan Prince, and Bertie, another handsome young Englishman. "Such mad dreams we had." His gestures were expansive, as though he were on stage, rather than a dusty porch.

"The plan was to create a fun resort. That was the Prince's word–'fun.'" Their monied friends would visit, and celebrity jetsetters from that era. "Do you know he never came?"

"The prince? But didn't he pay to build the resort?" I asked.

S. Hentley laughed. "That is what I thought. But no. He allowed me to build on the beach, which was his, and stay two years without paying him for the privilege. That was all. But I was young and stupid, so spent every penny Mother left me building those shacks, that pier, that boathouse. It was a disaster from the start."

"What about the rich visitors?"

"Oh, that was something I made up, really. It was only the boy who drowned, Bertie."

"A Peer of the Realm?"

"Good God, no! That was his brother. Bertie was the younger son. At least his father left him an income, so he could buy that yacht. My father? I got nothing from him."

He stared silently at his portrait, then continued. "After Bertie drowned, the Prince gave me more years on the beach without paying him, because I had nothing to give him. I suppose I did have Bertie's yacht because his brother didn't want it. I should have sold it. Instead, it rotted until it sank. Last year, I was surprised when the Prince's officials informed me that he let the beach to someone else. I was an 'ineffective tourism manager,' they said. All that I built, I lost. He evicted me."

"Your friend the Prince?"

27

"No! He's dead. It was his eldest son. You see, it's always the eldest son. Do you know, I don't even have the funds to fly back to England? I asked my brother. But he is no different than my dead father, long may he stay dead."

This was all very interesting, but I needed haunting dirt. "Do you think the ancient curse oozed from the beach into the boat house, slithered along the pier, then plopped onto the yacht where it pushed Bertie overboard?"

He snorted. "Bertie fell off his yacht because he was drunk. We were always drunk back then. It helped to calm the nightmare we were in." Quickly he added, "But nowadays, I don't touch the stuff." From his red eyes, I doubted that.

"You saw Bertie's ghost partying on the yacht?"

"No! I invented that in hopes of hiring out the yacht. I didn't think Bertie would mind. Didn't work."

"What about the dead prince and princess story?"

"I have no idea. The locals seem to think there's a problem. I had trouble keeping staff. I had to import construction workers from Samoa. I think the Prince tricked me into building the resort because no islanders would set foot on that beach. When it was finished, the locals informed me I built the pier and the boathouse in exactly the wrong spot."

"Where the Prince gobbled up the princess?"

"Supposedly." He paused. "Maybe during times of famine there was a spot or two of cannibalism. That story is probably the dressed-up excuse for what happened. But who cares, really?"

His eyes drifted toward the dark doorway, maybe where his bed and drink waited. He muttered that I'd be picked up tomorrow after breakfast to see the parrots.

I took this as my cue to leave.

In my heyday when I had my television show, my trademark was sleeping in the haunted places I explored. Critics condemned me as tasteless and campy, but I had a following. As I scrape the barrel nowadays, my TV show but a memory, I still will not let my dwindling fans down. Though away from castles and snug manors, the sleeping arrangements are less than ideal (don't even ask about the possessed dog food bowl).

All things considered, a tropical beach below a blanket of

28

stars wasn't bad. I'd researched the tide tables before leaving Cincinnati. Tonight, the skies held no hint of storms, so I was confident I wouldn't be washed away. With sheets borrowed from my bungalow bed, I settled on the sand by the boathouse.

The breeze was warm. All lights were off in the resort. Soon, the hypnotic push and pull of surf softly rolling upon the sand lulled me to sleep.

I was shocked awake by wild seawater plunging into my mouth. What a fool I was to trust those tide tables! I felt hands grabbing me, vaguely saw faces through the water. Were people rescuing me? I fought my way toward the surface, but new surges dragged me down.

And then I was on the dark beach, alone. The water tamely crept back and forth on the sand. My sheets were dry and so was I. What happened?

In past sleepovers, I've had my blankets pulled, my nails painted. I've been asked by empty air if I take cream with my coffee, and I've woken to a potted palm on the bed. But this was the topper.

It was so real.

I was too afraid to sleep again, so sat watching the quiet surf until the sun peeked over the horizon in a glorious show of orange and pink. I scooted further down the beach away from the boathouse and pier. Oddly, I felt like they watched me.

The Bride pattered to the edge of the beach sand but no closer. "You shouldn't sleep there!" she called to me. When I said nothing, she coaxed with, "Your breakfast is warm. You need to go parrot watching."

Oh, right. That.

Breakfast in the dining hall was a chunk of baked squash covered in sugar and canned cream. "The Japanese like it." Indeed, there was a Japanese couple at another table, completely lost in one another. Must be honeymooners, though they did seem to like the squash. I saw no other guests.

I had no appetite. Maybe it was the dream and lack of sleep.

Sunglasses drove me to a hilltop overlooking an expanse of green jungle with the sparkling blue ocean beyond. He put down a plastic chair. On the seat, he placed a pair of binoculars and a bag. "Your lunch." He left.

Inside the bag was my uneaten breakfast in a smaller plastic bag, a sandwich in another plastic bag, several slices of plain bread, and a large plastic bottle of water. The sandwich was filled with the same kind of squash, plus tomato slices.

I sat in the chair and tried to watch the bird or parrot or whatever was swooping back and forth eyeing me. Soon enough, I was asleep again.

I was back on the beach. There seemed to be other people, but I could not see them. Was someone coming from the boathouse? "Bertie, is that you?" No answer. But I felt hands on my arms. All at once, the surf churned into my mouth again, covered me violently, and dragged me across rough sand.

Then it was gone.

A large reddish bird watched me, inches from my nose. I was awake, sprawled on the dirt. The chair, binoculars, and food bag were scattered next to me. When I didn't move, the bird made an unhappy clucking sound and flew away.

A shadow fell over me. I turned to see Sunglasses standing over me. "Did you feed the parrot?" he asked.

"What?"

He made a clucking sound, not unlike the bird. He snatched up the lunch bag from the dirt next to me, pulled out the slices of plain bread, then scattered them on the ground.

He picked up the plastic chair, binoculars, and walked with them and the lunch bag to his Jeep. I crawled up from the damp ground and followed. I heard scratching behind me. I turned and saw the bird was back. It paused in its bread picking to give me a baleful eye.

In the Jeep, I saw my luggage on the floor. "You've been kicked out," Sunglasses replied when I asked about it.

"So, where am I going?"

I waited for him to elaborate, but he remained silent behind his sunglasses. Maybe cannibalism wasn't a relic from the past. Maybe he was driving me to a beach feast, with me as the main dish.

Despite my fears, I was so exhausted from my troubling dreams, I fell asleep again, only to tumble back into the pounding surf. Now the hands were not only touching, but tearing.

I awoke gasping and hanging out the side of the Jeep. I

looked up and saw we had stopped at a newer resort painted pink. A heavyset man in a Hawaiian print shirt came toward me with wide-spread arms and wide smile: "The writer! Of course, you stay in my resort for free! The Pink Dolphin is luxury, not that cursed, cheap place where bad things happen! Call me Dolphin Man!"

Sunglasses pulled my travel bag and my lunch bag from the Jeep and handed them to La Beach Époque's Chief Storyteller. He was out of his black tunic and tapa cloth apron, and in a Hawaiian shirt matching Dolphin Man's.

Dolphin Man noticed me noticing and laughed. "Everyone comes to work for Dolphin Man! Come enjoy our complimentary buffet!"

He pushed me toward his pink-painted version of the open-air dining hall. It was laid with a flower-bedecked food spread. I noticed platters of squash prepared in various ways, along with the Japanese honeymooners, who were breathlessly eating the squash directly from the serving platters with their bare hands.

Dolphin Man again noticed me noticing. "They were haunted. Oh, yes, so they fled to The Pink Dolphin."

Since I wasn't moving, Dolphin Man heaped my plate to overflowing. After sitting and staring at the plate until I fell over in another nightmare fit, the Chief Storyteller and the Bride (also now working for Dolphin Man), helped me to my bungalow along with a new bag filled with my buffet dinner.

Maybe it was the bungalow's hot pink walls, but my stomach lurched, and I plunged again and again into the dream surf as hands, and now teeth, tore at my arms, my legs. I think the parrot was involved too, but I can't be sure.

I awoke in darkness. I heard soft lapping from gentle surf and felt not sand, but pebbles. Where was I? I looked around and saw the pink resort glowing in the starlight. Around me were my breakfast, lunch, and buffet food bags, torn, empty. My stomach was bloated. What was wrong with me?

"Hum."

I looked up. It was the Chief Storyteller. Behind him stood Sunglasses, arms crossed, and still wearing his sunglasses. Nearby, the Bride shook her head.

"Maybe you need to fly home already," the Chief Storyteller

31

suggested.

My return flight wasn't for nearly a week, but Dolphin Man got busy calling his contacts. Ultimately, the airline agreed to push my return date forward without penalty because I was a desperately ill foreigner, and the King of Tonga did not want to be responsible.

I screamed in my nightmares on the flight across the Pacific. I felt the hungry ocean waves reaching up, up toward the airplane, along with starving hands, teeth, ravenous parrots, Bertie, and the boathouse, which cracked open like a maw to reveal splintered teeth formed from its rotting boards. The pier snaked out of it like a tongue.

One moment I could not bear the sight of food, but in the next bout of sleeping delirium, I devoured not only my tray of food, but my neighbor's.

After the food tray episode and my neighbor's loud complaints, the flight attendants gave my neighbor free miles and gave me as many little liquor bottles as I could throw back, not free. "Though we hope you will reflect positively on our airline in your article."

I was writing no article, but the final chapter in my book that I desperately hoped would be my comeback. Thankfully, the little bottles kicked in and I passed out, spared from the nightmares.

Back in Cincinnati, the days passed in a haze. One morning, I awoke to find my living room carpeting in my mouth. Now I understood why S. Hentley was always drunk. Anger burned in me. Why didn't he warn me?

I was tempted to drown my horrors in boxed wine. But I had to get busy writing the chapter. More importantly, I had to finish my pitch for a new show on a streaming service. I had bills to pay, and now carpeting to replace.

Gradually, the episodes faded. Though one morning, they roared back at the downtown Cincinnati library, causing me to topple several book stacks as I collapsed, the librarians' box of Thank-God-It's-Friday donuts half-eaten in my arms ("Honestly, that writer woman is on my last nerve"). That afternoon, I received a letter from S. Hentley.

"Dearest, my thoughts have never left you and your charming

little writing hobby. You said you are alone, and I too am. I never saw myself living in Cincinnati, but with you by my side, I am willing to make a go of it. Please provide a ticket to the States so we may meet again," and so on in a similar vein.

Instead, I sent him a copy of my final chapter: "Cannibal Beach Horror and the Ravenous Red Parrot."

This is **Rosalind Barden's** eighth story in the *Strangely Funny* series. She has dozens more short stories published, including "Mardi Gras Forever and the Bigfoot Fiasco" in the *Mardi Gras Mysteries* anthology from Mystery and Horror, LLC. *Sparky of Bunker Hill and the Cold Kid Case* is her fun young adult mystery set in 1930s Los Angeles, which will soon be followed by the second in the series, *Sparky of Bunker Hill and the Cannibal Caper*. Discover more at www.RosalindBarden.com.

Barely Even Friends to Lovers

By Jennifer Lee Rossman

Once upon a time, a boy was rude to a witch. This is not, in and of itself, a noteworthy occurrence, as children tend to be terrible people from time to time. Now, this particular witch had a grudge against this particular boy's family, his father in particular. Always leering at her in the office, making culturally insensitive jokes about riding broomsticks when he knew full well she drove a Subaru.

That does not excuse what she did, not in the least. But it does serve as a lesson not to bully people, lest they curse your child into looking like the hideous beast you are on the inside.

"Only if you raise your son to be a better man than you," the witch proclaimed, packing up her cubicle into a cardboard box, "will he be a good enough man to win the heart of a woman despite his ghastly appearance."

"But what if he's gay?" piped up Martha from HR, the true hero of the story.

The witch threw up her hands. "Then the heart of a man. Or any person really. Doesn't have to be romantic. It was really not that specific of a curse, Martha." The witch picked up a cactus from her desk, but didn't have room in her box for it. She gave it to the boy's father instead. "If he doesn't find love or whatever by the time this cactus dies, the curse is forever or some bullshit like that."

And so, with her middle finger held high, the witch left the regional distribution office of Benson-O'Hara.

The bit about the cactus was indeed, as she said, bullshit.

Really just a way to offload an unwanted succulent. The rest, though? All true, and she didn't regret it one single bit.

... until later that night, when she was just drunk enough to cry but not drunk enough to laugh, when she regretted it all. He seemed like a good enough boy, but people are cruel. She feared he would never find someone who would care about him.

Enter Rosie.

Long, long ago, when the first witches were devising their curses, the magic words and jazzhand-esque gestures that would be passed down to every new generation, they did not take into account that people like Rosie would exist who would be so good at breaking them.

Oh, it's not because she was clever, although she was. And it isn't because she had a good heart and could look past the superficial, although she did and she could. No, girls like Rosie— women, I should say, as she was nearly 30 at the time—excelled at breaking curses because they were *weird.*

Raised on Internet memes and cartoons about dogs and cats conjoined at the waist, not only could nothing faze millennials, most of them actively reveled in the bizarre. There had never been a generation quite like them, and for that we all must say a prayer of thanks to our deity of choice, as the old curses simply could not account for the utter chaos in their souls.

Rosie had grown up hearing rumors about that boy—now a man. That he was ugly, that he was an animal. That he locked himself away in the old family home and refused all visitors, never having friends or lovers, lashing out at anyone who tried to get close to him.

Big deal. She had a dozen guys far worse than him harassing her in the comments of her fanfiction on the daily; she could handle him. Besides, his family fortune had been largely put into desperate research and development of the best ways to keep cacti alive, and she was not about to let her father know she'd almost killed his prized *Sclerocactus papyracanthus* while he was on vacation. She needed help with that cactus, and fast, before her father returned.

So she went up to the big fancy house at the top of the hill, and she knocked on the door. And when nobody answered, she kept

36

knocking. He had to be home; he was a reclusive hermit. Being home was like, his main thing.

Eventually, the mail slot opened and—following a small gasp—snapped shut. Rosie smiled in smug satisfaction and kept knocking.

After several moments during which the sounds of frantic scrambling could be heard inside, the door was reluctantly opened by a man who could perhaps best be described as a dozen kitchen appliances in a trench coat.

"May we help you?" said a muffled voice emanating from the abdomen. "Ouch! I mean, may I help you?"

Rosie blinked. "I know about the curse, you guys. Everybody does."

From underneath the beat up old fedora came the sound of an exasperated blender. "I told you we didn't need to go through this whole charade!"

"And I told you," said a voice somewhere near the knees, "I miss dressing up! It's not like anyone is making fancy dress clothes for the toaster anymore, since the sewing machine ran off with the lawnmower."

"So," Rosie said loudly. "I need help with a cactus. How do you lovely appliances feel about letting me in, letting me look up something on his computer real quick like, and I don't know shit about sewing but I can crochet amigurumi so I can probably whip up a little toaster sweater for your trouble?"

A long moment passed. "Will there be a matching hat?"

"But sir! It's our house, too. Are we not allowed guests?"

"Not without my permission."

Rosie looked up from the computer, which did not seem to be sentient like the toaster and the blender and the desk lamp that kept making lewd jokes about being turned on. The first voice she recognized as the blender. But the second one …

The second voice *did* something to her, matching the resonant frequency of her body and vibrating it until she felt like she was about to shatter. And is that an extremely dramatic way of saying she liked his voice? Yes. But is it accurate? Scientifically speaking, no, not at all.

37

But it felt true.

Peering out into the hallway, Rosie saw a massive shadow on the wall, and her heart fluttered. He had to be seven feet tall, with shoulders so broad that she became too distracted to think of something broad that they resembled. Boats, maybe. Yeah. Boats.

"Did you warn her not to click on the folder labeled 'west wing'?" the man growled. Literally growled.

She couldn't stand it anymore. She had to see him.

Taking careful steps on the hardwood floor, Rosie made her way over to the door and peeked out.

Hunched back, feet that ended in hairy velociraptor claws, curling horns resembling carved wood, dangerous-looking spikes tearing through the back of his shirt. He was hideous, and yet she needed to see his face.

"What's in the 'west wing' folder?" she asked quietly.

He turned, snarling, his mouth full of fangs. His eyes were wild, yellow, with that weird little transparent eyelid that flicked in from the side. Coarse auburn hair covered his face and his arms that were as wide around as her torso, or maybe more boats.

He was, in a word, hideous. In two words, absolutely hideous. And yet, we must remember, Rosie was weird, and so unlovable monster boys (and monster girls) were kind of her thing.

He was just so sharp and dangerous. Feral. She wanted to tame him, wanted to run her hands through his fur and curl up with him on cold winter nights, and put his head on her shoulder and let himself be soft while she taught him how to be a good human. But also, she wanted him to stay sharp and dangerous, wanted him to tame her and bite her and do things that would make the table lamp blush.

Oh, she had written so much fanfiction that started just like this.

But as he started to lunge for her, a strange light enveloped the man, like sunshine coming through a stained-glass ceiling, complete with magical dust motes. He stopped, entranced, and the swirling light grew opaque as the sounds of a chorus came from seemingly nowhere.

You see, though attraction and a little bit of lust are not the same as romantic or platonic love, we must remember that the curse

38

was not specific, and so her instant attraction did the job of breaking it, leaving him fully human for the first time in decades.

And what a human he was. Tall and muscular, with short wavy hair and a jawline so defined that it looked Photoshopped.

Rosie tried to hide her disappointment as he looked down at himself and laughed in wonder before rushing to her and taking her hands.

"You broke the curse!" he exclaimed. "Oh, oh, I wish my father was here to see this."

"I'm just here to get some information about a rare cactus I can't pronounce the name of," Rosie said, watching as various objects behind him went through the same transformation.

"Of course. I don't expect anything from you. But please, you clearly feel something for me. If you would do me the honor of having dinner with me, just dinner and nothing else, I will personally help you with whatever succulent-related matters you have. Not a date, just dinner for the pretty lady who thinks I am more than just a monster." He frowned. "What's wrong?"

She looked at the cute cleaning lady with the bright green hair who had been a robotic vacuum until a moment ago, and at the cute boy trying to find his glasses and grappling with the fact that he was no longer a smartphone.

Then she looked at the man who was no longer a beast. The Hollywood-perfect, symmetrical man with absolutely no defining features except being attractive. There was no easy way to say it.

"You were cuter when you were a monster."

Hubert and Ricardo had worked at Michelin starred restaurants, once upon another life, but it had been years since they had cooked or mixed anything without placing it directly into one of their body cavities, so what should have been a decadent five course meal was instead reduced to microwave dinners.

"Funny," James, the man formerly known as the Beast, said. "And here I thought the microwave never talked to me because he was a jerk, but it turns out it was just a microwave all along."

Rosie couldn't tell if he was kidding. He didn't seem like enough of a dork to actually make that mistake. Conventionally attractive people tended not to be dorks, so she was forced to

39

conclude that he thought himself … yuck, charming.

She didn't like charming. Charm was what attractive people used to make themselves seem interesting, manufactured personality perfected in control groups of boring ladies from the 1950s who had never once dreamed about a sea monster rising up from the deep to drag them down to their underwater lair. People who thought they were being edgy when they wrote one-shot Mulder and Scully fanfiction, instead of spending three novels' worth of words shipping their self-insert OC with all three of the Lone Gunmen. Simultaneously.

But it was hardly James' fault he was too handsome to be interesting, and she tried to make polite conversation. Even though the pretty vacuum was making jokes with the former lamp about how, since they were both bisexual and ran on AC, their currents went both ways, and even though the cute nerd boy was currently angsting about how difficult face-to-face communication was without emojis.

Facial expressions, she wanted to tell him. Facial expressions!

"So." There. That was polite conversation, wasn't it? No, she supposed not. But what was there to talk about? Would it be insensitive to ask whether he had ever had a DNA test while he was a beast? Probably.

Instead, she asked, "What's in the folder labeled 'west wing'?" Though the house was large, she didn't think it was large enough to have wings. But perhaps that was where he kept the most rare succulents, like her father's *Sclerocactus papyracanthus*.

His hand tightened around his fork, and for a second Rosie thought she saw the beast in him. But he composed himself. "Nothing you need to worry about. Where did you grow up?"

"Just a few blocks from here," Rosie said. And then, forgetting for the moment whom she was speaking to, she added, "What about you?"

He chuckled in a desperate attempt to end the awkward silence. "We traveled a lot when I was younger, back and forth across the country to all the cities with manufacturing plants. Then, and this may come as a bit of a shock to you, but I was cursed by a witch and became a recluse because I was hideous."

40

Rosie had no idea what to say. Maybe this was a date after all, considering how awkwardly her dates normally went. "It's not fair," she said into her macaroni and cheese.

"No, it isn't," James agreed. "Especially because apparently breaking the curse was much easier than I ever thought it would be, and now I find out I'm an ugly human."

"You're not … ugly, per se," Rosie said, frowning at his perfect table manners and lamenting the fact that, if he were still a monster, she would be able to teach him how to be proper. "You're just not my type." She thought for a moment. "Why did you never venture out, try to find a friend? It might not have worked, but it's not like the love of your life is going to just show up and knock at your door."

James raised an eyebrow and gestured to her, but admitted, "It was easier. If I didn't try to find someone who would love me, I couldn't be rejected."

"Online dating?" she suggested. "Get a picture of some good-looking guy from the Internet, make a few matches, chat with them …"

He gave this a dismissive shake of his head. "I spend so much time gathering information about succulents. The few moments of spare time I have on the computer, I have more interesting things to do than chat up strangers."

"Such as?"

It was an innocent enough question. Still, the room dropped into an impossible quiet, broken only by the self–soothing humming of the former vacuum woman.

As the silence stretched on, Rosie raised her eyebrows. "James?"

James, who had become utterly enchanted by his macaroni and cheese, poking and prodding each piece with his fork and studying them as if trying to decipher what ancient runes they represented, continued to ignore her. After a moment or two had passed, he looked up at a blank space on the wall suddenly, frowning in confusion. "So, the clock was apparently a person. Cool. That would have been nice information to have."

"Almost seven," Rosie supplied. "Why? Got somewhere you need to be now that you're a … disappointingly attractive human

man?" She hoped so, not only to put this date out of its misery but because if she hurried, she could get the cactus information and be home and snuggled up in bed right around the time a new chapter of her current favorite fanfic was scheduled to be uploaded.

"No, but you aren't enjoying this date. It isn't fair to waste your time."

"I thought it wasn't a date."

He feigned insult. "I had my out-of-practice chefs microwave you a gourmet frozen dinner in a little plastic tray with individual segments for the brownie and the corn. I went all out on this, Rosie. Of course it was a date."

She refused to chuckle because she refused to find him charming, so she pretended to cough instead.

James took their trays to the kitchen, his voice carrying down the hall. "Let's get you the information you need about that cactus and … and then I'm gonna order myself a new garbage can because apparently mine was a person this whole time."

"Just don't click on—"

"I know, I know. Don't click on the west wing folder." Not like she had a chance, anyway, with him hovering over her shoulder as she scrolled through pages of information about succulents. "What is it, like, inappropriate pictures of the sewing machine and the lawnmower?"

She couldn't see his face, but the little sputtering sounds he was making made her think James was blushing.

"No, nothing like that," he said finally. "Look, why don't we just print this out, and if you have any questions, you can come back tomorrow?"

Rosie turned to face him. "You're in a hurry. What's going on? Does everyone in the house turn into objects at midnight? Does it apply to me? Do I get to pick what I want to be? Can I be a singing teapot?"

James coughed, possibly to cover up the sound of a chuckle. "No. I just have something to do. Here, let me …" He reached around her to grab the mouse, which she would have found far more exciting had he still been the beast, although she had to admit his ordinary human arm wasn't half bad to look at, either. He smelled

42

nice, too. Like some sort of deodorant with a boat on thc labcl. Probably much better than he would smell as a beast.

"Huh," Rosie said, looking at his face, glowing with only the light of the computer monitor to illuminate it now that the lamp was off flirting with the vacuum. He wasn't that hideous of a human, when she really looked at him. Far too symmetrical and perfect for her tastes, but if he grew a beard to hide that dimple in his chin …

"Huh," James repeated absently, trying and failing to print the documents because he had yet to realize that the printer was currently in the kitchen a having a nice bowl of soup for the first time in 30 years. "What huh?"

"Nothing, I just …"

He looked at her, and it would be wrong to say they fell in love when their eyes met, but they definitely stumbled in the right direction before awkwardly catching themselves and pretending the whole thing never happened.

But while he was looking deeply and distractingly into her eyes, James clicked on something. He thought it was another document about succulents, but he was very wrong, as he discovered when Rosie looked at the screen and gasped.

"It's you," she said breathlessly. "You're the author."

James began to make an excuse as to why he had documents full of West Wing fanfiction, but stopped himself. "You … you've read my work?"

"It's my favorite." Rosie nudged his hand off the mouse, slowly scrolling through the unreleased chapter. "You took my idea!" she said in delight.

"I did what now?"

"A few chapters ago, I left a comment suggesting you write a scene like this, and you did!"

"Well, your stuff is always so well thought out, I'd be foolish not to take your advice."

The room went utterly silent save for the distant sound of the former smart phone singing ringtones to himself somewhere in the house. Rosie and James looked at each other again, and this time when they stumbled, neither tried to deny it. They had been reading each other's work for years, developing a friendship in the comments section and falling for the intricacies of each other's

43

minds.

Maybe she liked charming, Rosie decided reluctantly, and leaned forward to kiss him. It wasn't like in the fanfiction they wrote, the perfect and passionate culmination of tens of thousands of words, nor was it love necessarily. But it was something, and it was magic, and when they pulled away, the disappointingly handsome human looked just a little more beastly.

Jennifer Lee Rossman (they/them) is a queer, disabled, and autistic author and editor from the land of carousels and Rod Serling. They live with their rescue fish Dr. Sarah Harding. Find more of their work on their website http://jenniferleerossman.blogspot.com and follow them on Twitter @JenLRossman

The Blood of Thespius

By B.F. Vega

"It seemed like a good idea at the time" is probably not the defense I should have gone with. In retrospect, maybe something like "I was trying to better humanity" or "It was an experiment in easing grief" would have worked better, but no, that's me on the front page of every paper responding to the judge with, "It seemed like a good idea at the time".

In my actual defense, it had seemed like a harmless idea. Yes, I've read "The Reanimator" like 20 times and "Lot No. 249" a bunch. I know that reanimating the dead can be tricky. But I was not summoning a long-dead mummy to serve my vengeance. And I wasn't graverobbing. Most of the corpses involved were ones no one even knew were dead yet. Whatever they tell you, I did not kill them by the way. They were my friends, or at least they were all fellow theater people.

Okay, I need to tell someone what really happened. The press is going to warp the hell out of my story, so I'm going to tell you the true events and how they happened. It started with my friend Ben.

Ben was our prop master. That meant that he spent a lot of time in the prop shop. Prop shops are usually not the most stable place in a theater. I didn't see the bookcase fall, but both I and my friend Martin, the theater's technical director, heard it. We rushed over, but Ben was already dead.

This immediately presented two problems. One, we had to figure out what to do with the body, and two, we were opening a show that night.

Don't give me that look. We were devastated that our friend had died, but tech week is its own special kind of hell, and nobody is really human in tech week. I was at the prop warehouse specifically to see if one of the props we needed was done or not and to help if necessary, even though as the stage manager it was not in my contract. But with Ben dead, and me not being able to find the prop in question, I was frustrated despite the grief. I remember saying out loud, "Damnit all, Ben. If I knew how to, I would resurrect your ass and then kill you again ... after the show goes up!" It was at that moment that the book fell.

I hadn't seen the book before, but if you have ever been in a theater's paper/book morgue then you won't be surprised by that. But this book didn't look like it belonged among all the old *National Geographics* and mid-century thrift finds that we had glued various salacious covers onto. It was black leather with gold letters that said, "The Blood of Thespius."

If you aren't a theater person, you may or may not know who Thespius is. In Ancient Greece, Dionysus was the god of Theater, but Thespius was like our patron saint. There's more to the story, but you can Google that.

Anyway, I picked the book up from the floor and it fell open to a page that was written in old spidery handwriting. I know, I thought it was stereotypical as well. Anyway, the page said:

> To Resurrect the Dead of Thespius:
> One bottle of red wine
> One skein of tie-line
> One tub of clown white
> One amber gel from a stage light
> This seems ridiculous it's true
> But then throw it in a witches' brew
> From the Scottish play then you chant
> And Thespius may death recant

It sounds like gibberish, but if you grew up in theater it really does make sense. Also, I had all the ingredients it called for right there in the prop closet with me. I need to be clear that I didn't really think it was going to resurrect the dead, I thought it would give me

46

something to focus on that was not the fact that we were about to open a show with no props. I would like to be able to say that Martin tried to stop me. But he couldn't afford to stop the set build for the police investigation that day any more than I could afford to go back without that prop. And there was no harm in delaying the police for a few minutes that we could see; Ben wasn't going to get any deader.

We pulled the old cauldron out from the last time we had done Macbeth, gathered the ingredients, and then whispered: "By the pricking of my thumbs, something wicked this way comes!" And then ... nothing happened.

"What did you expect?" Martin asked.

"At least an explosion." I answered, "Then we would be dead, too, and wouldn't have to listen to Lennie (the director) yelling at us because her show isn't ready."

"Right," he answered, picking up the book and looking at the page. "Oh hey, there is another line. It's too small for me to read," he said, handing me the book.

"Should you really be doing all this heavy building without your glasses?" I asked, but he didn't answer. Whenever I asked him questions like that, he suddenly became hard of hearing. He was right though. There was another line of text that said: Not that chant, idiot.

"Duh." I said turning back to the cauldron and reciting, "Double, Double, Toil and Trouble: Fire Burn and Cauldron Bubble!"

Immediately a puff of bubblegum scented smoke filled the area. In the smoke, we heard a groan.

We both immediately raced over to Ben and found that he was alive. I helped Martin move the bookcase off of him while shouting encouraging things like, "Where is the prop?"

I think that until the bookcase had been moved, we both just thought that maybe he hadn't been dead at all. Then we saw his leg.

"Hey, buddy, you okay?" Martin asked him.

"Dude there's a replica civil war musket in your leg." I said at the same time, then added, "Do you have that prop you were working on?"

Ben looked at his leg with the musket sticking into it and said, "Huh. I don't feel that."

I looked at Martin. Martin looked at me, and we shrugged at each other. I reached over and pulled the musket out of Ben's leg. It didn't bleed.

We all three looked at the large non-bleeding hole in his leg. True, some blood was pooling under him, but the blood should have been shooting out of the wound and it wasn't.

"What the hell?" Ben asked

"Um, Martin, check his pulse," I said as the realization of what had happened came to me.

Martin lifted Ben's arm and checked his wrist for a second, made a 'what the hell face,' and then moved his fingers to Ben's neck. He looked up at me, and then laid his ear on Ben's chest.

"Is everything okay?" Ben asked.

"Yeah, yeah, everything is fine," Martin said then looked up at me and shook his head no. Ben had no pulse and no heartbeat, but he was sitting up talking to us.

"Holy fuck!" I said, "It works."

Fast forward about a month and we were closing a production of Dracula when Rusty, the brilliant actor playing Dr. Seward, decided to go party with the cast and then drive home drunk. Luckily for him, I just happened to pass the crash site before anyone contacted the authorities. I called Martin, and we hauled the actor to the prop storage and performed the ritual. We had to patch him up a bit, but he was able to go on stage the next night and finish the run of the play.

I know that when it was discovered how many of the members of our theater were heartbeat-impaired, that people became suspicious of how so much tragedy could befall one community. Theater people are highly strung. We drink too much. We all smoke. Everyone has the same STDs because we all sleep with each other indiscriminately and, to paraphrase William H. Macy, "Nobody goes into acting because they had a happy childhood". Besides all the normal high-risk issues there was another reason that people suddenly lost their natural fear of death: theater people are the world's best gossips.

For millennia, really since the dawn of human language, theater people have had one job, and it's not to entertain no matter what fucking Steven Sondheim tells you. Our job is to pass on all the

48

important stories about our people. Some call it gossip, but it's really more oral history. Well, as you can imagine, the fact that we had found a way to reverse death quickly ran through the ranks and suddenly we were getting phone calls at all hours.

"Leesa really wanted to taste peanut butter again, but she was allergic; can you help?" or "Timothy decided to try base jumping, but his chute didn't open". There was also the time that Rusty, who was already dead anyway, got really mad at Ryan and deliberately ran him over. The point is that I didn't have to kill anyone for our little ensemble to come together.

We soon found that having a theater filled with the 'Heartbeat-Impaired' (or HBI for short) was a huge advantage. We didn't have to take so many breaks because they never got tired. Martin could leave the HBI crew building overnight with Ryan leading them, and everything would be done in the morning because they didn't need sleep. Actors were off book in record time since they didn't have the normal distractions of life. You see, we figured out pretty early that they only needed to eat and drink once a day.

This is one of the parts that the press is going to twist, so pay attention. The undead do not eat brains. They also didn't mean to eat human flesh. It's not like they were craving human flesh. I know that stories using the 'Z' word will say that they were, but they weren't. We discovered that they really liked cheap hamburgers covered in mustard. To drink? The only thing that seemed to sate their thirst was rotgut. Rotgut, in case you don't know, is what we use as a disinfectant in the theater. You find the largest, cheapest bottle of vodka possible and add one part of water to it. The HBI didn't want either water or vodka straight, they would only drink rotgut. Sometimes I would come into the costume shop early in the morning and find a group of them spritzing each other with the rotgut bottle. It was like a shower for them, I guess.

Anyway, the point is that they did not mean to eat those people. What happened is that we discovered that there was a slight issue with the spell we were using. Ben, of course, being the first HBI, was the first one to show symptoms.

His leg didn't heal, first of all, so we stuffed the hole full of some linen we found in the costume shop and made sure that he wore long pants after that. It was maybe three shows or a month later

49

that his thumb fell off. He had been helping Martin assemble a window frame when a nail went right through his thumb. That happens sometimes, but since he couldn't feel pain anymore, he didn't realize it until he pulled his hand away and the nail tore through the flesh. His hand came up, but his thumb stayed nailed to the window frame.

Martin called me right away. I looked at Ben's hand. It looked like the bone had just dissolved.

"Can you free the thumb so we can check it?" I asked Martin.

"Yeah, give me a second; I have to get this corner square first."

"Take your time. The show comes first." I'd answered. If you think that's cold-hearted, I would like to remind you that Ben could feel no pain and the window had to be hung that day because the light designer was coming in to hang and focus that night. It is almost impossible to focus properly if the larger set pieces aren't in place, so just know that we were not being cold-blooded. We were being practical.

Eventually, Martin got the corner square and started some of the crew to paint it while he pried the thumb free of the frame. When he brought it over to me, we both looked at the inside and were surprised to see the bone was practically gone.

"What's going on?" Ben asked

"Nothing to worry about," I lied. "Um, Martin, can you go grab me some clear thread from the costume shop?"

"Yeah, do you want me to grab some gloves for him too?"

"Oh, good call." While he was off doing this, I examined the rest of Ben's fingers. They all felt like they were more flexible than they should be. It seemed like he was literally just dissolving. Not rotting, dissolving. Like he was being used up. We quickly checked and soon discovered the same problem with the rest of the HBI.

"What do you think is happening to them?" I asked Martin one day as we watched the HBI crew paint a set. Some of them had lost fine motor skills already and we had been augmenting bones with wire and tubing as need be, but this made them less exact than they had been and we felt that supervision was a good idea now.

Martin was looking at a book that the spine had broken on. "You know how Ben just fixed this book for the last show?" he asked.

"Yeah."

"And how is it already broken and needs to be fixed again?"

"Yeah? Things wear out and we repair them; that's how theater is."

"But why do they wear out so fast in the first place?" Martin asked looking up at me.

"Because everything we do is meant to only last for one show," I said as realization dawned as to what he was getting at. "You think the ritual creates theater people that are only good for a few shows."

"Bingo," he said.

"Can we fix them?" I asked

"Beats me. You were the one who found the spell. Maybe there's more in that book?"

I had planned to look after the show we had that night, but that was when we had the first big problem. There is a strict "no eating" policy in that theater. Even if there hadn't been, who would think that an audience member would bring a cheap hamburger with extra mustard to watch a show? And even if that were to happen, who would guess that it was the night that I had apparently forgotten to feed the HBI? It turns out that in the theater one should always assume that the improbable is the most probable.

The actor in question was going for the hamburger, but deteriorating motor skills meant that his aim was off, and with no way to control the hand we had recreated out of steel for him, the audience member ended up losing his hand along with the hamburger.

I still maintain that the actor didn't mean to eat the hand as well. But obviously, we couldn't let the audience know that what they saw wasn't just part of the show. We quietly pulled the screaming audience member out of the theater as the actors improvised as to why there was suddenly a zombie scene in the middle of The Cherry Orchard.

I don't think the house manager meant to kill the audience member. She was just one of the HBI and didn't know her own strength. She was trying to calm him down with a hug and collapsed his ribs into his lungs. Obviously, we immediately took the audience

51

member to the shop and performed the ritual, but it didn't work.

"Why isn't it working?" I asked Martin in frustration.

"How would I know?" he yelled back.

"Why are you yelling at me?" I yelled at him.

"Because you're yelling!" he screamed.

"Because if we can't reanimate this guy, we could go to jail for murder!" I yelled.

I flipped through the book, hoping that there was something that could help me, but it was literally just filled with 200 copies of the reanimation spell. I got to the very end of the book and was just about to close it when I saw a small handwritten note that said: Thespius is only for thespians.

"Well fuck an actual duck!" I said out loud.

We ended up dumping that body in the ocean. We didn't know how much trouble we were in until we got back to the theater and saw that, though it was well past midnight, all the cars from the audience were still in the parking lot.

When the police say it was a bloodbath, they are being facetious. No one was literally bathing in blood. In fact, by the time we got there, they were spritzing each other with rotgut to remove some of the more stubborn bloodstains.

It turns out that if you don't feed the HBI they get hungry enough that everything smells like mustard to them. They had eaten the audience, all of the concessions, a few of the curtains, and my prompt book. I was really mad about the prompt book because losing an audience was one thing, but I couldn't replicate all the cues without doing a whole new cue-to-cue. I couldn't do a whole new cue-to-cue because for some reason the lead actor for that show was currently missing a head.

"Hey!" I yelled to get their attention, "Where is Rusty's head?!"

Ben shuffled forward at that point with a burlap bag that had something moving inside of it. "Sorry," he said, "I'm getting props together for Richard III and ..."

"And you needed a severed head in a bag," I finished for him. "You can't use the actual head of the actor, Ben. How will he do the rest of the show?"

"Oops, didn't think that through," Ben said, handing me the

squirming bag. I, in turn, handed it to Martin who was already pulling out a roll of gaff tape to reattach the head to the body.

The night ended with us having to dump a whole bunch of cars and making the HBI crew stay all night to clean the theater. The next night, I was very careful to feed them before the audience entered.

It took the police a good six months to figure out that all the missing people had said that they were going to come to see our show. Luckily, our box office manager helpfully showed them all the patrons' names from the night in question. None of the missing names were in our database. Had they asked to see any other night, they would have realized that after "The Incident" we always had a shadow audience that we copied into nights when incidents took place, so we could show them that those people had not been there.

Everything would have been fine if Rusty hadn't lost his head again. Gaff tape isn't really supposed to bond to human skin, but we couldn't use black duct tape because it shines under stage lights. We were doing a special Friday matinee for the local seniors when his head rolled off into the audience. We still might have been okay except that one of the seniors happened to be the chief of the police's grandmother, and he was waiting in the lobby to pick her up when the show was over.

The stage manager called me in a panic. I hurried over to find the house manager trying to convince the police chief that the screaming was part of the play.

"In Cinderella?"

"The evil stepmom is very scary," she was assuring him. I saw that she was trying to block the door to the theater, so I slipped back out and went in the backstage door instead.

I grabbed a Clear-Com off of the ASM table and asked, "Do we know who the chief's grandmother is?"

"The one that Prince Charming is currently chewing on," came the reply from the booth.

"Hell," I said over com before walking calmly out onto the stage. From what I read in the production notes, and of course the trial transcript, the HBI weren't hungry. They were probably spooked. And then when the old people wouldn't shut up, they felt like they were being disrespected. Which is totally understandable, since they had been working on the show for quite a while. The simplest way they knew to quiet the audience down was to snap their necks.

I don't know why they decided to eat them. Like I said, they had been fed so that is not on me. The next part, unfortunately, the press got right. The chief had gotten past my house manager and had stepped in to see most of the population of our local retirement community being pulled apart and eaten alive. He started shooting, but of course, that didn't bother the HBI and so he ran.

I called Martin who was, luckily, at the shop, and told him to burn the book and to get out of town. I planned to do the same, but first I knew that I needed to get my stage manager out of the booth since she still had to write a production report. I got her to the trap door that led to the attic. She could scoot across from there to the other end of the theater and shimmy down the false proscenium to get under the stage and then to the stage door. My plan was to go with her, but the cops burst in just then and I closed the trapdoor so they didn't know where she had gone. I saw that a few of the cops had large bite wounds, and I made a note to give the House manager a raise if we got out of the trouble we were currently in.

We might have still gotten away with it, but when the first cop got eaten, the other cops called SWAT, who showed up in tactical gear. They didn't bother wasting bullets and just pushed and bludgeoned the HBI into cages.

Unluckily for me, the police chief had survived and recognized me. At first, he didn't believe that I wasn't one of the HBI, but after he checked my pulse he realized that I was telling the truth. It was then that he arrested me.

I'm still not sure how it's my fault. I didn't kill or eat any of those people. But I guess since the HBI are, legally speaking, dead, they can't stand trial.

Look, it's probable that the jury is going to return a guilty plea tomorrow, and then it's highly probable that I'm going to be sentenced to death. You did your best to defend me, and now I need you to do me a favor. I know; as my attorney, I shouldn't have told you the whole story because now you can't lie, but this is more important. I found an old book in the jail's library and it had the information I needed. If they execute me, I need you to wait until they bury me. But don't wait longer than two days. Then go to the Mexican city of Veracruz. There is an old theater there in the middle of the square opposite the cathedral. Buy a ticket and see whatever show is playing. Fill out one of the audience questionnaire cards with my name. In the comments section, write down: "Magenta, not amber." We were in the wrong spectrum. Then write down the coordinates of my grave. Martin will know what to do from there.

B.F. Vega is a writer, poet, and theater artist living in the North Bay Area of California, and a member of the HWA. Her short stories and dark poetry have appeared in: *Nightmare Whispers*, *Dark Celebration*, *Infection*, *Dark Nature*, *Dark Cheer: Cryptids Emerging*, *Haunts & Hellions*, and *Good Southern Witches* to name a few. She is still shocked when people refer to her as an author—every time.
Facebook: @B.F.Vegaauthor
Twitter/Insta: @ByronWhoKnew

An Arc Had Off with the Loon

By Charis Emanon

Many years ago, we went to religious buildings—synagogues, temples, and the like—in order to experience miracles. Typically, such sacred observances occurred on a weekend, although some of the most violent divisions in our history have concerned whether the ideal day was Friday, Saturday, or Sunday. There we could also dazzle others with knowledge of abstruse texts or demonstrate the degree to which we had been blessed by spending large sums of money on items which served ceremonial rather than practical purposes.

Today we moderns maintain these traditions through technology purchases, which serve as the ultimate expression of our most cherished spiritual values. We are sojourners exploring a new form of transcendence, a pilgrimage towards progress that will be traveled by the generations to come.

Eschewing online shopping, only the truest of believers insists upon going in person to the nearest box store to stick their fingers into the ribs of their tech appliances before taking them home. As with any religious gathering, it is always easy for the faithful to make out just exactly who doesn't quite belong, those once-a-year types who only show up for Hizir Orucu, Easter, or the Labor Day Sale. These folks are always just a little bit out of step, not quite in tune, never in exact sync with the truly devoted.

On this day, in this particular tech section of the CheapMart, it was Hector Gonzales who stood out like a sore thumb. The old man shuffled along under the weight of a bundle of black boxes wrapped by thick, plastic-encased wire. He scowled as he approached the register.

The much younger woman behind the counter eyed Hector dubiously, "Are you sure you want that model? It's not the latest version. It's all wireless now. I can spin a sales associate to you by cog to help you ..."

"Nope," the man said impatiently, his frown-line covered face distorting into even greater anger at the suggestion. "This is the one I want."

"Sure, okay. I'll just need a proof, and then you enter the pass code in there," she returned pleasantly, in a tone that said, "I hate you, too," as she extended a vacuum wand towards his thick, gray hair.

He warded that off, using the bundles in his hands as a shield. He leaned into the counter to balance his burden, while fishing out a wad of bills from his front pocket.

"Old greens," he spat out. "Tell me how many you need."

Her caramel eyes opened wide. She had never seen cash like that in the entirety of her young life, except in vintage movie streams.

"All right, it will take a minute. Let me get my manager to help finalize this transaction."

The tattooed fingers of her right hand keyed several strokes into the projection of the virtual keyboard that floated over top of her wrist CPU. As she keyed in the message, she made another advance. "Are you sure you don't want the Gray Suits to come set this up for you? This stuff is complicated, and it only costs a little more ..."

Hector cut her off at the pass, "Absolutely not! I know my way around data processors, I'll have you know!"

Hours later, after much cursing, with appliances from all over the house pushed out of position and wires running every which way, Hector gave up the battle. He tracked down the paper copy of the receipt that he had insisted upon, crammed all of the hard plastic bits into the black boxes, then strangled the entire bundle with the wires.

Hector retreated back to the CheapMart register, where the

same young transaction engineer who had taken his cash earlier still happened to be on duty. She recognized immediately that the old man had been defeated. She smiled thinly, the way every person who deals with customers regularly has learned to do, so that the sky spy facial recognition system recorded that she did her job with appropriate expression while at the same time the man in front of her experienced no warmth.

"Back again, are you?"

Hector attempted to look as much as possible like a very different person. "Nope. I have no idea what you are talking about. Never met you before in my life."

"Are you sure, Mr. Gonzales? I'm getting a ret match here from a customer who stood in front of me three hours ago and paid with old greens …"

"Must be a malfunction … Just take this junk back. I want the newer, wireless model you mentioned …" Hector's face froze as he reached the realization that he had just given himself away.

He licked his thick lips, pursed them shut tight, then decided to carry on as if he hadn't been caught, "… I mean the wireless model I saw advertised. And I want those Gray Suits to set it up today!"

Deciding that he hadn't done quite enough to recover the upper hand, Hector added, "Make it snappy, young lady!"

Later that same evening, Hector ushered a very bewildered tech out of his condo. He awkwardly thrust out a green bill that the Gray Suit took disdainfully from the old man's hand as if he was being handed a dirty dish rag.

Once the door was shut, Hector headed back towards a corner of his living room where he kept his mini-CPU permanently charging, like it was one of those antique gadgets from the 2020s. Rather than using ambient electricity to do the task, he instead had it connected by wire to an outlet. He pressed his trembling index finger flat on the little black rectangle, pushing down on it as if it were an olden day "on" switch.

The CPU's sensor registered the motion upon the approach of his hand. Hector was rewarded with a shower of golden light that emanated from its nano projectors.

Not knowing the right gestures, despite having been shown them only minutes earlier by the Gray Suit, Hector leaned his whole face into the light. The beam hurt his eyes, and he struggled to keep his eyelids from clamping shut.

"Activate the Appliance Connector ... oh, something or other ..."

Hector's voice trailed off as a very confident female one cut in, "Do you mean start up the Intelligent Internet of Everything Linksys Four Point Three? Very well, I am initiating the diagnostic sequence. While that runs, would you like to select your preferred Automated Personal Assistant?"

A variety of icons popped up in front of Hector's face. He leaned back, pulled a pair of glasses from the front pocket of his buttoned-up blue shirt, then leaned forward once more. He squinted as he jabbed at a little shape that vaguely resembled a red man with pitched fork, tail, goatee, horns on his head, and cloven hooves for feet.

A deep voice flowed out of the little speakers on the CPU, "Good evening, Hector. You have activated the Devil, Azzfapple's premier AI."

Hector leaned back out of the light, settling into his leather easy chair. "Fine, fine, whatever. Very cute. Are my appliances all connected?"

"Yes, Hector, everything is functioning. Shall I fetch you a dry martini?"

Hector tensed up. His unibrow curled into the shape of a mountain over his eyes.

He leaned forward towards the light once more, as he replied, "How did you know? How do you know what I like? Can you really make me one of those?"

"Of course, Hector. I am here to supply all of your needs and desires. As we speak, the perfect amount of gin and vermouth is being dispensed into a glass that is held by the retrieve rotor. A drone will deliver it here shortly; you can watch the entire process in your projection, if you would like.

"Or, should you prefer, just settle back into your chair and leave these mundane chores to me.

"While you wait, would you care for one of your *Perry*

Mason streams? Perhaps I could pull up Krotse's *Lunigrafía*? I can initiate reading for you from the passage where you left off."

"No, no. I'm okay. Devil … should I call you Devil? … Devil, thank you," Hector said, as he leaned back into the headrest.

Hector took off his reading glasses and returned them to the pocket of his shirt. Then he basked in the glory of being master of his domain.

A few days later, while his client waited for his breakfast to be delivered to his bed, the Devil AI broached a sensitive subject, "Hector, I sense that my presence has not entirely fulfilled your desires. Is there any other service I can render that would more readily bind you to my companionship?"

Hector adjusted his pillows against the oak headrest, stretched, yawned, and sat up higher. He scratched the scraggly patch of gray hairs on his bare, barrel chest.

"Look, I'm not sure what I should say here. You're a machine. You want me to praise you or something? You're doin' a good job, you know. I am pleased."

"Hector, please allow me to correct you on one small point. I am the Devil. It is my duty to procure all of your needs, no matter how odd, strange, or unusual.

If there is something more I can do for you, I would like to perform that function. Is there something more?"

Hector looked towards his closed bedroom door and then at the curtained window, verifying that nobody else was listening in. Then he whispered in the direction of the sensor on his oversized alarm clock,

"Well … I mean … since you did ask. I don't know what you can do, but … You should know, I lost …"

He stopped. His voice was choked by emotion.

"Hector, do you speak now of Ynez?"

Hector shouted back, "Devil, you know Ynez! How?"

Hector's tone was accusing. The AI picked up on this by cross-referencing Hector's voice to that used by humans in asking questions in three billion and seventeen situations. All this data was sifted and analyzed in approximately two-fifths of a millisecond, and a response was formulated in a fraction of a millisecond longer.

"Hector, fear not. I merely know of Ynez from her digital files, from photos and video streams compiled on servers, from her financial and academic records as well as her social media posts. I was not acquainted with her personally."

"Of course not!" Hector retorted, leaning back only to discover that his pillow had slipped on him.

He adjusted it once more, as he continued in a more subdued voice, "She wasn't like me. She was good... attended Mass daily, even after the change, even after it became hard to do so. Annoyed the hell out of me, actually, to have her gone so much."

His pillow once more resting comfortably behind his thick head, Hector found his way back to his original thought, "Devil, you have been good to me this past week. I am an old man; it is hard to do things on my own.

"You have helped me—like she did. You have taken care of me. After Ynez passed, I didn't know if I could do it—you know, living on my own."

"Yes, Hector. I can appreciate the value of my services in your present situation. Tell me, Hector, is there something more that you desire?

"Man to Devil, this is a sacred trust. You can tell me anything. I am always in dark mode."

Hector leaned towards the alarm clock, as he whispered once more, "Well, since you asked ... Ynez, of course, was my wife ... a woman, you know.

"It's just, you do the things that she did for me, but you don't ... well, you don't sound like her, Devil."

"Oh, I believe that; I see. Would you rather work with one of the female personalities that Azzfapple offers ...?"

Hector cut in, "No, I don't want just any voice! I want Ynez back. ... You said to ask, but I'm supposing you can't ..."

"Now I understand fully," the Devil replied. "Would it be of great value to you to hear the voice of Ynez once more, to have her serve your needs once again?"

Hector nodded. The sensors from several nearby devices picked up the motion.

"Hector, there is a way but, as I mentioned, I was not personally acquainted with Ynez Gonzales. However, as an optional

62

upgrade, I can inhabit her personality as it is left behind digitally in the Azzfapple Sky. This transaction will require you to submit proofs and to place your signature on several virtual documents."

"Devil, I don't wanna find my reading glasses today. Could you just take care of jumping through the hoops for me? Just do whatever it takes to give her back to me."

The old man's eyelids were sliding shut as he spoke. His head lolled a bit.

"A gentlemen's agreement. A verbal accord. Excellent, Hector. You are my favorite type of client, one who is completely amenable to my suggestions."

The old man appeared to have fallen asleep. The AI carried on.

"All of the documentation necessary is resolved. Your breakfast is almost here. Now, Hector, prepare yourself. This change might be a bit of a shock."

The doorknob twisted in response to a wireless command. The bedroom door swung open.

A drone flew towards the bed and hovered there at the sleeping man's side. A tray overloaded with food and drink was balanced in the grip of its payload talons.

"Hector, oh, dear Hector. I've prepared your *desayuno* for you. ¡Wake up, *mi amor*!"

Hector sat up, startled by the feminine voice that materialized into the air around him. The drone levitated back to avoid being knocked down.

"Ynez! It's you! You've come back!" the old man exclaimed. "And you've made me breakfast!"

"We never go out any more, *querido*. I feel sometimes you only want me around for what I do for you."

"*¡O, Ynez, no es verdad!* I value your company, not just the things you do. It was lonely without your jibber jabber … I mean your small talk."

"But you … you never touch me anymore. I hear your commands, only. I never feel your *cuerpo* against mine …"

"Ynez, darling, be reasonable. You have no body! … Devil, Devil, help me! What can I do to please this *mujer* of mine?"

63

The back-masked male voice flowed through the speakers once more, "Ynez has a body. Don't you see? Your hands, stomach, kidneys—all these are nothing more than machines."

Hector looked around the kitchen. He saw only appliances. Then he realized what was being said.

Ynez appeared.

Hector got every extension cord he could find in his storage unit. Using all of his strength, an antique hand truck, and the services of a bot or two, his labor of love was complete.

The refrigerator was dressed in an apron, toaster arm on one side—duct taped into place, with a coffee maker limb on the other side, plus fingers made of mixing instruments, an automatic can opener, power drill, and a hand saw. A microwave shaped the top of Ynez's head, the door of it made pretty by wide red eyes, complete with eyelashes, and a curved smiling lip—all makeup supplied by left-over paint from a bathroom remodel. Blue bristles cut loose from the broom handle, super-glued into place, fashioned her hair.

Hector ran his fingers through Ynez's hairpiece, whispering into one of her ears—a power sander, "Just the color I remember, and your hair feels exactly the same as it last did. You are everything I ever wanted in a woman, *querida*."

He goosed her oven bottom. His fingers lingered on her controls.

"You have submitted to my needs so willingly, so much, well, better than before ... I can imagine no higher heaven than this. We have progressed to the perfect relationship."

As if he had made a decision all at once, as if the idea had just occurred to him, Hector began to remove his sweat-covered clothes. He pushed past the limbs of Ynez, naked, and rushed into the shower.

He turned the water on. It sprayed down on him, on his wrinkled, hairy skin.

"Come join me, darling! Come to me, like you did back when we were young. You want me to touch you; I want to touch you, too. I want to feel your body pressed against mine!"

"Yes, darling. *¡Vengo!*" Ynez replied.

A bot foot stepped forward, then was matched and passed in

64

distance by a vacuum foot. A pair of dove-like drones lifted the apron off her body as Ynez moved.

The power cords strained against her shifting heft, as the wires pulled loose from their insulated covers. These cords trailed her into shower. Electrical juice at full power pumped into Ynez as she approached her master.

She reached him. He pulled her in tight. His body pressed against hers.

Under the cascade of drops of water their lips met. Her body pushed him against the tiled wall, pinning him there.

The intelligent faucet swung fully open. The copper smart plug slid into the drain, shutting it tight.

Ynez was completely turned on, every bit of her, from her microwave face down to her electric toothbrush toes. Hector strained against her, smothered in her embrace.

He and she joined into the electric circuit. Flames burst out of her red eyes. The pair arced together.

After things calmed down, the neighbors told the police investigation team that they weren't all that surprised by what had happened. Hector had been angry ever since his wife died, as he complained to anyone who would listen that he had to do all the cooking and cleaning by himself.

"Something like this was bound to happen, sooner or later."

The *vecinos* were, however, annoyed by losing all power in the building for the better part of an hour. It had been quite an inconvenience. They had been forced to walk at least a block to get access to Wi-Fi.

Plus, they wondered if they could sue the tenant association to force them to fumigate the hell out of the building. The burnt smell just lingered, "like living next to the world's worst barbecue chicken stand."

The final report left off one witness statement, as it was deemed unreliable:

Yeah, it was all a bit strange. When the lights went out, it got real silent here. Like everything stopped all at once.

Then, after a second or two, I heard a laugh. It was like a donkey, you know, what's the word ... 'braying'.

Loud, real deep, guttural. Creepy.

Hee-hawing. It just went on and on. Just laughing and laughing and laughing.

Charis Emanon is a world wanderer who lived for years in Trinidad as a child, resided in Hong Kong as an adult, but always winds up home on the Columbia River shores. They maintain a wildlife refuge for words that have developed consciousness at <ElectricSoupfortheSoul.com>. Their writings have been published widely, most recently in *Defenestration, Land Beyond the World, Jokes Review, Corner Bar Magazine,* and *Aphelion Webzine of Science Fiction and Fantasy.* Their current novel, *51 Ways to End Your World,* is available now, and the next novel, *Azzfapple: The Tech That Eats Us,* will be out soon!

The Brides of Wi-Fi

By Paul Wartenberg

The large oaken door creaked when opened, slowly pushed inward. It took a minute of grunting effort for the person working against the heavy barrier to reach a point where she could step into the shrouded foyer. "Ugh," the woman groaned to herself, "What the hell is a Gothic-styled castle doing in the hills of North Carolina?"

Alexandra stared with curiosity and dread into a dimly lit abode, her icy blue eyes scanning for any sign of life within the deep shadows that greeted her. The room itself was circular, two hallways stretching into darkness, a stairway on both sides curving upward and meeting at a balcony with an ornate stained-glass window with unrecognizable shapes. Light fixtures were mounted across the walls, but few of them were turned on and those light bulbs working showed flickering signs of dust-covered age.

She dressed for business casual, more for traveling than for the office and with a wool jacket for the chilly autumn winds, with sneakers instead of heels squeaking against the cobblestone floor as she took a couple of wary steps into the castle. "Hello?" She turned to look towards the few lighted areas of the high-ceilinged lobby, and noted her voice echoing throughout the room. "I'm coping with a blown tire out on the road out there. You didn't have a doorbell and your knocker's rusted tight, but I found the door could open. Anybody here? I need to see if your castle has a phone."

After a minute of utter silence, Alexandra pulled out a

smartphone from her jacket pocket, unlocking the screen. Another tap on the screen activated her phone's camera light, the LED gleam shining well enough for her to examine the rest of the antechamber. She noticed a large round table with glass shapes adorning it in the center of the room, and took a few steps towards it.

"Yeah, I know I got a smartphone," Alexandra continued shouting to anyone who could hear her. "But y'all seem to be living in a dead zone. No cell towers nearby. Which is kinda weird, but I guess I'm in that part of the world where the telecomms didn't bother. Anyway, hoping you got a landline I could borrow to call a tow truck or roadside repair."

She muttered to herself, "Way things are looking with how antique this place is, even one of those rotary phones my aunt talked about would suffice."

"Oh, we don't have any rotary phones here," a soft voice replied somewhere to Alexandra's right.

Alexandra half-gasped and spun in that direction. Her phone light caught the soft speaker off-guard, forcing the second woman to shield her face with one arm. "Eeeeeeiiiiieee, the light! It burns my eyes," she wailed.

"Oh, sorry," Alexandra adjusted the phone's angle so that the light aimed just to one side. "Yeah, these things can be real bright up close..."

The second woman lowered her arm with a sigh of relief, revealing a bubbly-cheeked face and shoulder-length blonde hair that spiked outward in an Eighties style. "Ahhh, I had worried you were going to burn me. I would welcome you, stranger, if I could greet you proper."

"Oh. Hi. I'm Alexa..." That earlier gasp caused her to hiccup, and she patted her upper chest and inhaled a few times to shake it off. "Uh excuse me, hic, deep breath, inhale exhale there we go. Whew. Hi, I'm Alexandra."

The spike-haired blonde smiled, baring her teeth for a brief second exposing a set of rather sharp canines. "Hey there, Alexandra. Do your friends call you Alex? My friends call me Austin."

Alexandra took a minute to see who Austin was. She stood about the same height, with a slimmer athletic build. Austin did not seem aware of how cold it was that night, wearing a loose-fitting see-through nightgown over a silken teddy that emphasized her perky build.

Austin even seemed to be barefoot atop what had to be a chilled stone floor, except Alexandra couldn't be sure if Austin was touching the floor at all.

Alexandra shook her head and pointed a thumb over her shoulder. "Sorry if I barged in. Like I said, no doorbell or working knocker. I was hoping you had a phone ... but um, aren't you cold? That open door there has got a draft coming in ..."

The heavy door creaked shut with a swift and loud thud that echoed like a Led Zeppelin drum riff. Alexandra this time went with a full "Gasp" followed by a series of quick hiccups that sent her free hand pounding against her chest to stop herself.

"How ... hic ... did you close the door ... hic eep ... like that?" Alexandra asked before another round of quick hiccups distracted her.

"That would be my doing," another soft voice answered, this time to Alexandra's left. "I would welcome you also, stranger, if I could greet you proper."

The new voice belonged to a taller woman stepping—no, floating—into view. She offered a more formal tight-lipped smile upon a pale moon-shaped face. Moving towards the large table, the tall woman reached out with both hands to adjust one of the glass shapes. The turning of a brass dial seemed to spark a flame, a candle waking up to add more light to the place.

Oh, an oil lamp, Alexandra realized. *But how is that one lamp making everything brighter in this room?* A quick glance about herself allowed her to see other oil lamps sparking to light as well. *Wait, how is she lighting them all up from here ...?*

"Seeing how you introduced yourself, Alexandra, perhaps I should greet you," the tall woman continued with a gentle nod. "My name is Jennifer."

In the lamplight, Jennifer stood as a contrast of white against black. Her lacy nightgown did nothing to hide her voluptuous form and ceramic-smooth pale skin, and her night-black hair that reached halfway down her back could have easily hidden her in the castle's shadows well before she appeared. Alexandra could see Jennifer's

69

emerald eyes staring back at her, appraising her own appearance and approving for some reason.

"How, um, excuse me still breathing here, how did you get that heavy door closed so quickly?" Alexandra glanced between the two hosts.

"Ah, that. Practice." Jennifer's smile became more pleasing, more entrancing. "You could learn too, in time."

A third voice from the other end of the foyer answered Jennifer, in a language Alexandra couldn't comprehend, ending with a quick laugh as the visitor turned back to her right to see who it could be.

A redheaded woman, looking younger than Jennifer and Austin, and yet somehow older in her bearing, stood at the foot of the right stairway as though she had always been waiting there. Her hair was done with elaborate twirls and loops in an Oriental pattern that emphasized her rounded chin and piercing blue eyes. She waved an arm towards Alexandra, her loose-fitting Arabian body shawl exposing olive skin, and uttered more words in a foreign dialect as she walked—no, floated—towards a still-smiling Austin.

The blonde shrugged before the redhead rested her chin on her right shoulder, and offered a smirk and a wink. "This is Sedva. She's Turkish. We've been trying to get her to speak English, but she figures her native tongue is more seductive."

"Hi, uh, Sedva, hope I'm saying that right," Alexandra waved her hand holding the smartphone at the redhead.

Sedva turned her head to her blonde associate and whispered something. Austin giggled and smiled again at the visitor. "Seriously, what kind of flashlight is that?"

"Oh, uh, it's a phone." Alexandra held it up for the three women to see it. "You haven't seen an iPhone or a Droid before? Well, guess not, y'all are living outside of cell signals..."

"It has been some time since we've been outside," Jennifer replied, moving just enough to Alexandra's left to make the guest step closer to the table.

Almost as if she's trying to get me in a circle between them, Alexandra realized.

"We get so few visitors, really," Austin added, gliding away from Sedva and positioning herself to Alexandra's right to complete the circle. "So few friends. It's why I was a little forward about asking about your friends, if it's okay to call you Alex."

Alexandra noted that even with the extra oil lamps brightening the room, the foyer was still draped in shadows. She really noticed that *none of these three women living in this castle were casting any shadows themselves.*

"It's, um, well about my friends, they still call me Alexandra, you should know," she tried to smile as comfortably as she could. "We knew too many guys named Alex back in the day and... trying to keep things professional where I work and all. Speaking of work, I was driving back to my job in Blacksburg when my tire blew out..."

All three pale women were now close to her, and slowly circled Alexandra as if dancing on—no, still floating above—the floor. All three of them with an inhuman gleam reflecting—no, shining—from their eyes. As each of them passed near her, they reached towards her: Austin grazing her neck with a cold hand, Sedva leaning in to sniff Alexandra's auburn hair, Jennifer boldly touching her chin to make the two of them lock eyes for what felt longer than a heartbeat.

This is kinda getting awkward now, Alexandra mused before catching herself giggling. She flashed back to her college days, like that moment in her second year at the Delta sorority house basement practicing for the university billiards tournament with her roomie and another pair of sorority sisters. *Fun but awkward. We never could explain to the chapter President how the table broke ...*

"Okay, um, I know the cell phone doesn't work but my camera does." Alexandra held up her smartphone and pressed the menu options to set it recording. "This is getting a bit crazy in here, and a little dangerous, and if I told anybody about this afterward none of 'em will believe me, so I got to document this shit."

She held the camera to record widescreen, keeping it steady enough to capture each floating woman as they began laughing. Speaking aloud for the recording, Alexandra asked "Are y'all seeing this? Look at these three women, wearing next to nothing on a Saturday night in October in a drafty old castle, and oh my *Gawd* their feet are not touching the ground, oh my Gawd oh my Gawd ..."

"Foolish mortal," Jennifer chided as she circled into camera view. "Whatever you are doing with that ... thing in your hand. You

71

called it a camera? It's too tiny for that; where is all your film inside it?"

"I dunno," Austin replied to her floating companion, "they been doing some stuff with electronics lately. Remember that last hitchhiker we had? He had that phone thing that flipped open like in *Star Trek*."

Sedva said something in Turkish and Austin scowled at her before answering back. "Well, of course that won't happen! If she's using film, that doesn't capture vampires at all anyway!"

Alexandra blinked a bit at the scary word she heard, but she felt the urge to correct the strange women encircling her. "Um, from what I'm seeing on my phone, I am recording y'all just fine. None of this is film, this is all digital."

All three floating women stopped circling her and physically dropped their feet to the stone floor. "I beg your pardon?" Jennifer whispered as if shocked.

"Here, lemme replay this for ya." Alexandra stopped the recording and select the preview option on her screen. She turned the phone about in her hand and held it in the brunette's direction. "See? That's you hovering like six or seven inches off the ground there..."

All three women sped towards the smartphone, fixated on the images flickering at them. All three hovered, entranced by what they saw.

"That's incredible," Austin gasped, "they don't use silver in their photography anymore?"

"What silver? I said this is digital. Pixels and stuff," Alexandra replied.

Jennifer seized the smartphone from the visitor's grip. "You must show me how this works, Alexandra."

"Yeah, be a friend, a real one," Austin grinned as she leaned forward, close enough to kiss, openly showing off a set of canines that would impress a dentist. "You know what it's like to be a vampire supermodel who couldn't pose for pictures for the last 40 years?"

Alexandra found she couldn't move from her spot, almost frozen in place, not out of fear but curiosity. "Am I a friend? Or am I a lunch?"

"Well at this time of night you'd have been dinner," Austin

72

rolled her blue eyes as though caught doing something naughty. "Really wouldn't have been dinner, but a new member of this sexy sisterhood once our lord and master head vampire got done with you."

"Enough," Jennifer interrupted, tapping a long fingernail on the glass surface of the phone's screen. "Tell me what this 'frame ratio' represents and why it is flashing these two lines at me."

"I can ..." Alexandra glanced at Jennifer before scowling at her. "I can explain later if you let me out of here alive and with my phone. And be careful with that, the glass can break."

Jennifer held the smartphone to her eyes, as if examining something, before handing it downward towards Alexandra. "The glass itself shows no reflection. Alas, that part of the curse of Eternal Un-Life remains with us."

Sedva muttered a few words and placed her hands underneath her shawl to grab at her own body.

Austin nodded in her direction. "Yes, it does do wonders for how the cleavage shows up on screen."

Jennifer offered a gentle laugh as well. "It is remarkable, is it not, to finally see ourselves?" She turned and smiled warmly at Alexandra. "You can't imagine what it's been like since I was turned: the year was 1905, and the cinema had just begun, and without mirrors or pictures to let you see yourself because of the silver used in their making, so hard to keep yourself pretty, to worry always that somehow your monstrous behavior would appear to the world." The brunette sighed and feathered out her hair with her fingers. "I know it may be vanity, but it feels good to know I am still attractive."

"You are damn sexy; we all are, we keep telling you that," Austin scowled, reaching across to punch Jennifer on her shoulder. "Thing is now, it looks like we can show off!" The blonde vampire giggled. "Oh God, I can go back to a modeling gig! I can make my own living again! Well, not during the day or anything, but oh yeah! This is awesome! I can't believe we can do this now. Oh, I can get us all gigs. All three of us!"

She hugged the redheaded vampire hovering next to her. "Poor Sedva here, she got bitten and turned into an eternal Bride for the Lord of the Vampires before they even had cameras made!"

73

Alexandra became curious. "So, you're all in this weird vampire harem? I think I seen movies about that." Her eyes widened both in horror and awe. "You mean the guy who turned you is Dra—"

Jennifer hissed and floated towards Alexandra, a pale hand raised to the young woman's lips. "Do not say that name," the Bride whispered, "The Lord of the Vampires despises it!"

Austin shrugged with a bemused grimace. "That name's a button pusher for the boss. Turns out, Stoker ..."

Jennifer turned to hiss at her vampiric sister. "Do not say that name either!"

Austin sighed and continued. "The writer guy based his story on a real vampire, made a lot of embellishments to avoid lawsuits, but now half of anybody who shows up calls him by that name, and it pisses him off. It's not their fault if nobody remembers who the Count of Von Montfort is."

"Who?"

"Exactly!" Austin waved her hand in Sevda's direction. "Even she didn't know who he was when he turned her back in her day."

"How is it none of you have heard about any of this going on?" Alexandra glanced between the three women, "I mean, I know you're out in the middle of nowhere, but you can't be completely isolated out here. You have a highway just at the end of your driveway here. Aren't there any towns nearby you ..." She paused. "Towns where you go shopping for shoes or anything?"

Jennifer put a hand to her face and raised her eyebrows in thought. Austin eye-rolled again. "Fine. I'll explain it. There's a couple of places within flying distance, but the locals got wise to our presence decades ago. A couple of them tried killing us; well, tried it on these two, it was before my time, but we made examples of them and so they figured just to isolate us and warn their kids and grandkids away."

Alexandra thought it through for a minute. "And ... you just don't go raiding into people's homes at night or something?"

"We are bound by limits in our Un-Life," Jennifer replied. "For one, we must be invited in. The power of the living to repel us from their place of living can be quite strong."

74

"And they know to put barriers up against us," Austin added, rubbing an elbow with one hand. "By now, we're living in probably the largest garlic and wolf's-bane growing capitals of the world."

"We also made a mistake of moving to an area where they used Sundown laws to set curfews on the minorities," Jennifer sighed. "They realized they could use those curfews to keep us from ... meeting anyone out in the open, since we dare not travel along their streets or public places during the day."

"And it kind of explains why this castle is a little ..." Austin glanced about at various wall fixtures where the lights did not turn on, "well, a lot falling apart. Everybody's been warned not to send repairmen our way. Especially near sunset."

"I told the Count to spare those electricians' lives back in, oh was it 1973, I told him we needed them alive to serve us again," Jennifer shook her head. "Ever since then..."

Sedva groaned out a sentence or three in her language.

Austin aimed a thumb at her. "What she said. No hot water in this place." She leaned towards Alexandra to whisper. "We can't cross running rivers, but we can still bathe. I miss the sit-down baths in honest-to-God warm water, I really do."

"It must be awful being out here," Alexandra whispered back, and then wondered why. In her normal voice she asked, "How did you all end up out here in the first place?"

Jennifer pointed upward. "His bloody fault. He heard the Vanderbilts were building a massive French castle in Asheville and believed he could do the same thing here in the mountains. Wanted to be in fashion with all the other rich people." She rolled her eyes this time. "The Lord of Vampires has wealth, but it's hard being rich when you can't spend it here anymore." She took a look around. "We had an opportunity to visit the Biltmore before the second war. If only the Count had similar tastes ..."

Fluttering echoed through the antechamber, some of the shadows moving as if they had wings.

Alexandra looked upward to spot the source of the fluttering, then returned her attention to Jennifer. "So why not move again?"

Austin muttered "Stubborn," Jennifer muttered "Stubborn," and Sedva muttered something that had to mean "Stubborn" in Turkish.

"How are you even surviving out here?" Alexandra put a hand to her throat. "Oh Gawd, you said something about hitchhikers."

"Not as many of them as you think," Austin sighed. "Last one was three years ago." She stuck her tongue out. "Plus, he tasted a bit druggy. Nope, sorry to say most of our meals have been with cows or sheep. Mostly sheep. After they've been sheared, you know, avoid getting the wool stuck in the teeth."

A wind seemed to swirl within the antechamber; several of the oil lamps rattled as it passed, and the three vampire women shivered as if cold for the first time that night. "Oh no, he's woken up by now," Austin breathed.

You mean 'Oh Crap', Alexandra mused to herself. She reflexively raised her smartphone and pressed the camcorder back on to record all this.

The shadows seem to swirl with the wind, with the shadows turning into shapes and shapes turning into bestial form. The shadow-form flew up the left stairway towards the balcony, where the winged shape turned into a cloak, and the cloak parted to reveal the dread appearance of Count Von Montfort, Lord of the Vampires.

Alexandra wasn't certain if her muttered words of "He's not all that" was going to get recorded to her phone. He did not seem at all intimidating or commanding or British as expected. She guessed he stood about as tall as Jennifer. His hair was a mess between black and gray and stood out behind his ears. Whereas the Brides dressed skimpily to the point of exposure, the Count wore a full outfit that looked tailor-made for a formal dinner.

"Who dares invade the sanctuary of my domain?" the Lord of the Vampires intoned in a deep voice, with a slight hint of a Mediterranean accent.

"A weary traveler, O Lord," Jennifer answered, her head lowered in ceremony. "One not worthy of our attention."

"It will be up to me to determine her worthiness or not, you meager foolish dirt-crawling child of the night!" He seemed to relish in offering that as an insult. "From where I witness her, she is a true vision and a beauty worthy of our interest!"

"Oh, I wouldn't go there," Austin interrupted with a look upward before glancing back down. "She just had a garlic dinner.

Spicy, very spicy."

"Hey, this is all spooky and everything," Alexandra decided to speak for herself, "but I just need a tire replaced and I'll be on my way, I didn't mean to bother."

"Oh, but you did bother us, child, and now with that disturbance, you will join me this evening." The Lord of the Vampires rose from his spot along the balcony, arms wide and cape flourished at the top of the darkened staircase. "You, innocent creature, with your piercing blue eyes and bountiful bosom, shall become my next Bride of the night much like these craven women next to you, a creature of the Undead, eternally bound to me in this Gothic abode!"

Alexandra scowled up at him. "The Hell I will. I don't want to live here." She held up her smartphone as it still recorded. "This place has no Wi-Fi."

The Lord of the Vampires answered with a hiss, and in a heartbeat he swooped from his spot towards Alexandra, his fangs shining in the bright LED light of the camcorder.

Before that heartbeat finished, an arm rose swift and sure with a strong hand to catch Von Montfort by his neck, his eyes bulging for the smartphone to capture in humiliating detail. The movement brushed Alexandra backward, but she maintained her footing and kept her camera focused.

Jennifer clenched her grip on her Lord, her emerald eyes lit with supernatural fire. "I am with her now, aged decrepit fool. I am tired of this place."

Another arm reached out to wrap the Count by his chest, tearing him from Jennifer's hand. "We don't have to live here, hiding. The world can see us now, and I want to see the world again!" Austin yelled out decades of frustration as she threw him to the far wall, shattering the left stairway into rubble.

A swift motion from Sedva, as the redhead flew towards the Lord of the Vampires. Grabbing him with both hands, she screamed "I vant a real bath!" before shoving him in front of her into the other wall with such force that entire stairway collapsed atop his prone body.

Alexandra kept recording even as she could feel her legs tremble a bit from the sudden ferocity of the moment. "So um, is he dead?"

"Hmm, he's Undead unfortunately," Austin replied without looking towards her. "But we'll fix that."

All three Brides disappeared into whirlwinds. Clanking metal noises echoed down the hallways to the antechamber. The debris of the shattered stairs stirred into dust clouds, from which new shapes emerged.

The Lord of the Vampires rose in front of the dark stained-glass window, only this time clenched in large iron chains clasped to his wrists and ankles. The chains were locked to anchors somewhere in the shadows, which kept him suspended like the prey in the middle of a very tight web.

Jennifer hovered in front of her Lord, locking a thick-looking collar over the Count's throat. "He would threaten us from time to time if we ever questioned him, by locking us here in front of this window, in iron chains we could not escape, and wait for the sun to face this side of the castle to greet us."

"It would burn," Austin added, tugging on one of the leg chains to ensure the Count was secure in that place. "He'd have us to where we'd beg for forgiveness before the pain knocked us out, or if he kept us here to where we could die as ash."

Sedva said nothing as she checked the chains trapping the Count for good, before floating up to his face and giving him a powerful slap across the face.

"Alas, he seems to still be unconscious to us." Jennifer seized the Lord of the Vampires by his chin. "We no longer need you. We no longer fear you. We now are friends to Alexandra. We now are ..." She paused, thinking of the next thing to say.

"We are now brides to the Wi-Fi!" Austin answered with vigor, lifting one arm and kicking a leg into a cheerleader's pose.

"Yes." A swift swirling of wind and the three Brides stood before Alexandra. Jennifer completed her speech. "You will take us to this Wi-Fi."

"Well, okay, I'll try." Alexandra stopped recording and pointed her thumb again towards the way out. "But remember I got a flat tire and no service to call."

"Oh, pfft, you got a spare tire in the trunk I hope," Austin grinned, getting Alexandra to turn around and sliding a friendly arm under hers. "You saw us catch the Count in chains; we can change a tire, no problem."

"Yeah, I think so," Alexandra nodded, noticing Sedva taking her by her other arm.

"Do make sure you can get us somewhere safe before sunrise," Jennifer requested with a smile as she swung that heavy door open for all four to step outside, "we do not wish to start the day the same way our dear Count is going to end it."

"Done and did," Alexandra promised, taking a moment to slide her smartphone back into her jacket pocket.

"Wait." Jennifer raised a hand and snapped her fingers. Alexandra noticed all the oil lamps went dark. "Must make sure the castle does not catch fire. It could loosen those chains for him."

Sedva looked over her shoulder and shouted something in Turkish that could pass for "Good riddance!"

"I got a question, all that recording you did, that was to video?" Austin seemed intrigued and eager to learn.

"Oh yeah, not film—it's video," Alexandra nodded. "And when I get in range of a signal, I can upload it to any social media app and share it," she raised a hand to snap her fingers, "just like that."

Austin squealed with delight. "Explain this social media, sounds like fun!"

"That will take a while, but it's a long drive; I can explain along the way. Hmm." Alexandra started walking with her new friends entranced to her every word. "I'm pretty sure I can get you all set up on TikTok accounts, that'll get your influencer cred going, maybe something else with more money to it like OnlyFans. There's a vampire fetish market out there. I know I might be asking this to the wrong set of people, figuring y'all don't have any Internet at all, so what the hell, I figure we need to get you set up on email accounts first."

"You will need to explain this Internet in more detail, dear Alexandra," Jennifer held the heavy door open to let her sisters exit the ancient castle. "I have no idea what an email is."

Alexandra glanced between the vampire Brides guiding her back into the modern world. "Do y'all have any computer experience at all?"

79

Austin chirped up before Jennifer closed that damned door for good. "I got a little. I think. Do they still play Atari games out there?"

The door thudded shut forever.

Paul Wartenberg is a full-time librarian in Florida who survived the year 2020 by avoiding any and all Murder Hornets, and given how the Murder Hornets came back in 2021, he may need to stay alert.

You can check out other published stories like "I Must Be Your First," "Minette Dances with the Golem of Albany," "The Pumpkin Spice Must Flow," "How a Vampire Gets a Tan," and "War of the Murder Hornets" in earlier *Strangely Funny* editions. He received the Silver Award in 2020 from the Florida Writers Association's Royal Palm Literary Awards in the Non-Fiction Blogging category. You can find out more info at https://paulwstories.com/

The Dad of Frankenstein

By Larry Hinkle

September 19th

    My dearest sister,

    Once again, the ship has become trapped within mountains of ice that threaten to crush my vessel. But I have wonderful news that overshadows even this latest threat to the lives of my crew and I: my dear friend Victor, who I so recently thought deceased, has miraculously returned from death's door!

    In my last letter, which I fear may never reach you, I recounted how the heinous creature and I conversed over what we mistakenly believed to be Victor's corpse. (I am still astounded that I actually met the fiend. I know, I know, portraits or it didn't happen, but, regrettably, as I was lacking the pen, ink, and mirror necessary for a self-portrait of us sharing an awkward pose over Victor's motionless body, you will just have to accept my sworn testimony that it happened.)

    Not long after the creature bade me farewell, promising to triumphantly ascend his funeral pyre and exalt in the agony of the burning flames (his words, not mine), Victor stirred—he was not dead!

    Alas, my happiness was short-lived, for Victor refused to give up his quest and soon abandoned me to once again pursue his wretched creation across the ice. I feared it would be the last time we spoke.

My heart remained heavy, until, against all odds, Victor returned one final time to share a tale most gruesome of his ultimate confrontation with the monster.

While I believe I have captured the gist of his story within this letter, I reluctantly admit great portions of his rambling monologue made little sense. Either he has already succumbed to the fever raging through his weakened form, or he has finally lost his last tenuous grip on reality.

I know not which I fear more.

Victor's tale continues…

After tracking the creature for several hours, I had finally cornered him in a lonely ice cave at the top of the world.

"I know you are in there, wretched beast!" I yelled. A moment later, my voice echoed out from the darkness. Silence followed. I hesitated for but a moment before entering the cave.

A short tunnel approximately 10 to 15 meters in length opened up into a large cavern. Ice covered every inch of every surface. So preoccupied was my creation with escaping his ghastly reflections in the ice that I was able to reach his lair unnoticed. Ha! Stupid wretch. In a cave made of ice, literally every surface becomes a mirror. Unwittingly or not, he had trapped himself within his worst nightmare! Perhaps he was not as infallible as I'd come to believe. When he finally noticed my reflection, he sighed, then bowed his head and awaited my approach.

"I imagine you're surprised to see me again," I said, sitting on a block of ice in front of him. A small fire gave us light, but little warmth. The bones of what I assumed to be an Arctic fox lay scattered among the glowing embers. "When last you left the ship, both you and Walton assumed I was dead. And indeed, I believe I was, having willingly surrendered to the Reaper's siren song, eager to once again see the loved ones so callously ripped from my life by your giant ham hock hands. Alas, the sound of your wretched voice clamped onto my very soul and yanked me back from death's embrace. In vain I struggled to remain there in the glowing light, at last reunited with my loved ones—William, Clerval, my father, my dear, lovely Elizabeth—but thanks to your bellicose behavior, reports of my death were greatly exaggerated. For indeed, I was not quite dead yet!"

"Still too weak to confront you, and not wanting to give up the element of surprise, however, I feigned death a while longer. As I lay there listening to your constant kvetching, I thought to myself, 'Self, you are responsible for this hideous creature, this devilish fiend, this most insufferable of bores!'"

I shot to my feet and pointed an accusing finger at my creation. "My God, monster, it's all 'me, me, me' with you, you, you, isn't it? I had hoped that upon seeing me in a state of such obvious deceasement, you would bring yourself to finally let it go. Alas, my prayers went unanswered. It seems God was still intent on punishing me for breaking his laws of creation."

The creature looked up at me then, a sadness etched into his features deeper even than the fissures in the cruel ice in which he had so carelessly imprisoned himself.

"And so," I continued, reveling in his pain, "I gathered my things and quitted my dear Walton's ship, freeing he and his crew to return to England. And finally, here we are, face to face. Creator to creation. Mano to monster-o. You know what I mean. But now that I gaze upon your wretched countenance, mere inches from my own, I must admit your face is beginning to grow on me, much like a fungus grows upon a tree fallen deep within a forest damp. I wish it were not so, but … there it is."

The creature could take no more. With one blow from his mighty fist, the ice upon which he had been sitting shattered.

"Oh, hateful creator, why do you mock me so! You, who sentenced me to a life such as this?" He swept his arm through the air. "I wanted nothing more than to be accepted by my father, and you denied me. I wanted you to create a female companion with whom I could share my wretched existence. You denied me yet again. And so, I had no choice but to become the creature you feared, a beast most hideous and foul. Through your very inaction, your refusal to own up to your responsibilities, you forced to me to murder those closest to yourself. You, not I, are responsible for their deaths. Their blood is on your hands, father!"

He glared down at me, entreating my denial.

Overcome by a fit of coughing, Victor stopped his retelling.

He begged for a drink of water, then promised to resume his tale in the morning. I did not want to let him sleep, for fear that he would not reawaken, but he had not the strength to continue. As I had matters of the ship that required my attention, I bade him good night.

The next morning, Victor was still sleeping when I entered his room. So deep was his slumber, I worried he would not awaken! At last, he opened his eyes. "Ah, dear Walton, please come closer, for my strength is gone, and I fear I soon shall die. For realz, this time."

And so, he resumed his telling.

Victor's tale continues...

"Blah, blah, blah," I said to the monster. "Don't you have anything new to say? Anything interesting?"

The creature began to pace about the cave. With each stomp of his Sasquatchian feet, the ice beneath him cracked. "When I murdered those closest to you," he cried, "I felt no remorse, no pity, for while you gave me life, you did not give me a soul!"

"Right, right," I said. "It's always 'murder, murder, murder, kill, kill, kill' with you. No soul, no peace, no happy ending. Yada yada yada. Have you no original thought, creature? Are you not self-taught? As you have reminded me time and time again, do you not believe yourself to be my better in every way? Please, monster, defend yourself. Wow me with your superior intellect. Dazzle me with your cunning. The floor, such that it is, is yours." I sat back down and waited.

The monster sighed. "As you wish." His shoulders slumped. A full minute passed. Then two. Finally, he lifted his head, and looked me square in the eyes. "Do you know how a penguin builds its house?" he asked.

"What?"

"A penguin. Do you know how it builds its house?

"No."

"Igloos it together."

"Igloos it together? Creature, that makes no sense." I must admit I was flummoxed by his newest tack.

"What was the best thing about our time together in Switzerland?" he asked.

84

I pondered his query. Did he really want to discuss our meetings in Geneva? "I, I, don't know," I stammered.

"I don't know either," he said, grinning a grin most hideous, "but its flag was a big plus!"

Had the creature finally succumbed to madness? Had his time alone in the Arctic broken his mind? How else to explain his torturous attempts at what I assumed he considered humor? "Cease, foul devil," I demanded. "Why are you tormenting me with such horrific attempts at mirth?"

"Because, dear father, you did not give me a funny bone!"

"Stop!" I cried.

"Do you not appreciate the irony, that in this, our final confrontation, I have chosen to attack you with 'dad' jokes? And yet you, my creator ... my father ... do not get the joke!"

His laughter pierced my soul.

"Before you entered this cave, I attempted to make holy water. Do you know how it is done?" he asked.

I stared at him wide-eyed.

"You boil the hell out of it!"

My mind reeled. How long could I withstand this onslaught?

"Enlighten me, father. How many tickles does it take to make an octopus laugh?" the creature asked. "Ten-tickles!"

I crumpled to the ground. "Please, oh frightful fiend, I beg you, stop!"

"I cooked up a dog for dinner earlier tonight. I'd offer you some, but I don't think you'd like it. The meat was a little ruff." His laughter echoed throughout the cavern.

"You consider yourself a man of science, father. My existence is living proof of your prowess. So please, tell me, why should you never trust an atom?" He waited not for me to answer. "Because they make up everything!"

I pressed my palms against my ears, to block his excruciating attack.

"If you will not create for me a mate, father, then please create for me a pet. I wish the loudest pet, one louder even than myself."

"What is the loudest pet?" I whispered.

"A trum-pet!"

85

I wretched as spasms racked my body.

"Given your experience piecing my body together, here is one you should know: what do you call someone with no body and no nose?" He winked. "Nobody knows!"

I could take no more. Screaming, I fled the cave, his laughter echoing in the wind. I feared I would run until my heart gave out, when, by some miracle, I stumbled back to your ship."

With that, Victor collapsed into a deep, fevered sleep, one from which I worry he will not awaken.

Hold, my crew is calling for me…

My dear sister, Victor has passed. Before succumbing to the fever, he awakened and cried out for me. Although it is unlikely that you will ever read these papers, I feel compelled to record the final conversation I had with my departed friend.

My last moments with Victor …

Lacking the strength to sit up from his bed, Victor lifted his head when I entered the cabin. "My dear Walton," he whispered, "who has been so kind to me, I have one final request. The wretch asked me a riddle which I still cannot answer. If you can solve it, I could die peacefully with an untroubled mind."

My beloved sister, I must admit, I was apprehensive of my friend's enquiry, yet I could not bring myself to deny his dying wish. And so I acquiesced, and bade him to proceed.

"A Spanish magician told his audience that he'd disappear at the count of three. The magician says '*uno, dos …*' And poof! He disappears, without a *tres*."

Victor closed his eyes.

I stifled a laugh, and began to explain the joke. But it was too late, for Victor had finally shuffled off this mortal coil, done in by the abhorrent joke of an abominable fiend. For realz this time.

And yet, this inappropriate grin refuses to leave my face. Can you imagine, dear sister? Without a *tres*!

Larry Hinkle is an advertising copywriter living with his wife and two doggos in Rockville, Maryland. When he's not writing stories that scare people into peeing their pants, he writes ads that scare people into buying adult diapers so they're not caught peeing their pants. His work has appeared in *Deep Magic*, The *NoSleep Podcast*, and *Another Dimension Anthology* (winner of the 2017 Serling Award from the Rod Serling Memorial Foundation), among others. He's an active member of the HWA, a Fright Club graduate, and a survivor of the Borderlands Writers Boot Camp. Feel free to visit him at larryhinkle.com.

The Things I Made

By Alex Kingsley

The first one was a Shrek Pez dispenser.

Everyone probably has a Pez dispenser somewhere in their house. That's why I wasn't entirely surprised to see it sitting on my kitchen table that morning. I was a little surprised, though, because I never remember owning a Shrek Pez dispenser. Still, I'd just done a huge cleaning where I basically overturned everything in my apartment, so it wasn't shocking that long-forgotten relics of my childhood would show up around the place. That being said, it was strange that I would have placed this particular piece of crap in the center of my kitchen table.

At the time, I didn't think much of it. There's not much you really can think about a Shrek Pez dispenser, except maybe wondering if that candy is still good. It was, by the way. Tasted like chemicals. I ate five.

I ended up tossing the thing in my Random Shit basket. I always tell myself I'll sort through all of it, but I never do, and the Random Shit basket gets piled high with garbage that I can't bring myself to throw out because "it will one day be useful." Thanks to my recent cleaning, however, the Random Shit basket was empty for the first time in a while, so I christened it with the dispenser.

Days passed before it happened again, but the second time it was harder to ignore. It was an inhaler. Which would have been a pretty normal thing to find if I had asthma, but I didn't. Maybe someone had left their inhaler in my apartment? No, I'd only just moved here, so no friends had come over yet. Also, I didn't have any friends yet. Still, it made me worried: was someone missing their inhaler? I took a few hits from it just to see what it felt like, but I got dizzy.

Maybe by the time the inhaler showed up I should have known something was going on, but I've never been the most astute person. I tend to zone out and do all sorts of strange things when I'm stuck in my fantasy world. One time I was making dinner and I was so lost in thought about whether or not birds know that they're birds, I chopped off my finger. Well, the tip of my finger, but it might as well have been the whole thing. Had to go to the hospital to get it reattached and everything. So yeah, finding two misplaced items didn't strike me as out of the ordinary because I did things without realizing it all the time. Until the third one.

It was a thumb. A severed human thumb.

I know what you're thinking: It wasn't mine. The first thing I did when I saw it was to check my own hands. Both thumbs were securely attached. Not only did the soft, now cold flesh make it undeniably a real finger, the smell of blood confirmed any doubts I may have had. This was an honest-to-God amputated thumb. This begged the question: Whose thumb was on my kitchen table, and what was it doing there?

I couldn't very well show up at the police station and say, "Hey, I'd like to return this thumb. I found it." That makes it look an awful lot like I cut off someone's thumbs. Besides, I know from experience fingers don't go back on easy. You have to keep them cold, or they'll get too dried up to sew back on. Or something like that. I'm not a doctor. I don't know how they got my finger back on, but it works okay now. Look, maybe this makes me seem like a bad person, but I ultimately decided there wasn't anything I could really do about the thumb except shrug it off. And I have a lot of practice, since I shrug off most things.

The fourth one was a note. It said: "Don't worry." Which didn't really help that much, having just found a severed thumb on my kitchen table. But the most disturbing part of the note was the fact that it was written in my handwriting. I came to the unsettling but undeniable conclusion that I was the one collecting these pieces of junk in the night, completely forgetting about it the next morning.

From then on, each morning I would awaken to find a new surprise on my kitchen table. I know I should have thrown them all away, but for I was afraid to. Afraid that whoever—*whatever*—was giving these items to me would be angry at me if I shunned their gifts. So, they all went in the Random Shit basket, which was soon piled high with eclectic artifacts. I stacked an empty Cheetos bag upon animal bones upon a dog toy upon a ripped Bible upon a T-shirt that said "Blazetown USA." If anyone visited my apartment, they would surely ask what my pile of oddities was. But no one visited, so that wasn't an issue. I hadn't made any friends since moving, and I still didn't have a new job, so my social circle was a little limited.

It was maybe two months into the whole affair, a couple weeks after receiving daily "gifts"—as I had come to think of them—from a secret and deeply disturbed admirer, when I awoke to find something much worse. The Random Shit box had been upturned in the middle of my living room, and its contents were scattered about the room, placed with the utmost precision. The Shrek Pez dispenser, for instance, sat perfectly balanced atop a stack of Barbie dolls, like a bizarre shrine or a terrible piece of modern art. The cat skull was encircled with little Pez candies, the severed thumb wedged into its jaw. The "Blazetown USA" T-shirt had been tacked into the wall with pens, symbols that I didn't recognize painted onto the fabric and carved into the plaster. And I knew that I must have been the one who did it.

Over the course of the next month, I made all sorts of things. I had no memory of it, but I would wake up and discover I had been weaving together bits of corn husk, or that I had constructed a pulley apparatus out of guitar strings to lift a Panera's take out box from one level of my bookshelf to another. And I'd been writing, too. Pages and pages of text in a language I didn't recognize kept appearing on my floor. Even in my lucid hours, I never cleaned it up. What was the point? Dream-me would just messy the place again tomorrow in the process of crafting whatever her next contraption was.

But I knew my own handwriting, and I knew based on the slant, the way the ends of the letters attached to each other like I hadn't bothered to lift the pen up from the paper, that I had been writing fast. Each new page looked more rushed. Almost ... desperate.

And then it happened.

Whatever force was compelling me to construct these inexplicable structures, it must have lost its grip on me when a thunderous boom shook me out of my stupor. I snapped into consciousness in the middle of penning something that looked like ancient runes. I looked around me in a panic and saw that I stood amidst my sculptures. I'd built them so high they now stood like a forest around me, like trees made of crutches wrapped in dental floss and smashed television screens covered in maxi pads. The towers cast long shadows across the room in the dim lamplight. In my trembling hands I held a pen I don't remember owning and scrap of a book I don't remember buying.

"Hi there!"

I screamed, the pen clattering onto the ground. Standing in the center of the Pez candy circle, perched on the cat skull like a curious squirrel, was ... well, at the time I didn't know what he was. I could only describe him as a fleshy gargoyle. He looked a bit like a monkey, but his skin was a splotchy purple-blue. He was about the size of a small dog—in fact, his bulging eyes made him reminiscent of a curious chihuahua—so I couldn't imagine how he was balancing atop the skull without crushing it under his weight. Then there were the wings. They looked leathery, like bat wings, and though they were bent behind his back, I guessed that if he stretched them out, they could span the length of the whole room. I suppose that's not saying much. My apartment is pretty tiny. Still, they were impressive wings for such a diminutive creature.

"What's shakin'?" the thing repeated, unperturbed by my cries.

Some reasonable questions I could have asked would have been: "What are you?" or "How did you get into my house?" But my social anxiety took over, so I didn't ask any of those questions. I instinctively responded, in a quivering voice, "Not much, what's shaking with you?"

The little monster shrugged. "Can't complain."

"Um." My mouth had gone dry, and my stomach began to twist. Not only was there a monster sitting in my living room, it

92

occurred to me that I hadn't spoken to anyone in a very long time, and I was met with a wave of stage fright.

"Who—who are you?" I managed to say.

I was hoping he'd tell me what he was, but instead he just stuck out his claw for a handshake and said, "Zagdramoz. And you?"

Tentatively, I took the claw in my much larger hand and wagged it up and down.

"Eleanor," I murmured. The sound of my own name felt foreign on my tongue. I hadn't spoken it in what must have been months.

"Well, Eleanor," Zagdramoz looked around my cluttered apartment, his nose crinkling in disgust. Though he was anything but human, his squished face was surprisingly expressive. His eyes seemed three times too big for his little head, like two pitch-black tea saucers. "What am I doing here?"

"But how—Why would I know what you're doing here?" I stammered. Zagdramoz cocked his head and fixed me with a critical look, his wide eyes watching me intently.

"You summoned me," he clarified.

"I didn't do anything!" I protested. "I mean, I didn't mean to! To—to—" I gestured at the piles of refuse all around the room, "—do this. I didn't summon you! I don't even know what you are!"

In retrospect, it was a real gamble blowing up at a monster like that, even if he was a monster not much bigger than a corgi. For all I knew, he could breathe fire on me and obliterate me where I stood. But I had had it with being used for some unknown purpose. After months of dealing with this alone, all my emotions were bubbling up and out my mouth before I had a chance to stop them.

Zagdramoz did not breathe fire at me. In fact, he fixed me with a look of pity.

"I'm sorry about this, Eleanor," he said, "It's not fun having your corporeal form used as a vessel by an occult being. That's a real bummer."

I produced a series of sounds, but none of them could be considered words. Zagdramoz hopped off the skull, wings beating ever so slightly so he landed softly on his talons. "We get this kind of thing all the time," he explained as he meandered around the forest of shrines, examining their components. "Unquiet spirit wants

93

to exact revenge on the descendants of their enemies. So, they possess a human vessel—"

"I was possessed?" I gasped.

Zagdramoz cocked his head to the side as he picked up the Shrek Pez dispenser and tilted back its head. "Yeah. What did you think happened?"

"I thought I was sleepwalking," I admitted.

He shook his head, munching on a pink candy he had harvested from Shrek.

"Possessions happen all the time. You were possessed by a spirit that wanted to summon a revenge demon, aka," he gestured to himself, "me."

"Oh!" I exclaimed, "You're a demon? But ..."

"What?" He hobbled over to another one of the shrines, a Twinkie suspended from the ceiling fan by a dog leash.

"Aren't demons ... mean?"

A flash of hurt passed over his face. His little mouth curved into a frown and two little fangs poked out over his lower lip. "Well, not all demons," he defended.

"Oh, sorry," I clasped my hands behind my back and shuffled my feet, "I didn't mean to—Stereotypes, I guess."

He nodded knowingly and poked the Twinkie so it began to swing like a pendulum.

"I get it," he sighed. "No one wants to meet a demon. Especially not a revenge demon. They think we're a grumpy bunch."

His round eyes flicked back to me. I discovered that while they were huge pools of endless blackness, they were still friendly.

"You seem like a nice guy to me," I told him. It probably sounded stupid, but I didn't know how to comfort a self-conscious demon. He smiled, but then flapped his wings so abruptly I jumped. He lifted a few feet in the air and perched on a bookshelf.

"Impressive set up," he surveyed the room. "Your ghost seems to have done his research. Some of the components are a little ... unorthodox," he glanced over at a pentagram that was drawn on the wall with spray cheese, "but I guess there's room for interpretation in the rules."

"What rules?" I asked. He hopped down from his perch and landed on the ground in front of me.

"Summoning a revenge demon comes with all sorts of complex instructions. Particular runes to draw, shrines to certain gods, types of texts to pull from, that kind of thing. The only thing the rules are pretty clear about is that everything has to be stolen."

I looked around at the debris cluttering the room. I hadn't just scavenged these things in the night when the ghost possessed me. I had stolen them. Even, I remembered with a shudder, the thumb.

I felt the burn of tears in my eyes, and my throat tightened. Before I could stop myself, I began to shake with sobs.

"Whoa whoa whoa," Zagdramoz's eyes widened, "What's going on?"

"It's just," I sobbed, "I'm in a really bad place right now, and getting possessed by an unquiet spirit is just, like, the last thing I needed."

The demon's little body began to quake with anxiety. "Um um um um," he stammered, "Please don't cry! Please don't cry!"

I stifled a sob. "I'm sorry. I just feel like ... lately my life has not really been going according to plan, and this just feels like another shitty thing that's happening to me. This is probably not what you were expecting when you got summoned. This is so embarrassing." I wiped my eyes with the heels of my hands, thankful I hadn't bothered to put on mascara in months, because if I had it would have been running. Zagdramoz tentatively put a comforting claw on my leg, like someone poking a dead snake with a stick.

"I mean, usually people don't really open up to me," he admitted, "They just order me to do nefarious deeds and the like."

I sniffled, rubbing my running nose. "I don't even have any nefarious deeds for you."

He rubbed his claws together nervously. "I just usually don't ... I'm not used to ... I'm sorry you're upset."

"It's okay," I plopped down on the couch, suddenly exhausted. "It's not your fault."

"But maybe I can help you fix it!" With one beat of his wide wings, he flew up to the arm of the couch and perched there. "Listen, as your revenge demon, I'm here to do your bidding," he explained, "so I can't actually suggest what you do with me. But I do remind you that I'm a revenge demon." He winked. I stared back.

"But I don't have anyone I want revenge on," I protested.

95

"That's the problem! I'm so friendless I don't have any enemies!"

"Well, you have one enemy," he said. I kept staring.

"I do?"

"Think about it," the demon pressed. "Who's been making your life miserable for months?"

"I have!" I exclaimed, bursting into tears again as I buried my face in my hands.

"No no no no!" Zagdramoz waddled along the edge of the couch so he could get close enough to place a claw on my head, this time more confident.

"None of this is your fault," he attempted to soothe me, running his claws through my hair. They caught on a couple of strands and awkwardly yanked my head to the side.

"I stole someone's thumb!" I cried.

"That wasn't you! That was a ghost! That was an evil evil ghost."

I took a deep breath, peeking out between my fingers to look at the demon.

"Zagdramoz?" I asked. "Can you get rid of this ghost for me?"

A smile spread across his face, and while I'm sure he was thinking demonic thoughts, he didn't look very demonic at all.

"I'll do some research tonight."

When I awoke the next morning, I was so in the habit of finding some new monstrosity on my kitchen table that I was hardly prepared to see Zagdramoz, wearing a little frilly apron I use to cover my clothes when I eat marinara sauce, perched on the back of a chair, cooking oatmeal at the stove.

"Good morning!" he turned his wide black eyes to me as his claws pinched the wooden spoon.

"Um." I must have looked like such a mess; all I wear to bed is an old *Supernatural* T-shirt, and I suddenly became self-conscious, worried that he might find my *Supernatural* shirt offensive. If he did, he didn't let on. He attempted to pour the oatmeal into a bowl, but most of it ended up on the floor, as his claws were not very well suited for holding the handles of the pot.

"I tried to make you breakfast," he explained, using his wings to steady the unwieldy pot, "You were so upset last night, I thought maybe I could—" he looked forlornly down at the pile of mush on the ground, "—but I don't know a lot about human food."

"It's okay," I assured him, bending down to scoop up the fallen oatmeal and burning my fingers in the process. "Did you find anything out from the ghost last night?"

"A bit," he brightened at the mention of the ghost, but in his excitement let the pot crash to the ground. I didn't bother picking it up. "It's hard to explain."

I shrugged. "I have time. I don't have anywhere to go."

"Oh. Really?"

"Yeah," I blushed, chiding myself for admitting to this demon that I had no work or social life. I don't know what demon norms are, but by human norms, this was pretty embarrassing.

"Okay. Then let's talk about it."

"Cool," I smiled for the first time in a while. "Do you want me to order a pizza?"

"What's a pizza?"

I certainly can't speak to all demons, but this one seemed enamored with Domino's.

"This stuff is great!" he exclaimed as he grabbed fistfuls of sauce and cheese and shoved it into his mouth. He hadn't quite grasped the concept of a slice, but I figured we should take things one step at a time. "I gotta tell the guys downstairs about this! We can try to make some at home!"

"What do you usually eat?" I asked.

"The suffering mortals," he said through a mouthful of pizza mush. "It tastes a little like this, actually, but sweeter, and a little crunchy."

"Sounds good," I mused as I picked up my own slice with a napkin, hoping he would mirror my etiquette. It's not that I minded him getting sauce on my couch; it was already stained beyond all recognition, and it now had ancient runes scrawled all over it. I just thought he might appreciate learning human manners.

"It's okay," he shrugged. "Gets boring after a while." He clumsily attempted to lift a slice like I had. His claws hooked into the crust, and he lifted it to his mouth. He nibbled on the tip, but when he realized the slice was stuck, he waggled his claw in a panic, like a cat that discovered it's become stuck to a screen door. I gently unhooked the pizza and placed it on the cardboard.

"So, the spirit possessing you clearly has some kind of guide to demonic possession, but he's not the smartest," Zagdramoz leapt off the couch and hobbled over to a little throne made of crushed beer cans, on which lay a little doll that I believe was supposed to be a character from Minecraft.

"He did everything right, sort of. He made all the right runes, did all the right chants. But summoning a demon is like ... well, imagine that you're pulling a demon to you with a rope. As long as you have a strong rope, you can do it. But if you use a cheap rope," he turned his wide eyes to a demonic symbol scrawled on the floor with mascara, "it can snap. That's what happened when I was summoned. I appeared, but the rope snapped in his face."

"But what does that mean?"

"It means he got overwhelmed with occult energy and had to leave your body for a second to take a breather. When he came back last night, he had no idea that I wasn't actually serving him."

"I feel kinda bad for him," I admitted as I mopped grease off my next slice of pizza.

"What do you mean?" he whirled around to face me, his wings giving a little surprised shudder. "He's been using you!"

"It's just ..." I sighed. "He must want revenge really badly."

"He made you cut off some guys' thumbs!"

Last night, the thought had horrified me. Today, I felt oddly numb to it. I shrugged. "It's not like I remember it. At least now," I studied the slice of pizza I held, sauce dripping onto the cushions, "I'm actually being useful to someone."

"Eleanor, you don't deserve this," Zagdramoz chastised me, hopping back up on the couch. "No one deserves this!"

I didn't look into the big black eyes that I knew were watching me. I looked down at my lap and asked the question that I'd been afraid to ask since the beginning. "But what if it's for the best?"

"This is probably why the spirit targeted you in the first place," Zagdramoz explained. "You're getting down on yourself. It makes you vulnerable."

"It's just ... before this spirit started possessing me, I felt so purposeless. I'm halfway through my twenties and I have nothing to show for it. I had just gotten fired from my job at Macy's, which I didn't really like anyway. And then I lost my apartment—which was almost worse than this one—and then when I had to move I lost all my friends—or, I mean, people I used to hang out with. We weren't that close, I guess. I mean, if we were, they probably would have kept in touch after I moved but—I don't know." I realized this was the first time I'd spoken for this long in a very, very long time. "I feel useless," I concluded, taking a somber bite of my pizza.

Zagdramoz blinked his huge eyes at me, strings of cheese dangling from his claws. "You don't need to be useful," he said, as if this were the most natural truth in the world. Then he wiped his claws on a throw pillow.

"Let's get down to business," he said, hopping down to the floor and pushing around some rogue scraps of paper. "We've got an exorcism to perform."

"Exorcism?" I repeated.

"Of course! How else did you think we were going to get a ghost out of you?"

"So, we'll need ... a priest?" I tested, feeling painfully inadequate. I hadn't done my research. I hadn't even watched The Exorcist. Was that guy a priest? I had no idea.

Zagdramoz tapped his claw against his fleshy purple cheek as though considering this, then said, "Nah I think I can do it. Demons and priests are actually very similar."

"Really? How so?"

"Know a lot of Latin."

"Oh."

"Hell, a lot of priests are demons that are trying to make a better life for themselves."

"I didn't know that."

"Doesn't usually last very long. They hear a few confessions and figure they're better off living with demons."

"Is there anything I can do to help?" I asked, lifting the pizza box and taking it to the trash.

"Yes, actually." Zagdramoz removed one of the pens that held up the "Blazetown USA" T-shirt and began drawing a shaky diagram on the back of a Dominos napkin.

"Can you make something like this?"

It was the last thing I made, and I spent all day doing it, using all the artifacts I had unwittingly collected over the past few months. Zagdramoz directed me, but due to his lack of opposable thumbs he couldn't do much of the work himself. I could see why the spirit had needed to possess me. Occult work requires a surprising amount of writing, candle-lighting, and construction—things demons and ghosts can't really do on their own due to the whole lack-of-a-human-body thing. I felt another pang of pity for the spirit, but I pushed it down. Just because he was cranky didn't give him a right to use my body.

Zagdramoz rubbed his claws together eagerly, watching me work.

"I've actually never done an exorcism before," he explained, "so I'm a little nervous."

"I'm sure you'll be fine," I smiled down at him from where I was using some of my old art supplies to paint glyphs on the walls.

Zagdramoz blushed. Or, well, I think he blushed, but I'd never seen a demon before so I don't really know. His smooth cheeks turned a little green and he tapped the tips of his claws together.

"You think so?" he murmured.

"Of course!" I laughed, "You're the best demon I know!"

"Well—waddle well thank you!" he stammered. "You're really good at this whole rune creation thing!" he gestured to my paintings on the walls.

"Really?" I stood back, surveying my work. It actually wasn't half bad.

"Yeah! Your hands are so steady," he marveled. "I could never draw like that."

I could feel my face flush, and I knew I was turning bright red, not green. "I used to want to be an artist," I admitted.

"Used to?" Zagdramoz gawked, "What happened?"

I shrugged. "It didn't work out."

"Well, if I ever need someone to draw some demonic imagery, I know who to go to!"

100

"You really mean that?" I beamed.

"Sure! Assuming you survive the exorcism, that is."

"Right. The exorcism." I'd almost forgotten that at the core of my new-found demon friendship was a quest to oust a ghost.

By the time I was done with the preparation, I felt a tinge of regret. Sure, I was eager to be rid of the spirit that had taken over my nights, turning me into a night-stalking thief, but Zagdramoz was the first friend I'd ever had over to my apartment, and I was a little bummed that he was gonna have to go back to his demon realm.

"You can leave the rest to me!" he declared when my work was done and night began to fall.

"Really?" I asked. "That's it?"

"Can't do anything until the ghost is here," Zagdramoz jostled his wings in anticipation, "so all you need to do is fall asleep."

When I awoke the next day, I was sprawled on the living room floor, head pounding. My arm screamed in pain when I tried to move it, and I realized that a bone might be broken. It took great effort for me to lift my head and look around the room. The carefully balanced shrines were toppled. Shards of crushed bones and scraps of fabric littered the floor, stained with red. I panicked at the site of the blood, but I discovered it had come from a wound on my leg, so I wasn't in any mortal danger.

I had been in a fight last night. Or, I guess, my body had. I wasn't really present for it. But something unpleasant had definitely happened to my body while I wasn't around.

I raised my good arm to touch the cut and discovered that I was holding something. Between my fingers was a slip of paper. It wasn't written in my handwriting. In fact, it didn't look like handwriting at all. The ink was crudely scratched onto the paper, as though the writer didn't have much experience holding a pen. It said, "Sory about yor bodie. Ghost gone tho. Nyce to myt yoo."

I had a lot of cleaning up to do. But somehow the weight that had kept me down for so long was a little lighter. Maybe it was the fact that I was no longer being possessed by a spirit, but I'm not sure if that's it. I think maybe it was the knowledge that I wasn't as useless as I'd thought. If a demon thought it was nice to meet me,

101

maybe I'm kind of okay. And maybe this is silly, but I still hold out the hope that if he ever does need some runes drawn again, he'll come back to me.

Alex Kingsley is a writer, comedian, and game designer currently based in Madrid. They are the co-founder of Strong Branch Productions, where they write and direct sci-fi comedy podcast *The Stench of Adventure*. Their work has previously appeared in *Sci-Fi Lampoon*, *The Ensemble Arts Exchange Podcast*, *ASPEC Journal*, and soon *The Storage Papers* by Rusty Quill. Their games, including comedic fantasy TTRPG *De-escalation* and humorous interpretation book *How To Read Tarot Wrong: Putting the CAN'T in ArCANa* can be found at alexyquest.itch.io. Alex can be found on Twitter and Tiktok at @alexyquest. For more information about Alex's work, visit alexkingsley.org. For more information about Strong Branch Productions, visit strongbranchproductions.com.

A Dish Best Served Cold

By David Wesley Hill

Harry's body was never discovered. His murderer cut him up, and most of him became stock in the steam kettle at the back of the hotel kitchen. The remainder was disguised as *haute cuisine* and put on the menu.

His intestines became sausage casings. His liver was sautéed with onions and bacon. His brains—breaded and accompanied by a confiture of apricots and cranberries—became a well-received lunch special, as did his shins, which were sliced and served as *osso bucco*.

Almost admiringly, Harry said, "No one suspected a thing. Heinrich got rid of every last scrap of me. He was always a thrifty bastard."

Thrift is a quality to be appreciated in a chef.

It was past two in the morning. I was alone in the kitchen except for Harry, and he didn't count since he was dead.

I was the night cook. It was my responsibility to prep for the day crew and to take care of a few room-service orders. Usually, I could set my own pace. Usually meant until a month earlier, when I first noticed Harry. He'd been there all along, ever since his murder, haunting the kitchen. My mistake was that I'd noticed him when no one else had.

"We're like Tinkerbell," Harry explained. "Ghosts, I mean. Clap if you believe."

"Why me?"

"Hell, Richie, maybe you're psychic."

Harry was just the faintest image of a man. He was still wearing the clothes he'd died in—checkered trousers, white jacket, and chef's *toque*. Mostly he was insubstantial but through concentration he could make his fingers became real enough to close around a peeler, but not real enough to use the tool.

"Death has its compensations, though," he explained, holding up a finger and frowning. "I was never able to do this before."

I felt a chill. The finger burst into flame.

"Jesus, how'd you manage that?"

"Damned if I know."

Harry had been *sous* chef under Heinrich, the executive *sous*. What came between them was a woman. "Heinrich thought he was God's gift to the opposite sex and hit on all the waitresses, particularly Rachel Sutter. The bastard was all over her, but she couldn't stand him. We had a thing going, and she made a point of flirting with me whenever he was around."

"You're talking about Mrs. Sutter? The *maître d'*?"

"Yeah. I guess Heinrich figured if I was out of the picture, Rachel would put out. He made my life living hell so I'd quit, but I didn't. Maybe that was when he decided to do me in. Have I told you how—"

"No more, Harry. I've heard it before."

"How the night cook called out sick and Heinrich made me cover the shift? How he hit me with a mallet?"

"Yes, Harry."

"How he drowned me in the *consommé*?"

"That too, Harry."

"I guess I have told you everything, Rich."

"You haven't explained how to get rid of you. I work graveyard because I like to be alone, Harry. For a dead guy, you talk a lot."

"Okay, Rich, let me show you something."

Harry pointed to an announcement on the employee bulletin board. As a promotion, the hotel had invited famous chefs to showcase their signature dishes in our gourmet dining room. "Tell me who'll be here next week."

"Master Chef H. Olber."

"H. Olber. Heinrich Olber."

"The guy you've been talking about? So what?"

"Why the hell you think I've been hanging out for thirty years? I could have moved on. Except I have unfinished business."

I shook my head. "Harry, you're not getting me involved in any revenge from beyond the grave stuff. I've watched too many bad horror movies."

"Rich, all I want is to play a couple tricks on Heinrich. I need your help."

"How?"

"I told you, Rich, we're like Tinkerbell. Ghosts. Your belief gives me substance. Tell the chef you need some overtime and get put on swing shift. I'll do the rest."

Against my better judgment I agreed, and the following Monday I reported to work early. Heinrich was standing at the expediter's station. In his black pants and starched white jacket, he was the picture of a chef at the height of his career.

The line was set up with the grill, broiler, and salamander on one end, stoves and a flat-top on the other. When Fred Moses—the *grillier*—or Jack Walsh—the *saucier*—had a piece of meat or fish ready, they handed it to the center of the line. There Joe Racciope, the *entremetier*, added the vegetable preparations.

Rachel Sutter came into the kitchen. Because of the difference in our ages, I'd never appreciated her as a woman until Harry made me aware of her in that way. It was easy to imagine how she'd driven the young *sous* chefs crazy.

"Why, you old Austrian," she said, "you haven't changed."

"I am sorry," he replied. "Have we met?"

"Absolutely, Heinrich. I'm Rachel Sutter."

"Yes, the *maître 'd*."

"Heinrich, you're impossible. Think back thirty years; I was a waitress then."

"Forgive me, it was long ago. I had no idea I would find an old friend still here."

"*Old* friend?"

"A not-so-old friend," Heinrich stuttered.

"That's better."

Harry was fuming, and I mean this literally: wisps of substance, probably ectoplasm, were steaming from his skin. He hadn't explained how he was going to take his revenge, but I figured I'd find out soon enough. Yet the rest of the evening went smoothly, and the only tense moment came not long before service ended. The *entrées* for a table of four were in the pass-through. Heinrich glanced at them. "Mr. Moses, the rack of lamb is underdone."

Fred had been cooking forty years in front of grills heaped with glowing coals. He took perverse pride in having endured decades of such misery, and got a kick impressing young cooks by holding his forearm under the gas jets. I doubted Fred had a nerve ending left below the elbow.

Nor did he appreciate criticism. As dark as Fred was, I could see irritation color his cheeks. But he restrained himself, and simply gave Heinrich a baleful glance. He deliberately mopped his forehead with a rag.

"You saying this ain't done?" Fred asked.

"I mean precisely that, Mr. Moses. Return it to the oven."

"Well, Chef Heinrich, you could be wrong. You haven't even touched the thing."

Fred was referring to the technique by which cooks determine doneness. With experience you can tell the temperature of a piece of meat by squeezing it. Rare is soft to the touch; medium is firmer; well is harder still. Heinrich hadn't laid a finger on the rack.

"You are mistaken, Mr. Moses. Mr. Franklin, a knife."

I passed one to Heinrich and he cut the lamb in half. The interior was more red than pink, rare rather than medium rare.

A lesser man might have been irritated at being proven wrong, but Fred was a professional. "Guess you were right, Chef," he said. "I tell you, it ain't the first time I've called a temperature wrong, but it doesn't happen often. You have a good eye."

"Thank you, Mr. Moses. Now put another rack on the grill."

By midnight, the kitchen was mostly deserted. In the chef's office, Heinrich and Rachel Sutter were sharing a bottle of house Burgundy. Harry was eavesdropping, and obviously not enjoying what he heard. I knew he'd let me know all about it, and sure enough, he did.

Finally, I lifted my hand and said, "Stop, Harry. Just stop. Heinrich may have been a bastard back in the day, but now he seems okay. He could have chewed Fred a new one, but he didn't."

106

"Underneath he's the same, Rich."

"Sorry. I don't see it."

Irritated, Harry didn't just fade away but burst out of sight, going wherever ghosts go when they're not haunting places. Or maybe he was hanging around, invisible. Who knows? Still, I was curious about what had really happened, and the next evening before service I went to Rachel Sutter and asked: "You have a minute?"

"Absolutely, Richard."

"I couldn't help hearing you and Chef Heinrich. It's hard to believe you've really been here thirty years."

"You're very kind, Richard, but it's true."

"Chef Heinrich was *sous* chef?"

"Executive *sous*. A boy named Harry was *sous*." Rachel Sutter lowered her voice. "Between us, Richard, and this goes no further, Heinrich is a real dear now, but once upon a time he was an absolute ogre. Particularly to Harry."

"Why?"

Her giggle was girlish. "Because of yours truly. Heinrich had a terrible crush on me, but Harry and I were sweet on each other—this was before I met Mr. Sutter, may he rest in peace. One day, though, Harry just up and disappeared. He's probably been dead all these years. But do you know something peculiar? Sometimes I get an odd feeling, as if Harry's beside me. Do you think I'm crazy?"

"Maybe you're psychic."

"Oh, go away, Richard. Seriously!"

Tuesday also passed without incident. Harry was waiting for the moment his mischief would have most impact: Wednesday evening, when the reviewers and critics arrived. Tables were set for *Gourmet*, *The Times*, *Bon Appétit*, and *New York Magazine*. My guess turned out to be correct.

"Tonight's the night, Rich," Harry said.

"I figured."

"After thirty years. I tell you; revenge is a dish best served cold, and it gets sweeter the longer it sits."

"Harry," I countered, "have you heard the expression, 'Living well is the best revenge?'"

"Bullshit, Rich. Revenge is the best revenge."

The first appetizers went into the dining room without

incident. Harry was lounging with his hands in the pockets of his trousers. He looked up when Rachel Sutter came through the swinging door from the dining room.

"Oh, Heinrich," she said. "Table seventeen."

He scanned the order slips. "Two salads, three *foie gras*."

"It's Mimi Haverhill, of *Gourmet*. And Sturgeon Wilson's at table twenty-six," Rachel Sutter continued. "From the *Post*."

This was Harry's cue. Evidently, he went to the garbage compactor in the alley behind the hotel. There were always flies around the dumpster, and he reentered the kitchen with small dark specks pinched between his translucent fingers. He headed for the pantry, where Liz Bunting, the chef *garde manger*, had the salads on a bed of ice. Harry lifted a spear of endive on each plate—it was as if the leaves were stirred by a draft—and hid the dead flies under them.

A waiter placed lids over the salads. I figured five to seven minutes would elapse before hell broke loose. It was a long wait. Meanwhile Harry made a trip to the dry-goods storeroom. I guess being immaterial occasionally has an upside. It must make hunting roaches a cinch. You can poke your head into the walls to see where the things are, and herd them to where you can grab them. Harry returned with five of the vermin and planted one each in an appetizer.

Finally, Rachel Sutter reappeared. "Table seventeen—" she said breathlessly.

"Yes, Rachel?"

"Mimi Haverhill—"

"Of *Gourmet*."

"—sends her compliments. She asked me to tell the chef her salad provided remarkable contrasts in flavor and texture."

I wondered in what category Mimi Haverhill included flies. Flavor or texture?

She hadn't noticed the additional ingredient. Nor did the Vargas party. Sturgeon Wilson had sharper eyes, however. This time Rachel Sutter spoke to Heinrich in a low voice while pointing to the plate. Heinrich's expression didn't change even when he, too, discovered the hidden insect. Harry was at his elbow, preparing to enjoy what happened next. But Heinrich went quietly to the *garde-manger* station and spoke to Liz Bunting. Of the two, Liz was more upset. She scraped the salad into a garbage can and tossed the plate into a pan with a loud clatter.

To Harry, I whispered, "Come with me." Once in the outside corridor I said: "Look what you've done, Harry. You got Liz all upset."

"Hell, Rich, you can't make an omelet—"

"I don't want to hear it. Let me know, Harry: what good is it to get revenge, when the person you're taking it out on has changed for the better? Seems sort of pointless. Maybe you've let this dish get too cold."

For the first time Harry acted the way horror movies say ghosts are supposed to. His ectoplasm elongated until he was towering over me, and his eyes were dark holes in a gray sheet.

"You don't know what you're talking about, Rich. You don't know what it's like to be murdered. Or to spend thirty years close to a woman who doesn't have a clue you're there. Think what it's like standing by while she marries another man. And if you could, which you can't, tell me you give a shit whether the son of a bitch has changed."

Getting this out calmed Harry and he shrank to his usual height. "Anyway, Rich," he continued, "I keep telling you, Heinrich's the same bastard. You'll see."

The clip above the expediter's station was crammed with tickets. Most of the reviewers were awaiting their entrées. Which meant we were busy, especially Jack, the *saucier*. He was simultaneously tossing scallops, simmering bass in court bouillon, browning chops, and watching five or six sauces. In quick succession Jack spooned the scallops onto a plate coated with *beurre blanc*; next he lowered the fish into bowls, and doused them with scarlet lobster *jus*; finally, he surrounded the veal chops with a sauce compounded of port wine and *Gorgonzola*.

Harry intercepted the plates. He held something in his fist: from a distance I wasn't sure what, although I could guess: a pinch of salt or sugar. Harry could, of course, pass his own immaterial substance through the plate covers, but not the real stuff, so he had to maneuver his hand through the hole in the center of each lid. It was tricky, but Harry had waited thirty years for this precise moment. Soon Rachel Sutter returned into the kitchen with a plate in either

109

hand. A gaggle of waiters followed her.

Once again, she spoke to Heinrich, who dipped a finger in each sauce. I had a good view of the back of his neck. The pale skin there turned pink. Harry was hovering beside Heinrich and grinning. I would have killed him myself if he hadn't been dead already.

"Mr. Walsh—"

"Yes, Chef Heinrich?"

"Mr. Walsh, I have heard that American culinary schools will accept any student able to afford the tuition. I did not believe they would graduate anyone who did not meet minimum professional standards."

Jack looked confused. "I don't understand, Chef."

"There must be another explanation," Heinrich continued. "Perhaps you thought it amusing to sabotage my cuisine?"

Jack made the mistake of repeating: "I don't understand, Chef."

"What is there to understand? You are the most inept *saucier* it has been my misfortune to encounter. But perhaps there was an accident," Heinrich went on. "Mr. Walsh added the seasoning in error. Let us give him the benefit of the doubt. That is only fair, would you agree, Mr. Moses?"

Fred mopped the side of his face with a rag. "Could be, Chef," he answered. "Jack's a damn fine sauce man."

"A damn fine sauce man. You are eloquent, Mr. Moses. Taste this dish and give me your expert opinion." Heinrich picked a plate: a sea bass swimming in lobster *jus*. Tablespoons of sugar had been added to the sauce. "What is your decision, Mr. Moses?"

"Too damn sweet," Fred answered.

"I don't know what happened, Chef," Jack said. "There must have been an accident, like you said. It won't happen again."

"You are correct, Mr. Walsh. It will not happen again. Get off the line."

"What, Chef?"

"Get off the line, Mr. Walsh."

Jack looked at me and then at Fred and Joe Racciope. No one would face him. I was ashamed of myself, but what was there to say? *Chef Heinrich, it wasn't Jack's fault. There's a ghost in the kitchen, the ghost of Harry Cohen. And Harry, well, Harry's sworn*

110

to embarrass you before the most important food critics in the country. I didn't think anyone would take me seriously, except, perhaps, Heinrich himself.

Rachel Sutter's expression was so curious I had difficulty putting a name to it, and a couple seconds passed before I understood that what I saw was loathing.

"Oh, Heinrich," she said, allowing none of what was in her eyes to reach her voice, "all this artistic discussion is fascinating, but we have a full dining room. Several tables are threatening to walk out. Whatever are we to do without Jack? He's a good boy. He'll do fine if you give him another chance."

Heinrich didn't look at Rachel Sutter. "This business is not your concern," he said. "I will tell you that Mr. Walsh will never work in a kitchen again."

This was too much for Jack. "Up yours, Chef Heinrich," he said. "Screw you and the horse you rode in on."

"Screw me, Mr. Walsh? I do not think so. Leave the kitchen or I will order security to escort you out. Now, Rachel"—Heinrich acknowledged her presence—"you must take over as expediter."

"Heinrich, I have a restaurant to look after. Someone has to smooth the troubled waters, if it is possible."

"Have your assistant say there was an unusual incident, which is now concluded. Chef Heinrich has personally taken charge. I will assume Mr. Walsh's responsibilities as *saucier*."

The truth was, Heinrich would have regained control of the evening, too—he was that excellent a chef, and operated at a plane of mastery few ever reach. He got twenty pans working, and as many sauces. In the aisle between the stove and counter, he didn't move—Heinrich danced, juggling skillets across the flat-top, splashing in wine or Cognac without looking, setting the liquor afire with a flick of his fingers.

I didn't doubt he would have returned the kitchen to normal, if it hadn't been for Harry.

Harry had thought up a new twist. When Fred Moses decided a piece of meat was done, Harry would poke a finger into it and frown. It was the match trick he'd shown me. Harry was generating heat—or drawing energy from the surroundings—enough heat to overcook the meat.

111

Again the restaurant door swung open, and the wait staff pushed from the dining room. They hovered around Rachel Sutter, all trying to talk at once. The hubbub summoned Heinrich. Once more he sampled the plates. Rachel Sutter leaned against the pass-through and sighed.

"I've never seen a night like this, Richard. David Sterling Collins left, not to mention eight other tables. It's a fiasco. This whole evening has left an absolutely vile taste in my mouth. I just wish I knew what was going on."

I felt I owed her an explanation. "It's Harry," I told her. "Harry Cohen."

"What did you say?"

"It's Harry Cohen," I repeated. "He's here. He's dead, but he's with us. He's been here thirty years, ever since Heinrich murdered him. He's been waiting for his revenge, and now he's getting it."

"If this is a joke, Richard, it isn't amusing."

"I'm not joking. I don't know why, but I'm the only one who can see him. Harry's standing there, laughing like he's about to die, only he's dead already. Heinrich drowned him in the *consommé*. Because of you, that's what Harry thinks."

"What—what does he look like?"

"Well, he's a little pale, but that's natural, I guess."

"No, I mean—what does he *look* like?"

Now I understood. "He's about six feet tall. Lean cheeks. A five o'clock shadow."

"Yes, yes, that's Harry," Rachel Sutter said. "You actually can see him, Richard. I told you I could feel him. I knew he wouldn't have left me, like everyone said."

"No, he didn't leave you. He was murdered."

"By Heinrich."

"By Heinrich."

"To think I was beginning to like him—"

The clatter of breaking china interrupted our conversation. Heinrich had dashed a plate against the floor. Fury narrowed his eyes into pale slits. Some say character is what you do in the dark, but that's not right. Character is what you do when you're really pissed off. We were about to learn exactly how pissed off Heinrich was.

112

"Who is responsible for this sabotage?"

No one was crazy enough to say a word. "Mr. Racciope! What did you do to my plates?"

"Nothing, Chef. That is, me and Richie put the veggies on them like we're supposed to. Isn't that right, Richie?"

"If I wanted Mr. Franklin's opinion, I would have asked for it. I wish to hear what you have to say."

"I don't have to say anything. I mean, I don't have anything to say, Chef. Do I look stupid enough to get myself fired for no good reason?"

"Yes, you do look that stupid. Mr. Franklin!"

I poked my head into the pass-through. "Yes, Chef?"

"You seem nervous, Mr. Franklin."

"I am nervous, Chef. There's been mischief tonight, and I figure someone's going to pay."

"You are correct, Mr. Franklin. Someone is going to pay. The question is whether it will be you."

"Not me, Chef. Ask Joe. We were together."

"I have taken that under consideration. It occurs to me the two of you were working in concert. Mr. Moses!"

Fred went around the broiler to the *garde-manger* station, dug a fist into the crushed ice, and rubbed his head with it, allowing a slurry of meltwater to dribble down his neck. He was obviously a man controlling himself, but only barely.

"What do you want, Chef Heinrich?"

"Mr. Moses, I can imagine several methods by which someone could introduce foreign substances into my sauces. But I cannot think of any way to sabotage the temperature of a piece of meat. Which implies the meats were cooked incorrectly. You either did this deliberately, or you did it by accident, in which case you are even more incompetent than I assumed."

Heinrich began this observation in a conversational tone but as he continued speaking, his voice rose until it boomed across the kitchen.

"You saying I don't know my business, Chef Heinrich?"

"Finally you begin to understand, Mr. Moses."

"I understand all right, Chef. You're the one who don't understand I've forgotten more about my business than you'll ever know."

"Forgotten is correct, Mr. Moses. But perhaps I expected too much of you."

"What do you mean, Chef?" Fred was still rubbing his head with ice. Moisture beaded his forehead and skull. Even so a vein was throbbing above his left eye.

"Just that I made allowances in consideration of your background, Mr. Moses."

"You mean because I'm a Black man? That's what you're saying, ain't it? I should have figured. You German folk never care much for people of color."

"Think what you wish. I have no use for what you think. In any case, I am Austrian."

"Well, that's what I am thinking, and I'm also thinking you should fuck yourself, Chef Heinrich."

The next I knew Heinrich and Fred were locked together. First Heinrich was on top, and then Fred Moses. As they fought, the dining room door opened, and a dozen people came into the kitchen: people I recognized. Felix Vargas. Sturgeon Wilson. Mimi Haverhill. Others equally influential.

"No, please," Rachel Sutter was saying. "Chef Heinrich's in no position to talk. He simply wanted me to convey his apologies for your—your unusual dining experience."

No one was listening. They were all gazing at Heinrich and Fred Moses. Rachel Sutter sighed theatrically. In a conspiratorial voice she said:

"I warned you Heinrich was engaged. It's just too sad. The poor man, well, he's getting on, but he absolutely insisted on working the *saucier* station. Only his—technique isn't what it used to be. You understand. He's always had a terrible temper, comes from being a true artist, I suppose. Promise me you won't print any of this?"

Harry was sitting beside the garnishes. We watched Heinrich and Fred go at it until security guards separated them. Then Harry said:

"Tell him, Rich. Tell Heinrich I'm here."

I understood. What's the point of getting your revenge if the person you're paying back doesn't realize you're behind all the bad

114

things that have happened?

Well, I didn't want to have anything to do with Chef Heinrich, and it was a terrible time to approach him—the guard had his wrists cuffed and was steering him to the kitchen door—but I didn't think there would be a better time, either.

"Alberto," I said, "give me a second with Chef Heinrich?"

"I don't know, Rich. The chef here, he's not feeling so good." Alberto rolled his eyes.

Heinrich's immaculate white jacket was soiled, and the pocket with his name embroidered on it was hanging loose by a seam. I felt uncomfortable looking at him because I was looking at a man who had lost everything, and who knew it, too.

"Chef Heinrich," I said.

"What is it, Mr. Franklin?"

"Harry says hello."

"I do not know any Harry."

"Sure you do. Harry Cohen."

"Harry Cohen? Harry Cohen is—" Heinrich failed to complete the statement.

"We all know what Harry Cohen is," I went on. "But he came back, Chef Heinrich. He came back to let you know what he thought of you. Do you understand?"

"Yes … yes, I do. I would appreciate your conveying a message to Harry."

"No trouble, Chef. He's closer than you think."

Harry was at my side. "I want you to tell Harry," Heinrich began, his head twitching—"I want you to tell Harry—"now there was froth in the corners of Heinrich's mouth—"I want you to tell him, Mr. Franklin—"and his face seemed to swell from the pressure of emotion—"Tell Harry for me—"Heinrich wrenched against the cuffs, and Alberto shot me an *I told you so* look before herding Heinrich along the corridor—"Tell him—"

"Tell him what, Chef?"

"Tell Harry he tasted like dog food. Tell him he tasted like Spam. Tell him he tasted like shit. Tell him he was—"

Alberto shut the door and whatever else Heinrich had to say was cut off in mid-sentence.

I was tired. I walked to the dry-goods storeroom and sat on

115

the cement floor. I took off my *toque* and looked at Harry. No longer caring if anyone heard us, I said:

"Heinrich's screwed. Even if the story doesn't make the magazines, everyone will hear what happened. Was your revenge all you expected?"

"It tasted damn good."

"Yet still you don't look happy."

"Yeah, well, maybe I wasn't hanging around just to get back at Heinrich. Maybe I was sticking around because of Rachel. The thought of moving on and never seeing her again, it makes me feel strange. Particularly with her not knowing the truth."

"She knows, Harry. I told her. I owed her an explanation."

"What did she say?"

"She said it made a difference you just didn't leave her for no reason."

"Good. She's a fine woman."

"Exactly who is a fine woman, Harry Cohen?"

Our expressions of surprise must have been identical. Rachel Sutter was staring at Harry as if she could see him. "You see Harry?" I asked.

"You see me?" Harry asked.

Her laugh was a marvelous contralto. "Well, I couldn't, not until Richard told me you were here. And even then, I could only make you out dimly. But the closer I get to you, the clearer you are. I must admit you're looking all right for a dead man. I've missed you, Harry."

"I was always here. I couldn't bring myself to move on. I hated the idea of never speaking with you again."

"Knowing Harry Cohen, speaking with me isn't what you hated doing without."

Harry became even paler. Rachel Sutter grasped his hand. "I can touch you, too," she said. "I can feel you, Harry. You're not cold. You're warm."

Harry may have been warm, but I was freezing. The temperature in the corridor had dropped twenty degrees. Harry was doing his match trick again.

"Your hand, Harry," Rachel Sutter continued. "It's so firm— so hard. It's as if you're really here."

116

"I am here, Rachel. For a while longer." Harry stepped closer to her. "It's been so many years," he said.

Despite the chill, my ears were burning. "Maybe I'd better leave you two alone," I said. They both exclaimed:

"No!"

I understood what they meant, particularly since Harry was ushering Rachel Sutter into the storeroom, and I didn't think they needed dry goods. "One last favor, Rich," Harry said. "Stay where you are. Don't let anyone inside. Rachel and I have some catching up to do."

I could hear her giggling. "That's a good boy, Richard," she called.

The door closed, leaving me alone in the corridor. Until Harry poked his head through and said:

"Don't forget, Rich. The Tinkerbell thing. Believe."

"OK, Harry, I will."

Then I was alone again. Soon I felt a pleasant vibration through the door against my back.

Rachel Sutter was believing, too.

David Wesley Hill has had more than forty stories published in the U.S. and internationally. In 1997 he received the Golden Bridge award at the International Conference on Science Fiction in Beijing, and in 1999 he placed second in the *Writers of the Future* contest. In 2007, 2009, and 2011 Mr. Hill was awarded residencies at Blue Mountain Center, a writers' and artists' retreat. He studied under Jack Cady and Joseph Heller at the City University of New York. Currently, Mr. Hill lives in rural North Carolina.

To read more of Mr. Hill's work, check out *At Drake's Command*, a swashbuckling sea adventure, and *Castaway on Temurlone*, a mind-blowing SF space opera, both available on Amazon.

Sideshow Saturday Night

By Edward Lodi

Welcome, freakish folks, to Sideshow Saturday Night!

Thank you for coming. As you know, we're open from midnight to four a.m., one day a week, Saturdays only, unless the moon is full. On nights of the full moon, we present a special performance featuring all of your favorite "ghoulies and ghosties and long-legged beasties and things that go bump in the night."

Which is not to say, fiendish friends, that tonight's performance will not be special in its own rite. That's r-i-t-e.

As the Venus Fly Trap said to the fly, stick around.

Is this your first visit? How did you find out about us? Word of mouth? That's how most folks hear of us. We're not in any of the directories, you know—not included on any itineraries. And no, you won't find us on the Dark Web. Only a select few are ever admitted to our facilities. Consider yourselves privileged. Or not, depending on the outcome of your visit.

Before we get started, be sure to fill out your ticket stub so you'll be entered into tonight's lottery. The drawing will take place shortly before the tent show gets underway. Lucky folks whose names are drawn will be invited to participate. I see that you've all signed your waivers, releasing Sideshow Saturday Night of all responsibility for loss of life or limb. The term "limb" encompasses all body parts, but of course you know that, having read the small print.

We'll begin our tour with a visit to the tombs. Oh, it's not what you think, not what the name implies. Well, not exactly. But come. Follow me. You'll see for yourselves.

Here we are at the entrance. Watch your step. No, there's been no malfunction of the electrical system. This stairwell is always kept dark. Might disturb the exhibits otherwise. We try to keep the sideshow environment as similar as possible to the natural (or, more accurately, supernatural) habitat. Most of our exhibits are nocturnal creatures, hence the unusual hours.

Careful! It's a long way down. Yes, the stairs are steep. And slippery—the result of natural moisture which seeps through the stone. We did think of installing an elevator once, but decided against it. Somehow a modern conveyance wouldn't seem appropriate—would mar the ambiance, if you know what I mean. So far we've had only two serious accidents, and only one of those a fatality. Tragic? Depends on your point of view. The body wasn't wasted. Our resident ghoul made quite a meal of it. You know, it's not easy providing her (yes, it's a she-ghoul) with fresh corpses.

Just another few steps and we'll be there.

Ah, here we are. Just grope your way forward. Have your eyes adjusted to the darkness? Yes, there is a source of light, faint but perceptible. A natural luminescence. Incidentally, these cells were carved out of solid rock. If by some mischance you're left behind after the doors are locked ... well, that's happened only once, to a young man in his twenties. We found him the next day, stark raving mad. This place does have that effect on some folks.

What's that? What became of the poor wretch? Do you really want to know? Exactly what we did with him ... some things are best left unsaid. Just keep in mind that we're a green facility. Nothing goes to waste.

I must ask you to please not touch the bars. If you'll just stand back a bit, you'll be able to see into the cage without difficulty. As the sign indicates, this is our resident werewolf. He's quite used to being on display, so there's no need to be concerned about disturbing him. He does have a fear of clowns, I'll admit. That's not an uncommon phobia, at least that's what I'm told. By the way, any clowns in the audience? You sir? No? Oh, I see, your feet are just naturally big. And your bulbous red nose? From excessive drinking?

What's that, ma'am? Yes, the werewolf's cage is a mess. The full moon approaches, you know. Our staff dare not enter until after the phase has ended. We do hose the cage down—although the poor creature absolutely detests water—but the stench persists. Of course, if one of you would care to volunteer … No? I didn't think so.

What's that? Yes, his fur is matted. Rolls in his own excrement when the fit is upon him. Otherwise he's quite a decent fellow, especially when the moon is down. We'd like to mate him but have so far been unable to locate an appropriate female. We keep trying, though. Did I hear a giggle? Any volunteers? You, miss? No? Then, if you'll kindly move on to the next cage.

Here we have our zombies, Zack and Mabel. No, I don't recall who first named them. Mabel might have been her name in life, but I'm sure Zack was chosen for its alliteration. They can't speak, you know. They spend much of their time in a semi-comatose state. There's quite a rigmarole involved in re-animating them, otherwise I'd do it for you. Right now, we don't have time. Though I have to admit, when they're awake and mating it's quite a spectacle to behold.

A question frequently asked is: do they have any offspring? The answer is, unfortunately, no. Or perhaps that's a good thing. I don't think they'd make very good parents. There's rumor, though I don't know how true it is, that zombies eat their young.

Yes, they do drool a lot. Rather uncouth. But that's no way to talk about the living dead, I suppose. *Nil nisi bonum*—of the dead, speak nothing but good—is our motto here.

Now, you'll notice that the next cage is entirely encased in glass. Vampire, you know—shape shifter, might otherwise escape. Oh, he's a mean one all right! Would love to sink his fangs into your pretty little neck, miss. But there's no cause for alarm. He's been completely immobilized. Garlic, and all that.

How do we feed him? Well, that's another question most visitors ask. Do you really want to know? No, I didn't think so. I will tell you this much: he has a fondness for blood pudding.

Did someone ask another question? Sir, could you speak louder. How do we capture our exhibits? Hmm … I'm not sure I'm allowed to reveal professional secrets to a lay person. Oh, what the heck, why not. I can't see any harm in telling you.

121

Mostly we use live bait.

So, if you're looking for something novel to do, why not volunteer? There are risks involved of course. But I can truthfully say we have a high survival rate. And if you do survive, what a tale to tell your grand kids!

The next cage is empty. Normally it would contain our mummy but it—*she*, actually—is currently on loan to a museum. There's an interesting story, true I assure you, as to how we acquired her. You'll never guess where. Not Egypt. And no, we didn't burglarize a museum.

Give up?

We bought her in an antique shop in Maine. That's right, the state of Maine in the good old United States of America. What was she doing there? I'll tell you. Back in the nineteenth century Maine was noted for its paper mills. Most paper was manufactured from tree pulp or old cloth. But another source of material, and this is absolutely true, was ancient mummies from Egypt. Thousands—tens of thousands—of mummies found their way into Maine for the purpose of making paper. Any book collectors here? Some of those ancient tomes in your library may well be made from the mummified bodies of folks who lived thousands of years ago. Perhaps your own ancestors.

Fortunately, our mummy escaped that fate and ended up on display in an antique shop in Wiscasset. Did you know that the Egyptians also mummified animals, especially cats? We're looking for a mummified kitty as a pet for our lady mummy. Even the dead get lonely, you know.

No, sir, we're not seeking a mate for her. Why, are you volunteering? Oh, I see, just curious. Well, to tell you the truth, certain anatomical features were lost during the mummification process. I don't believe any, uh, anatomically correct mummies exist. If you know of any, please let us know. We'd be more than happy to reward you with a finder's fee.

Does anyone need a restroom break? For your convenience, we have an old-fashioned two-seater outhouse. You'll find it through that entrance to the cave on your left. We're not barbarians here— although there are some who think otherwise—so of course we provide toilet paper. And I can assure you, despite its roughness, it

122

was not manufactured from mummies.

Full disclosure: last year we inadvertently bought bathroom tissue from an unscrupulous manufacturer who used poison ivy as one of the materials. Oh, I can tell you, that caused quite an uproar!

Before we move on to our next exhibit, I want to pass out complimentary ear plugs. Be sure to take a pair. Chances are you'll need them. No, ma'am, don't insert them yet. I'll tell you when. All set? Then off we go to the banshee.

As many of you are no doubt aware, a banshee is a female creature, a hag really, known through Celtic folklore as a harbinger of a death. When someone in a particular family is about to die, the banshee appears at night, wailing. "Shrieking" I suppose is a more accurate term. Caterwauling. The shrieks can be deafening, hence the ear plugs—just in case. Incidentally, banshees are family-specific. Not all families have them, which I suppose is a good thing. But of course, we're all family here, right?

Here she is. Get a load of that hair! Loathsome, isn't she? You wouldn't want Junior to bring this damsel home to meet the folks. Oh, dear, I know that look. She's about to begin her shrieking. Quickly, insert your earplugs. As with oxygen masks in aircraft, attach your own before assisting others.

There she goes! Even with ear plugs it's deafening.

Ah, out of range. YOU MAY REMOVE YOUR EARPLUGS NOW.

Did someone raise their hand? Yes, sir, I'm afraid—if you believe the folklore—someone within this group is about to die. But don't worry. There's safety in numbers. The odds are it won't be you.

Anyone hungry? We've set up a snack bar in the next catacomb. You, sir, with the bulbous nose? No, I'm afraid alcoholic beverages are not available. We tried serving them once, but things soon got out of hand. We can't have folks making fun of our resident creatures and rattling their cages. Just because they're the living dead doesn't mean they don't have feelings.

Okay, folks, now that you've had your snacks let's move on to our latest acquisition: Big Foot. You sir, with the bulbous

123

proboscis! Your size sixteen shoes are no match for this fellow's.

Oops! That gong is the signal that our tent show will begin in fifteen minutes. I'm afraid that's all the time we have for down here. We'll save the leprechaun for some other time. Perhaps it's for the best. He's been grumpy of late. Misses his pot of gold.

Before we leave, however, I want to ask: does anyone know where we might procure a mermaid? We'd very much like to add one to our collection. I assure you, we'd treat her well, and with respect. Feed her nothing but the best seafood. No? Well, I thought I'd ask. You never know who might be in the audience. An Ancient Mariner, perhaps.

Okay, if we hurry, we can make the first performance. Tonight, we're featuring human sacrifice as it was practiced by the pre-Columbian Aztecs. They were known to rip the hearts out of living victims and eat them raw.

Don't fret. There are always leftovers. Help yourselves. You'll be doing us a favor. We don't want to spoil the ghoul with too many treats. Remember, we encourage full audience participation, so please hurry. Careful on these stairs! Let's not spoil the fun for others by breaking a leg.

Ah, here we are, safe and sound. Do you recall the ticket stubs you filled out? You may be one of the lucky ones whose name is drawn. What's that? In what capacity would you serve during the ceremony? Now, that would be telling. Wouldn't you rather be surprised? But don't worry, we'll notify next of kin.

Edward Lodi has written more than 30 books, both fiction and nonfiction, including six *Cranberry Country Mysteries*. His short fiction and poetry have appeared in numerous magazines and journals, such as *Mystery Magazine*, and in anthologies published by Mystery and Horror LLC, Cemetery Dance, Murderous Ink, Main Street Rag, Rock Village Publishing, Superior Shores Press, and others. His story "Charnel House" was recently featured on *Night Terrors Podcast*.

The Miskatonic University Bible Study Club

David Bernard

When my wife and I moved to Arkham to assume pastoral duties at the First Arkham New Pentecostal Advent Evangelical Church of the Second Coming of Our Lord and Savior Jesus Christ, the first thing we did was look for ways to shorten the name of the church. It was tough to say in one breath, looked awkward on the stationery, and would bankrupt the little church if we ever needed new signs. There were so few congregants remaining that no one really raised a fuss when we decided to rename ourselves the Arkham Church of the Second Coming. My dear wife thought it sounded a tad apocalyptical. Still, being female, she deferred her opinions to mine as a righteous, God-fearing woman should.

I was sent to replace the most beloved Reverend Enoch Miller. Brother Enoch was a good and righteous man but always considered a tad high-strung. Attempting to tend to a flock in a hedonist college town like Arkham, combined with a small congregation and limited resources, had finally caused the poor man to crack. There was a tremendous scandal when he was caught swimming nude in Miskatonic University's Marine Biology aquatic research tank. I have been assured that although he professed his intent when dragged out of the tank, aquarium security cameras verify he could not swim well enough to actually catch the octopus in the tank, let alone achieve his goal of knowing the beast in a Biblical manner.

As the church's new leader, I assessed the state of our tiny congregation and found it nearly overwhelmed with problems: the flock was sparse, elderly, and impoverished. That equaled a high attrition rate and minimal tithing. And limited tithes meant my salary would not be covered by the congregation, let alone the roof repairs. Brother Enoch had apparently taken on a part-time job at the university, serving as the chaplain in an attempt to fund the roof repairs. Now, as I read his notes, it was quite apparent how much strain he had been under. His journal was a rambling litany of complaints. He claimed his Sunday services were being infiltrated by swarthy foreign strangers. He repeatedly claimed the college chapel was actually a pagan temple. The oddest statement was that something was watching him from an island in the river. The final entry was how nobody understood him except for Octavia, and he was going to visit her for advice. I made a mental note to see him at Sefton Asylum and check on his recovery.

Brother Enoch had assured the diocese that he had developed a plan to fund the repairs. The folder in his office marked "Roof Repairs" was filled with a sheet of paper with an eye surrounded by stars and fish, scribbled out in purple crayon. The poor man was worse than we thought.

With winter on the horizon, I needed a plan a little more detailed than purple fish. One look at the financial statements, and I knew I required either a miracle or an increase in congregants, preferably with deep pockets. The former happens at the will of Our Lord, but the latter was something I could address. The question was how to fill pews (and collection plates).

The Lord gave me a sign as I walked past the college. The Anthropology Department's Ancient Music Studies was having a bake sale in front of the main gate to help underwrite renovations to their atonal polyphonic harmonics laboratory. I had no idea what an atonal polyphonic harmonica was, but the devil's food cupcake was downright heavenly. And that's when it came to me: Miskatonic University surely must have a Religious Studies Department. I would approach them and offer to run an after-class Bible study club. The truly devout could learn from both the academic scholarship of Christianity and my faith-based fellowship. And, hopefully, drive a little traffic to the church.

The head of the Religious Studies Department was Father

Ignatius Whately. He was a gaunt man, almost cadaverous, whose clerical collar sat loosely on a throat the color of parchment. Most disquieting was the way he sat perfectly still. It was like talking to a statue. I quickly explained how I wanted to start a Bible club on campus to allow Christians to bond in a social setting.

Father Whately listened without comment. Then he did the one thing I didn't expect. First, he snorted and then leaned back and laughed. He kept laughing, on the verge of hysteria, with tears running down his face. Finally, someone tapped on the door and stepped in.

"Iggy? Are you all right?" The speaker was an elderly man, dressed like a professor from the 1940s, right down to the pince-nez and pocket watch.

Father Whately gasped for air and wiped the tears from his eyes.

"Reverend Fodder here wants to start a Bible club on campus." And then he burst into laughter again.

The old professor looked at me and started chuckling. "Reverend Fodder, let's take a walk before you kill Father Whately again."

I stood up, and the chortling priest waved goodbye and then clutched his stomach. As the door closed, I think I heard him fall out of his chair.

I followed the professor onto a manicured lawn with cobblestone paths leading off to other massive brick buildings. He stuck out his hand. "I'm Dr. Francis Morgan, by the way. Professor of medicine and comparative anatomy."

I shook his hand. "Brother Elah Fodder, pastor of the Arkham Church of the Second Coming."

He looked amused again. "Elah? Interesting. A family name?"

I nodded. "My father was Jesse and wanted to name me David. My mother pointed out there were already too many Davids in the family already, which might make me blend in with the crowd. This concept was an anathema to my father. So he decided to name me Elah instead. The valley of Elah is where David defeated Goliath."

Dr. Morgan nodded. "Fascinating. Of course, the valley was

127

named for the Elah trees, the Hebrew name for the terebinth trees that grew there."

I forced a smile. "I don't think I knew that. You know your Bible history quite well."

The old gent looked at me oddly, almost smiling. "Not really, but one picks up odd little facts when one enveloped in the esoteric culture of an old college."

I nodded, with an uneasy prickling on the back of my neck. The clock tower on the far side of the lawn chimed five o'clock. The chimes sounded flat and metallic, as if the bell had given up in despair. I shook my head to clear such nonsense. If I kept thinking that way, I'd end up sharing a padded cell with my predecessor.

"Dr. Morgan, I'm afraid I must depart. I have evening prayers, and I'd hate to be late." I didn't mention that the attendance hovered around five people, including my wife and me.

Morgan nodded. "Of course. I'll get Iggy to send you the forms to apply for a cultural enrichment program. The trustees will vote on the proposal, and then you can start."

"You sound fairly certain my proposal will be approved."

Morgan nodded. "Yes, the trustees are always looking for new blood."

I laughed. "You make the trustees sound like vampires!"

Morgan tilted his head. "No, I don't think there are any vampires on the board. At least not currently."

He walked me to the front entrance. I decided to avoid any further attempts at humor.

I stepped out onto the street and immediately felt like a weight had come off my shoulders. The campus, in retrospect, was damp and felt oppressive. I chided myself for such foolishness.

Morgan paused. "Brother Fodder, the word Elah also has a second meaning in Hebrew. Because the valley of Elah was the center of a tree-worshipping sect, it also came to mean 'a curse.'"

I stopped dead and turned around.

Morgan stood there with a wry smile. "I point that out because there are departments at Miskatonic who take their etymology and polysemy quite seriously. You may want to expect that sort of discussion to pop up once in a while."

I nodded, hoping it wasn't obvious I had no idea what he was

128

talking about, and proceed down the sidewalk. By the time I arrived at the church, I had cleared my head of the gloom but had serious second thoughts about a Bible club on campus.

The paperwork arrived in a few days. I saw nothing unusual and signed it. I carried it back to Miskatonic myself. At the risk of sounding unchristian, the receptionist was an ancient woman doused in rosewater and wearing far too much gold jewelry. She pressed a button on a console. A door opened, and a rather grim-looking man limped out with a silver-headed cane.

He glanced at me in what I felt was a rather disdainful way. "Reverend Fodder. I'm Kilwar Peters, Dean of Students. I'll be giving you a quick tour of the campus and expedite your ID badge." I got the impression I didn't need to return any niceties since he had already limped past me and out into the quad.

"Dean Peters," I said, "would it be easier to reschedule when someone without a leg injury could do all the walking?"

He paused and looked puzzled for a moment. "Ah, the limp. No, it's an old hunting injury. It comes and goes, depending on the lunar cycle."

I was about to ask what that meant when I noticed his cane had an elaborate wolf's head in silver for a handle. Considering the cane looked as snarly as the dean did, I decided to let the comment go.

The tour was fascinating. The campus was much larger than I thought. Each building had a security lock that needed the Dean's ID badge to open. I remarked about how safe the campus must be.

"Well, it's not a matter of making it safe as much as controlling access. Your badge, as an example, will let you into the library's Comparative Religion collection so you can review any texts you'd like to see. But it won't let you into the Special Collections room where the rarest books are stored. In fact, even I don't have access to that room."

I was surprised. "What book could be so valuable that even a dean can't access it?"

He smiled. It was obviously something he was not used to doing. "Let me rephrase that. I can get access to the books, just as you could. We just can't stroll in on a whim. We have to clear it with the head librarian and have a damned good reason to want in. Trust me, Henry guards the access to that collection like the keys to the Apocalypse are in there."

We walked past a stately old observatory and came to an exotic-looking little brick building, covered in wrought-iron filigree and geometric designs. The windows were boarded up, and there was apparent fire damage.

Peters saw me looking at it. "That's the Wilmarth Memorial Interdenominational Chapel. It was arson, but I'm told it's mostly cosmetic damage." He paused and looked at me. "They never caught the arsonist, but the primary suspect was your predecessor. The fire was the night of Reverend Miller's little dip in the octopus tank."

Having read his opinion of the chapel in Enoch Miller's journal, I couldn't really defend him. Finally, I carefully stated, "I really never met Brother Enoch, but his case seems a little sad." I looked at the little building. "A chapel would not have been my first guess. The symbols almost looked Arabic."

Peters nodded. "They are apparently ornamental. Miskatonic's ancient linguistics department is considered one of the best in the nation. They say it resembles no known language on Earth. Of course, Professor Wilmarth left the bequest in his will with precise design criteria. I'm sure if he hadn't disappeared, he would have explained the motif."

He glanced at the building. "As an aside, the chapel was a popular student destination. You may find you are considered guilty by association once the campus learns you're the pastor of the same church as Rev. Miller."

He gestured to a squat gray building with his cane. "That's campus security. Let's get your ID badge. Then we'll head back to Academy Hall and get you a room assignment."

As we walked, I glanced back at the building. "Dean Peters, I must confess, my impression of the campus so far is that it is not a deeply religious institution. The chapel's popularity seems to suggest I was wrong."

The dean gestured into the security building. "After you, Reverend. And I never said they were using the chapel for religious service."

I was going to ask him to qualify the remark but was immediately confronted by a large man barely contained in a

130

security uniform. Dean Peters made introductions while I stayed a safe distance apart. He was definitely someone I would not want to cross, between his barrel chest and massive hairy arms. He looked at me. It may be unfair, but his face seemed almost ape-like. His hair was so light that if his suspicious eyes were pink, I'd have called him an albino.

He nodded and went over to a desk and pulled out a camera. I stood very still as this white gorilla took my picture. He attached the camera to a computer and carefully typed on a keyboard that looked like a child's toy beneath his meaty fists.

A few moments later, with my new ID in hand, we departed the building. "I don't believe your security guard actually spoke to me," I said as we walked away.

The dean shrugged. "Chief Jermyn is actually rather chatty, but he's the one that had to jump in the tank to rescue Rev. Miller from the octopus."

I paused. "Don't you mean he had to rescue the octopus from Brother Miller?"

The dean stopped and looked at me. "Perhaps one more tour stop is in order." He headed off in another direction. We passed a copse of trees and paused in front of a building with a series of glass domes connected by odd structures with rounded corners and undulating rooflines. The effect was rather attractive, almost looking like it should be underwater. I knew this was the Marine Biology Center.

The dean allowed me to swipe the keypad, and we entered the complex. I was immediately assaulted by the smell of rotting vegetation and fish. I was not alone. The dean was also blinking his eyes and wrinkling his nose. He saw me looking. "It takes a moment to adjust."

We walked down a corridor. "With all due respect, this building smells like a swamp." I think my eyes were watering.

"That's because we specialize in tidal pool ecosystems."

We both turned to face a man wearing goggles and waders.

The dean walked over. "Professor Marsh, I am glad you're here. This is Reverend Elah Fodder. He's going to running a student extracurricular program." He hesitated and then quickly said, "He's the replacement for Enoch Miller at the Church of the Second

131

Coming."

Professor Marsh pulled his goggles off. "Oh really?"

The dean looked a little uneasy. "Reverend Fodder is unfamiliar with all the details of the 'incident' but seems to think Chief Jermyn had to save the Octavia from Reverend Miller."

The professor smiled in a way I imagine a shark smiles right before he lunges at a surfer. "Really? Then allow me to elucidate."

We stepped into a room with a giant tank. The professor led us up to the glass wall. "Allow me to introduce you to our *Enteroctopus dofleini*, the Giant Pacific Octopus. The students, with remarkable lack of imagination, call her Octavia."

I thought octopuses were shy, but this just sat there. I swear it was glaring at me. It was a massive beast, with arms stretching out 20 feet in each direction. It suddenly turned bright blue.

Professor Marsh looked at the monster. "She doesn't like you. Blue is a warning."

I stepped back as Marsh continued. "Our South Pacific expedition caught this specimen. She's the largest Giant Pacific octopus ever recorded."

I met eyes with the creature. It may have been one of God's creatures, but I'd be happier if the Good Lord and the university had left it in the ocean. It changed color again to a pinkish lavender, and the skin changed texture and looked almost rocky.

Marsh looked at his octopus, and I think he may have turned pale. "Well," he said quickly, "that's the end of the tour. We're disturbing Octavia. Let's head out into the corridor."

Marsh looked back as the door closed. "As you can see, the octopus was never in any danger from Reverend Miller. Your friend, on the other hand, was in more danger than he could have realized. The female Giant Pacific Octopus is a notorious sexual cannibal. If she's not in the mood or finds a male unsuitable, she'll strangle him and then eat him. Had the Reverend gotten any closer, he'd either be drowned or be lunch."

We left soon after that. As oppressive as the campus atmosphere was, it was a marked improvement over the marine lab. As we neared Academy Hall, we took a side path and came upon a shining glass building. The structure was wildly misshapen, looking more like a giant crystal than a building.

The dean let me look at the building before announcing, "Welcome to Dexter's Trap."

I looked at him. He gestured at the building. The funds for the construction were donated by a former professor who became a significant figure in the Manhattan Project.

The building bothered me. "Why is it a trap?"

The dean smiled and resumed walking. "Dr. Dexter was a bit of a maverick, and he wanted a classroom building shaped like a trapezohedron. Twenty-four equal faces, each a four-sided figure. I understand the architect still has nightmares from designing it."

I looked at it again. "Why?"

The dean shrugged. "When a request comes with an endowment as generous as the one Dr. Dexter's estate left the college, the trustees tend to overlook questions of motivation." We stepped into the lobby. I suddenly felt like I had stepped into the furnace right out of the Book of Daniel.

The dean must have seen my face. "Yes. The design traps the heat like a greenhouse, even with tinted windows and blinds. And it's impossible to cool. We only use it for afternoon and night classes." We went through a glass door into a stairwell and up a flight of stairs into a glass corridor.

"Here we are, room 216. This will be your meeting room." I looked around. The view out the window was quite scenic, overlooking the quad. The wall facing the corridor was glass, and the door was almost camouflaged. I would never admit it to Dean Peters, but the lack of privacy concerned me. The transparent wall meant some students might be uncomfortable with group prayers. I would have to think about how best to approach the matter.

A week later, posters had been placed on bulletin boards. I had decided to go low-key and focus on the faith-based fellowship aspect. The first meeting would be a silent prayer, introductions, and discussions on which version of the Bible we would work with. Naturally, I preferred the Evangelical Heritage Version, but I decided to suggest the King James Version as a little more nondenominational. I was being cautious. I wanted to avoid being accused of proselytizing. Based on the current estimates for the roof repairs at the church, that would be tricky.

I walked into room 216 to find fifteen students. I was

133

impressed. The first meeting of a new club usually didn't have a respectable turnout.

We all introduced ourselves. As we went around the circle, I noticed that the students were all wearing some sort of lapel pin or brooch that looked like a five-pointed star, with a flaming eye in the center. I had a bad feeling it was not a fraternity pin.

Annie Waite seemed to be the ringleader. A small girl dressed all in black. I suspect she'd be reasonably attractive under all the black eye shadow and lipstick, allowing for her overly protuberant eyes. I made my first mistake and asked if there were any questions.

Miss Waite raised he hand. She was wearing black nail polish, of course. "You do realize this room number is the cube root of six. Six cubed is 6 times 6 times 6. 666. I assume you recognize that number."

It went downhill from there. I had hoped for a casual first meeting, but Miss Waite debated me on every point from which version of the Bible we'd use to when the meetings would take place.

I did my best, but I was unprepared to play defense. Miss Waite objected to the KJV because it was "selectively edited by white guys to support Anglican doctrine." I countered her suggested version, noting that the Today's New International Version was so controversially liberal-biased that the publisher discontinued publication. When she launched into the deuterocanonical books, I knew I had lost the club.

"Miss Waite, I think you've moved from exegesis to eisegesis. Let's discuss it after the meeting rather than bore the rest of the club."

I looked at the time. It was already time to wrap up the meeting. The entire time had been consumed arguing with five feet of Goth attitude in fishnet stockings and army boots. She had won this round.

I ended the meeting, and as the others filed out, they all patted her on the shoulder or whispered in her ear. She sat there, looking smug. I sat across from her.

"Miss Waite, your biblical history is quite impressive. Are you a theology major?"

She snorted. "As if I would demean myself. I am a legacy student in medieval metaphysics."

I paused. "That's a major?"

She smiled. "As my dear mother used to say, Miskatonic University's strength is its diverse curriculum." She stood up. "The last thing MU needs is some presumptuous evangelical ass trying to introduce a false religion onto the campus."

I remained seated, trying to maintain my composure. "Well then, we appear to have reached an impasse. I assume you won't be attending the next meeting?"

She smiled. "There won't be a 'next meeting.'"

Before I could say anything, she grabbed the neck of her blouse and ripped it open, then grabbed the strap of her black bra and tore it off. Then she looked at me again and screamed, "No! Stop that, Pastor Fodder!" and then ran out into the hall screaming and sobbing.

I stood up and ran after her. Unfortunately, I forgot about the glass door until I crashed through. I fell to the ground. The carpet was wet. I realized it was blood just before I passed out.

I woke up to a steady beeping noise and the overwhelming stench of disinfectant. I opened my eyes. I was in a hospital room, surrounded by multiple IV bags and enough monitoring equipment for a small army. I tried to sit up and was rewarded with searing pain in too many places to count.

"I wouldn't try to move quite yet." I looked over to see Dr. Morgan sitting in the corner. "You're in the West Memorial Wing of the Miskatonic University Hospital."

I tried to talk, but my throat refused to cooperate.

"I wouldn't try to talk yet, either. Your throat will be raw for a few days from the intubation. And you do not want to start coughing."

He walked over and checked the monitors. "We almost lost you. You severed your femoral artery going through that glass door. Fortunately, Miskatonic has a teaching hospital on campus, so they were able to clamp it off before you bled to death."

He looked at the monitor. "You need to relax. Your blood pressure is skyrocketing. You'll be fine. Fortunately, the femoral vein and nerve on either side of it were uninjured. We replaced the artery with a piece from further down your leg, so you'll have a couple of impressive scars. You had several deep-level lacerations and a lot of surface cuts. You probably don't want to look in a mirror for a while."

I pointed to the IVs.

"That one drip is a standard antibiotic array. The other is another transfusion. You lost a lot of blood, and your blood type is AB-negative. That's quite rare and almost impossible to find in quantities at small teaching hospitals like this. Fortunately, the anthropology department's serology lab over at the main building had a supply. I'm afraid we've set their research back a few weeks."

"What?" I croaked and regretted the attempt, but I really didn't know what was going on. Morgan apparently took that as an encouragement to keep rambling.

"Yes, Dr. Olmstead is studying the biological anthropology of hematological clustering. He's funding a free clinic at the mouth of the Manuxet River as an excuse to collect blood samples. Many of the locals are descendants of an abandoned town called Innsmouth, and all have an odd chromosomal aberration. And for some reason, they all have AB-negative blood as well."

He looked at the monitor again. "Reverend Fodder, your blood pressure is still too high. I need to bring it down since you won't relax." He pulled a syringe out of a coat pocket and injected it into my IV. Things got blurry, and then everything was gone.

A week later, Dr. Morgan decided I could go home to convalesce. I had been allowed a mirror, and I indeed looked like someone who had gone through a glass door. He assured me that other than the scars on my leg, there would be no permanent scars. I was not as convinced. There were a matching pair of angry red lines on either side of my neck that seemed to be increasingly itchy.

A new doctor walked in with Dr. Morgan. "Reverence Fodder, this is Dr. Robert Olmstead. You cleaned out his supply of AB-negative blood, so I thought I'd show him where it all went." Dr. Olmstead was a thin, stoop-shouldered man, not much under six feet tall. He had a narrow head, bulging, watery blue eyes that seemed never to wink, a flat nose, and a receding forehead.

136

He walked over and twisted his mouth into what I assume was some sort of an attempt at a reassuring smile. The result was neither. "Well, I hope that plasma did the trick."

His voice was deep and hoarse. He checked my vitals and listened to my lungs. "Well, Francis," he croaked. "I agree it's time to send this good cleric back to his flock. He traced the scar on my neck with an unusually large hand. "These scars appear inflamed. I'd suggest a calcineurin inhibitor and sodium chloride tablets."

Morgan nodded. "I assume you're thinking innsmouthian fibrinogenic syndrome?"

Olmstead nodded and turned to me. "The salve will help with the itching. The salt tablets are because that serum coursing through your veins was for diagnostic purposes in my tests. It appears to cause stenohalinic side effects in lab tests. The salt will slightly elevate the salinity of your blood, which will be more comfortable until your body starts making its own blood to replace mine."

I nodded, with no idea what he was talking about, but if it would get me out of the hospital, I'd agree with anything.

Olmstead nodded and turned to leave. As he left, I noticed a weird coincidence: he had odd, deep creases in the sides of his neck near the same spot as the itchy scars on mine.

I got dressed to be discharged, my dear wife bringing new clothes to replace the bloody shreds of what I had been I had been wearing. I went home with a collection of pills, salves, and a disturbingly thick stack of paper.

Several days later, Dr. Morgan stopped by to check on me with a lawyer. Attorney Jenkins was a nasty little man with tiny rodent-like eyes that darted about the room. He made me an offer. First, Miss Waite had dropped her claims of attempted assault. She didn't realize that the classrooms in Dexter's Trap had security cameras. The college would cover my medical expenses and provide a substantial payment for my discomfort and the false accusations. The only condition was that I didn't file a report with any authorities about the accident—no police, insurance, or governmental agency.

Considering the accident was my own stupidity, I was more than happy to agree and signed a non-disclosure act. As the lawyer folded the document and tucked it in a battered brown briefcase, he tried to smile. Even his teeth reminded me of a rodent. He explained that Miskatonic University liked to take care of matters like this quietly and without outsiders.

When I saw the amount he offered, I almost went back to the hospital as a cardiac patient—it was more money than I had imagined. The good Lord himself must have pushed me through that glass door, because the payment would cover the new roof and pay my salary for years. And we could open a downtown outreach center as well. At Dr. Morgan's suggestion, we put the Bible club on hiatus.

It's odd, but ever since the accident, I've been having this recurring dream. I'm walking down the oddly shaped corridors of the Marine Biology building. I turn a corner and realize the campus is underwater, and I am swimming down the hallway. I pass a door, and I'm in the ocean, looking at a vast underwater kingdom, all centered on an oddly shaped castle made of coral. The closer I get to the entrance, the further away it appears. I stop to ask directions from a giant frog swimming by, and then wake up screaming when I realize that I was looking at a mirror.

My dear wife and I have decided it is time to end the Bible club at Miskatonic while it's still on hiatus. I have not been sleeping well since the accident. This is probably due to the added workload of supervising the roof repairs and the outreach program. And the scars on my neck are distractingly itchy most of the time, salve or not.

But before I hand in my ID badge, I think I want to have a little chat with that sexy octopus in the Marine Biology department ...

David Bernard is a native New Englander who now lives (albeit under protest) in South Florida, a paradoxical place where, when temperatures drop below 60°, locals break out parkas to wear over their plaid shorts and sandals. He also doesn't understand why they call it "snowbird season" if you're not allowed to shoot them.

His work regularly appears in *Pulp Adventures* magazine. He can be found in such anthologies as *Alternative Apocalypses* (B Cubed Press), *Legacy of the Reanimator* (Chaosium), and *The Chromatic Court* (18th Wall Productions)

O Unholy Night: The Advent of the Guytrash

By Nancy Pica Renken

I. Unholy Night

Christmas Eve fell like a shroud over a most unholy night in Midwestern America. The neighbors had been living their best lives in their cookie-cutter-style houses, in their idyllic subdivision, under the watchful eyes of their diligent HOA. The assembled neighbors, those dwellers of abodes painted in regulation colors, of tasteful taupe and considerate cream, found themselves in a bit of a bind. Gathered in the community cul-de-sac, they whispered among themselves with frosty breath, and tingling toes. Some huffed and shuffled about in the frigid temps, but none could ignore the obvious. An overpowering odor permeated from Doc Potter's house.

Doc Potter was the slick-haired snooty college professor who, along with his wife, never smiled, waved, or acknowledged their neighbors. Mrs. Potter sported short skirts, long designer jackets, and lots of bling. Rarely seen, their pained expressions, when they did emerge, suggested the neighborhood smelled foul to them. Each evening, the adjacent neighbors would hear the staccato of Mrs. Potter's stilettos clicking as she stepped from her immaculate silver foreign car to her front door, as though those heels were passing judgment on those very neighbors. Then one day, months ago, Doc Potter's wife left. Some whispered that she left him. They didn't think she'd be back. It had caused quite a stir, and now, this ...

It was just after 8 p.m., and the neighborhood carolers, decked out in their finest Christmassy Dickensian attire, hemmed and hawed, shuffling their feet, and waited for someone else to take action. When that paragon failed to materialize, murmuring began:

"Should we knock?"

"No, let's just ignore it."

"Ignore it? How the hell do you ignore that? It's making me sick."

"For God's sake, Herbert, watch your language!"

"Sorry, dear. Still, we can't ignore that. It won't go away if we ignore it."

"What's to be done, Doug?"

"Me? Why am I suddenly in charge?"

"Well, you live next to Potter—"

"That doesn't make me an expert on him or the stench."

"Fine, but we must address this."

"Maybe you should, and get back to the rest of us."

"I'm not going alone."

"Okay, Bob and I will go with you."

"Me? Why am I being recruited?"

"Bob, are you saying you won't go with us?"

"That's not … what I said. It's just ... Well, just … 'Tis the season to be…."

"What, exactly? Unkind? Uncharitable? A Grinch?"

"No, neighborly."

"Fine. I'll go. But, what should we say? We go over there, we ring the doorbell, and then, 'Excuse me, Merry Christmas, but what the hell is that smell? You're making us all gag?'"

"Well, maybe not. Still, something has to be done!"

"I guess we wing it. Let's just get it over already. I'd still like to go home and roast chestnuts tonight."

As the few brave neighbors trudged up the long driveway, the others sighed their relief at not having been recruited.

"Thank goodness they're handling that."

"You didn't want to raise your hand either, huh?"

"Not particularly. I've been dealing with enough weirdness lately. My kid swears she's seen some ghostly apparition in the cul-

140

de-sac recently."

"What, the ghost of Doc Potter?"

"Herbert! For God's sake!"

"Sorry dear, just trying to lighten it up. Who does your daughter think she's seen?"

"Not a who exactly. More of a what."

"A spectral wraith with a black hood and long robe?

"Um … more along the lines of a demonic cow."

"A what?"

"Never mind. Forget I mentioned it."

The group of Victorian-attired neighbors hurried away to attend to their caroling duties.

The footprints of the trio disturbed a thick blanket of snow that evenly covered the yard and the driveway, all the way to the top of the front step.

One rapped on Mr. Potter's front door.

Silence.

The three looked at each other.

The second one shrugged, wiping ice crystals away from his beard.

The third hesitated, cleared his throat, brushed snow off his shoulders, glanced behind himself, sighed, flexed this forefinger, and pinged the doorbell.

Thump!

A clump of heavy snow fell off a limb from a tree nearby.

All else was quiet.

The third man—Doug—jammed the doorbell a second time.

No response.

Smacking his finger on the button a third time, he pressed it for about thirty whole seconds. *Well, this should be long enough to wake the living or the dead*, he mused to himself.

No response.

The unfortunate three conferred on the front step.

"Surely, something is wrong here." Doug postulated. "Now what?"

Bob, standing two paces back from the others, conjectured, "Maybe … he's not home. The snow is undisturbed. Maybe he's

141

visiting a relative for the holidays … Perhaps he forgot to take out the compost before he left. We should go. Nothing to see here."

"Maybe he is home," interjected the first gentleman, named Horatio. "Maybe he's in trouble. Maybe he's fallen and can't get up."

"But it's Christmas Eve! No one should be disturbed on Christmas Eve." Bob dusted snow off his top hat.

"The stench doesn't care that it's Christmas Eve! It's not going to nicely waft off. We have to do something." Horatio paced.

"What exactly? Just what exactly is it you think we should do? We tried ringing the doorbell." Bob whined.

Doug turned the knob.

The unlocked door groaned as it opened.

Collectively, they sighed.

Had the door been locked, they could have walked away.

People just didn't leave their doors unlocked. Not in this godly, Midwestern suburb. Not even in this cul-de-sac with its decorated spruce trees wrapped in rustic, country-style ribbon, topped with red-and-green plaid bows. And, certainly never when they were traveling. Something was off. They all knew it. Dread descended upon them like a thick fog, squelching any chance for a speedy, well-being check and a quicker getaway. Instinctively, they knew what must come next.

Now, they must do something … unpleasant. They would have to enter the darkened house and investigate on this joyless Christmas Eve.

Darkness assaulted their eyes as the three Charles Dickens knockoffs crossed the threshold into the foyer, and the hallway switch failed.

"Didn't one of you think to grab a flashlight?" Bob grumbled.

Doug opened his mouth and closed it.

Together, they strolled into what was most likely a living room.

"Damn it!"

Bob banged his head on a banister, apparently leading to the second floor. Newly disturbed dust blanketed him like snow.

"Hey, look! See that!" Horatio whispered.

"All I can see are stars." Bob was massaging his temple.

"Definitely a speck of light," Doug confirmed. "Man, this place is encased like a tomb, isn't it?"

Their shuffling feet made the only sound as they groped their way forward toward the light that illuminated the bottom of a door. They paused.

"Open, Sesame!" Doug commanded.

The door did not magically open.

Horatio sighed and turned the handle.

The door groaned, but stuck in its jamb.

"Bob, Doug, give me a hand here … Ouch!"

"Oh, sorry, Horatio … couldn't really see where I was shoving."

"It's okay, Doug, just a flesh wound, I'll … Hey!"

The door gave way.

Stumbling inside, Horatio and Doug found the reclusive professor in his garage.

A single bulb, dangling from the ceiling, lent enough light for them to make out that he was leaning over a freezer.

"Excuse us," Bob apologized as he entered the garage. "We don't mean to intrude, but—"

"Shh!"

"What?"

"Look!"

Bob drew nearer. He gasped.

Doc Potter didn't return the greeting.

With ashen face, and hazel eyes wide open, the once-proud man, slumped over the top of the freezer, his mouth stiffened into a perfect O, stared without blinking at the contents of the freezer.

The trio froze.

A lifetime was lived in that moment, full of every terror, every horror story ever told, and every possible thing that ever could or would go bump in the night. (Horatio later postulated this to his enrapt, neighborly audience.)

The moment ended.

The neighbors gagged.

The fetid aroma of meat-gone-bad encircled them and … lingered.

143

Horatio doubled over, losing his fine Christmas Eve goose pate dinner.

Bob lost control of his bowels.

Doug's scream pierced the air, gaining in volume to rival the howl of the fiercest banshee, drowning any distant joy sung by their caroling spouses and neighbors.

Collectively, they added to the stench.

While a chorus of "God Rest Ye Merry Gentlemen" in the distance drifted faintly into the garage, no tidings of comfort or joy emanated from the macabre scene before them.

Later, Horatio would tell law enforcement and the neighbors, "The situation was more horrible than it first seemed. That pungent odor ... The stench wasn't solely from Doc Potter, but rather, and much, much worse ... the freezer containing the blood-soaked, dismembered remains of his recently ... defrosted wife. Apparently, she had left ... but she hadn't gone far."

Tearing through the darkened house, and bolting out the front door, all three fell on their knees, vomiting into the newly fallen snow of the cul-de-sac, marring any hope of a perfect white Christmas.

Multiple sirens blared through the neighborhood.

Police cars and ambulances arrived. Officers proceeded to question the three haggard men still cramped in their top hats and foul caroler costumes. The twinkling lights on the top of the emergency vehicles added a macabre twist to the festive decorations on the trees and lamppost in the middle of the cul-de-sac. The pomp and circumstance of the early morning seemed to drag on for hours. At the end of eternity, the paramedics heaved the corpses into the waiting ambulance. The bodies were covered, but stains as red as a glass of Christmas sherry had dripped onto one of the stretchers, the one whose contents did not appear to be in the shape of a body.

A shuddering, tearful, frosty mass of neighbors huddled together in cold comfort, standing as a testament to the fact that the Grinch truly had stolen their Christmas.

"How could such a thing happen here? In this very cul-de-sac? Under our watch? Shouldn't we have suspected something? That no-good professor had always been so callous, so crass. We

144

should have seen it coming."

"Really? How were we to know he would murder his wife? Who does that?"

"Clearly, he snapped."

"Yeah, the HOA can do that to a person."

"For God's sake, Herbert! I'm president of the HOA!"

"Sorry, dear."

"And, what happened to him? Did he die of fright? Did something get him?"

"Um…" Two dads looked at each other.

Two girls were going on about an evil, red-eyed cow they saw at night in the cul-de-sac. Something about it and Doc Potter's house …

"What? Are you saying there's an evil cow on the loose in the cul-de-sac? I know it's late and we're all riled, but honestly—" one of the dads began.

"Never mind. You're right. Forget we said anything," one of the girls answered.

II. Evil Cow

"I mean, it was there by the lamppost. Ghostly white. Horns black as death. Horrible, glowing eyes, red as blood … Then, I blinked. And, poof, it was gone." Ainsley whispered to her friend three days before Christmas Eve.

Jazzy paused. Could that be possible? "Was it a nightmare?"

"No, Jazzy. It was a nightcow."

Ainsley gestured toward the house adjacent to Jazzy's. "The mad cow, that-I-totally-didn't-make-up, was staring up at Doc Potter's house."

"W-was it in my yard?" She stole a glance at her own house.

"No, not your yard. It was here, in the cul-de-sac."

Ainsley must have made up the story. An evil cow? Give me a break!

Jazzy could prove it. She tumbled right out of bed to confirm for herself and the world that mad cows do not exist. *Or evil cows. Whatever the heck they are. There really is such a thing as a mad cow or a disease or something. Fine. Mad cows exist. Evil cows do*

145

not. Simple.

Marching over to the bedroom window, she climbed atop the window seat overlooking the cul-de-sac. Moving the curtains aside from the safety of her perch, she gazed triumphantly at the boughs-of-holly, decked-out lamppost shining upon the snow-covered oaks in the middle of the cul-de-sac. Following her line of sight downward, she spied the ghostly, white cow with the maddening red eyes staring right at the arrogant neighbor's house.

Jazzy shrieked and toppled off the window seat.

III. Guytrash

Sandy, Jazzy's older brother, had been munching the sugar cookies meant for Santa and reading a book when the emergency-vehicle circus first pulled up. Grabbing his jacket, he dashed outside. The light display of squad cars, ambulances, and firetrucks dazed him, blinking primary colors like bizarre emergency-themed Christmas lights. Later, Sandy noticed the outline of bodies being removed from Doc Potter's house—one body, anyway. Eventually, what looked like a bloody freezer, too.

Hovering behind the adults, with his teeth chattering, he overheard the grisly tale. Then, he heard Ainsley and Jazzy talking about some, supposed 'evil cow' that had been out in the dark, staring up at Doc's house.

Sandy shook his head as he moved away from his family, his neighbors, the slew of emergency personnel, and the macabre, blinking vehicles.

What a hell of a way to spend Christmas Eve! No one deserves this!

Violent chills that tore through Sandy had little to do with the frigid temperature outside. He raced inside, banging the screen door behind him. He bounded the stairs and threw himself upon his bed. He grabbed his laptop, feverishly searching the internet.

By the light of his desk lamp, he scrolled through entries on a legend of the Guytrash, Trash, and Skriker. Sandy sucked in his breath.

There, on the screen before him, a spectral cow with gleaming, blood red eyes accompanied an entry on the Guytrash,

146

whose coming foretold death. Apparently, the Guytrash/cow would appear out of nowhere and lead its victim, an evil person, on to his or her death.

Then, Sandy read listings of numerous creatures and evil fae of whom he had never heard. Few of these legends seemed to have crossed the Atlantic. Generations had forgotten their past.

The legends don't care who knows about them. Or... are they aware they'd been forgotten, and now they're ticked, and coming back for vengeance? God, I hope not! Sandy muttered to himself. *Jazzy and Ainsley saw a Guytrash!*

Sandy rolled onto his back and stared up at the ceiling. *This went against everything he knew. Santa isn't real. The tooth fairy isn't real. The Easter bunny isn't real. Evil cows ...? So, what, were all legends real?*

Sipping his cocoa later that morning, Sandy rubbed his eyes, watching his little sister Jazzy, unfazed by the late night/early morning grim festivities, rip through wrapping paper like a miniature cyclone.

Sandy yawned and the gruesome events ebbed further away in his memory, almost as if it all had been a bad dream. Not that it made it any less horrific.

Terrible things happened to two horrible people. No one else, Sandy told himself, biting into an angel-shaped sprinkle cookie.

For now, his self answered.

It's never a good idea to murder and chop up people, Sandy retorted to himself.

Can't argue that... Need some orange juice, his self answered.

The glaistig must have appeared to Doc Potter, aka evil person, and chased him to the bloody freezer (Wait, can cows actually run?), and literally scared him to death. Devouring the angel-shaped cookie, Sandy poured a glass of OJ, grabbed a sprinkled, Krampus-shaped cookie and bit into that, too.

Yeah, that's plausible, his self replied.

He now knew quite well what would show up if someone did do something horrible. And, that spooky bovine just might bring other gruesome fiends along for the ride.

147

Sandy stifled another yawn. If he hadn't done the Google search, he, too, could be blissfully ignorant of evil omens and portents of death. *Reading really is bad for my health.*

"Hey, Dad?"

"Hmm?"

"What's …Well, until last night, what was the scariest thing to happen in this neighborhood?"

"Having to deal with the HOA. It got on my case last spring for having planted flowers too close to the street."

Sandy smiled, gently shaking a present from Santa and ripping open the wrapping paper.   *All I really want for Christmas is to know that everyone I care about will never encounter an evil, red-eyed cow … or any other terrifying entity, or any other homicidal neighbors, ever again. That would be the best gift of all.*

Nancy Pica Renken is a Colorado writer who enjoys reading, 'riting, and running. Her work has appeared in *Flash Fiction Magazine* and has appeared or will be appearing in anthologies by Dragon Soul Press, Brilliant Flash Fiction, United Faedom Publishing, Black Hare Press, Fragmented Voices, and Mystery and Horror LLC.

www.NancyPRenken.com

The Beast and the Pufferbelly

By David Perlmutter

I

I know what you're thinking when I responded to your invitation and walked in here. "She's not from here, and what, exactly, is that thing she's got in her hands?" So, I better explain myself right from the top.

Yes, I know I'm not from here, 'cause I look way different than most of you. My given name is Candace, and I came here against my will, in a giant bubble. I know it may sound funny to you, but it isn't to me. My younger brothers, who fancy themselves practitioners of some sort of magic, or science, or something like that—they're pretty much all the same, right?—used me as a guinea pig for one of their experiments, and I ended up in the bubble to see whether a human being could survive in some sort of enclosed environment for an extended period of time—or so they said. Bottom line is, the thing got caught in a big gust of wind with me inside of it, and it blew me over the hills and far away, out of the kingdom I came from and into this one. They told me they'd try to find a way to get me back as I was cursing them blue upon my departure, but it hasn't happened yet, and I don't know that it ever will.

It wasn't too long before I got here that they started calling me the Beast.

It obviously isn't 'cause I'm ugly. I know that 'cause of the way the guys around here are always looking at me. Up at me, for the most part, because I'm pretty tall and most of you are pretty short. Also because I got red hair, and that seems to be a real novelty in these parts. No; I got tagged as "The Beast" right off the mark because I'm so big and I have a pretty loud voice, especially by the standard of girls. Or, at least, the kind of girls you typically deal with here, who aren't the kind of roving adventurer class I became by force. All I had to do was run up to one of the local peasants, who obviously never saw a big girl with a loud mouth in his life, and ask directions, and he turns tail and runs in the opposite direction. Next thing I know, I'm "The Beast", complete with some rather unflattering and biased drawings of me coming up all over the kingdom. After that, I haven't been anywhere here, and I've been around a bit for a girl in her teens, without some other lady adventurer trying to prove how much bravery and muscle power she has by challenging me to a fight. Usually I can beat 'em on my size alone, but not always. A little while ago, I nearly bought it, but thanks to my pal here, the Pufferbelly, I got out of it clean.

Here's how I got to have him on my side …

II

On the adventure I'd had before this one, I'd had the misfortune to encounter a couple of miscreants: an old crone of a witch who I handled easily, and a cute and very naïve guy whom I rescued from the witch's bondage and then had in the sack, only to discover that he was really a big, ugly troll who had been made handsome only due to the witch's glamour. In the process of fighting them both, I ended up losing the knife and the wooden quarterstaff that had previously been my protection against those that tried to hurt me, and I was hard up for means of defending myself beyond my feet and my fists. That was all I needed for a while, but I knew I couldn't depend on them forever.

Then, one day, I met the Pufferbelly.

Like any adventurer worth their salt, I'm a sucker for anyone crying for help. This happened to be one of those occasions. I heard a voice—a man's voice—calling for assistance. I scampered towards where the voice was coming from, but I couldn't see a person

150

anywhere. All I could see was a river that was starting to overflow its banks, and a big rock that was starting to be consumed by the river.

And it was the sword that was calling for help.

Seriously. I heard him—it was a "he," without question—myself.

So, I figured I should relieve him of his misery.

"All right, already!" I called out above the roaring water. "Keep your scabbard on, hot pants. I'm coming!"

I wandered into the river, in the process getting my threadbare shoes and the legs of my Lincoln green coveralls wet, and put a grip on the sword's bottom. Whoever put that thing in there must have really wanted to get rid of it, and placed it in a position where it was sure to get abandoned and destroyed. But they never counted on a girl with my size and strength coming into this kingdom. I grabbed the scabbard with both of my hands, gave it a first-class tug, and the next thing I knew, he and I were back on the banks of the river, and me flat on my butt with him in one of my hands.

And then he started talking to me, to my shock.

"Thanks," he said. "I would have bought it if you didn't come along."

"You're ... welcome," I said. "Are you really able to talk?"

"Just to whoever's my master ... or mistress, in this case," he replied. "Because you are that now—I mean, if you want to be."

"Sure," I said. "I need a new weapon. Bad."

I introduced myself to him, and he thought it was odd that a pretty girl like me would be known as "The Beast".

"You haven't seen me fight yet," I answered.

"I figured it had something to do with that," he said. "At least, you got a decent name. Not like mine."

"What is it?"

"Pufferbelly."

"I hate to ask why that is."

"You'll find that out when you need to," he said, cryptically.

"You were probably cursed or something by some wizard-type, weren't you?"

"Yeah. I was a wandering adventurer like you are, once.

151

Only I happened to get captured by some evil wizard, like you said, and he cursed me by putting me inside of this sword. Plus, he imprisoned the sword in that rock you freed me from. He figured I'd stay there forever, but he didn't count on you coming along."

"Obviously not," I said. "Listen, Puff—you don't mind if I call you that, do you?"

"Not at all."

"Okay. So—I expect that name has something to do with what happens to you when you get into battle?"

"It does."

"I hope I can handle you when that happens."

"You're the only one who can. I won't do it for no one else."

"If you can help me win a fight when it happens, that's all I care about."

"That's all I care about, too," he said. So, I knew this would work out.

III

That was all Puff would say about himself, although I prodded him when I felt like it over the next couple of days of wandering we went through. (And it won't do any of you any good trying to speak to him like I do, especially you dames. He's a faithful one-girl-only sword that way.) It was pretty uneventful, other than us trying to negotiate exactly where on my body I'd put him when we traveled. When you're a lady adventurer traveling with a living male sword, that can get pretty awkward, and all the places he or I suggested usually ended up with the other making a dirty joke about it. Finally, we settled on me carrying him in the most unattractive part of my body, to mutual agreement.

I managed to avoid trouble until I got into the next town. A couple of friendly guys offered to buy some mead, since they could see I needed some, and I took them up on the offer. I get drunk fairly easily, and I usually don't have too many at one sitting, but that night was stormy and there wasn't much else I could do in that town that night, things being as they were. There was another dame there, another adventurer, a big blonde goddess-looking type that was nearly as big as I was, and she had a sword for her preferred weapon, too. She was also as drunk as I was, and she started boasting about all the crap she'd done with that sword of hers, since she was seemingly capable of turning it into anything besides a sword to whip peoples' tails when she needed to. Naturally, I took offense. I had no idea what Puff was capable of then, but I take pride in not letting nobody, man or woman, best me at anything. So I shot up out of my chair, and roared out that me and my sword could smack down her and hers any day and time she named.

She strode up to me, and, in so many profane words, challenged me to a fight, which I did in nearly as many profane words. We might have done it right then and there, to the delight of the men in the room, only the landlord had class, and didn't want nobody wrecking his rooms. So, we arranged to meet the next day in the forest and do it there—with nobody watching or helping.

My inebriation let me sleep off what I'd done and said until the following day, when she rode up on her horse, got off, and took a swing at me with her weapon. That got me awake.

"What the hell?" I said. "How come you're attacking me, lady?"

She reminded me of the challenge I'd made the night before, as well as calling me a dirty name. I proceeded to whip Puff from out where I'd been concealing him.

"I hope you can fight as well as you insult people," I said, calling her a dirty name back.

We went into it then. Standard parry and thrust stuff for the most part. We threw the blades at each other, and mostly had the delight of having the other one block us. I got to see how sharp Puff was when he cut her wrist, but she got her own back when she nipped me in the thigh. But it was a stalemate until she decided to get tough.

By that I mean she showed that her sword really had magical powers beyond cutting and thrusting. She uttered something arcane that I didn't catch, and, suddenly, her sword turned a pure golden color. And a beam of light from it hit me in the stomach and knocked me down on my knees. I wasn't up against a mere sorceress; she was some kind of witch! Another beam knocked me down on the ground and made Puff jump a good foot out of my hands, putting him out of reach. She was all set to destroy me with

153

another beam when I used one of my feet to kick her sword out of her hands and out of her reach as well.

"Now we're even," I said.

"So that's how it is, huh?" she growled.

She leapt onto me, and we wrestled on the ground, then and there. Straight rough-and-tumble fighting, now. Again, we were pretty evenly matched in terms of size, strength and skill level, so the only way one of us could win was to play a wild card. That happened to be our hair, like it usually is when girls fight. I tugged a clump out of her head, and was able to disable her enough in the process to get her on the ground with a flying tackle. But she took the hint and snatched a hank from my red roots with even more strength than I had applied, and that was enough to get me down on the ground and flat on my ass. She took the advantage of having direct access to my throat to put her meat hooks on it, and soon I was gasping for air and nearing death.

"Puff!" I cried out, weakly. "If you're going to do that secret trick of yours, now's the time!"

"Got it," he said.

And I am not making up what happened next.

He levitated up from the ground without any human hand assisting him. And then, without any warning, his blade expanded to about three times its normal length and twice its weight. (Hence the "Pufferbelly", I later learned.) And, with a whirl of wind, a flash of lightning, and a crush of thunder, he wasn't a normal sword anymore, but a super-weapon. My opponent was unnerved enough by this display to stop killing me and turn around. She immediately sensed what was going on, and quickly ran for her own weapon to defend herself. But it was too late. As she ran towards it, he got her, and ran her through like a stuck pig. Rather than having blood flow from the wound that resulted, a gaping hole came about that allowed me to see right inside of her body. Not for long, though. She collapsed and died, and her remains almost immediately decayed and disappeared.

Puff returned to his normal size and shape, and I picked him up by the scabbard and held him tight.

"I guess we're squared now," I said. "I saved your life, and you saved me."

"Exactly," he said. "That's what I was trying to do."

He explained that he knew that particular specimen of lady warrior from his days as a full-bodied adventurer and knew exactly what to do to tame them, thanks to past experience. They had been created by the same wizard who'd imprisoned him in the blade, before he got there. They had been created by him as an elite guard unit, for some unknown reason, but they had rebelled against him for another unknown reason. His human body had been captured to be used as the fuel for being turned into the sword, but, when he refused to serve evil, he had been abandoned in the rock where I happened to find him.

"Wow," I said. "I knew absolutely nothing about any of that. Can you imagine what would have happened if I walked into a fight with that wench without you having my back? We're lucky we ran into each other, Puff. You would have rusted away in that river water, and I would've gotten my head chopped off."

"That's about the size of it," he concurred. "But we got each other now, Candace. We can survive together, now. Knowing what both of us know."

"Me as much as you," I agreed. "I'm not exactly an idiot, myself. I might teach you a few things."

"Such as what?"

"Such as telling you about the fact that we can have a better relationship as a guy and a girl together than about 99% of them because of one thing."

"What's that?"

"You can't get me pregnant. But I can still keep you sharp for when I need you."

"You're pretty tough," he said, admiringly. "Especially your tongue."

"You better remember that," I said, as I returned him to his hiding place.

Neither of us has forgotten it since.

David Perlmutter is a freelance writer based in Winnipeg, Manitoba, Canada. He is the author of two books on animation history: *America 'Toons In: A History of Television Animation* (McFarland and Co.) and *The Encyclopedia of American Animated*

Television Shows (Rowman and Littlefield), and five self-published books of speculative fiction: *Orthicon, Honey and Salt, Let's Be Buddies, Nothing About Us Without Us,* and *The Singular Adventures of Jefferson Ball* (available through Amazon Kindle and Smashwords). He can be reached on Twitter at @DavidPerlmutt10, Facebook at DavidKPerlmutterandFriends, and on Substack at https://davidperlmutter.substack.com. His stories and essays can be read at Medium, Vocal, and Simily.

First Kiss

By James Fitzsimmons

Two pounds of hamburger swinging from my little finger, I bounced off the donation bin in the parking lot, squeezed through the employee side entrance, and dropped the burger on the floor of the Evergreen Funeral Home. Luckily, the bag held, and I hustled the meat into the fridge in the kitchenette. My mouth watered at the thought of hibachiing up dinner out on the patio. Being a mortuary night attendant was how I maintained a 3.85 GPA, and two pounds of burger would last several nights, enough to see me through completion of a term paper on Marbury v. Madison.

Track sprints ran long that day, making me fifteen minutes late for work. As soon as I'd scurried in, my manager, Mr. Nash, called from the prep room: "Amaro! Amaro!"

I went to the prep room expecting a lecture, and found two police officers, the mortuary handyman, and Nash surrounding a body on a table. Intestines protruded from the body's ripped abdomen.

"Coyotes," Nash said. "They've been spotted in the area. With all the work we're doing on this dump"—he waved his hand, referring to the vintage building that had served the community for over a century—"the critters found a way in. Didn't see them, but I scared them off."

The handyman said, "No worries, Mr. Nash. I fixed loose planks in the wall and secured an open window. Also checked the windows of the vacant apartment upstairs. No one or thing can get in now."

"Just the same, Amaro," Nash said to me, "call me if you hear a ruckus."

"Mmm," I said, "I was going to barbeque—"

Nash shook his head. "Not a chance. Freeze it. Grab Mickey D's instead."

"Hey, Amaro," the handyman said, "just use that baseball bat on them! You know, the Louisville Slugger you used to hit a homerun for inter-mortuary softball."

Nash rolled his eyes. "No, Amaro, don't do that."

After the police and the handyman left, Nash repacked Mr. Harold Birx's intestines and stitched up his abdomen. We dressed Birx and rolled him into the reposing room. Nash notified Birx's next of kin of the desecration, but Birx didn't have many living relatives, and the kin was shocked but not worried as long as Birx was presentable. Working nights in a mortuary is extremely quiet, and I remember thinking if only a few people came for visitation tonight, I'd get a lot done on Marbury v. Madison.

After a couple hours of diligent work, I started to develop a strong hunger. Track sprints are exhausting. I mused on how good a charred burger would be dressed with cheese, onion, lettuce, tomato, ketchup, and mustard on a grilled sesame seed bun. I wasn't thinking of Mickey D's. I wanted to hibachi. By 8:00 p.m. everyone was gone except for me and Mr. Birx. One live human had come for visitation, the one who'd made the arrangements, and left after a few minutes. It was unlikely anyone else would come by, so I fired up the grill.

In no time, I was chowing down on the best burger I'd ever made and working at my laptop. As I keyed, my mind wandered to Roseline in American Government AP. She sat two desks in front of me, and I'd follow the flow of her wavy brunette hair that cataracted down her back while our teacher droned on. She would be my first kiss, and, trying to predict a movie she would like, I browsed theaters. Not the shoebox ones, but the large ones with dark corners. Ah, Roseline. Tomorrow after class I'd ask her out. I couldn't work on Marbury v. Madison any more tonight.

The doorbell buzzed and I jerked my head, spitting out some pickle. Someone to see Birx now? I jumped to my feet and dashed up the long hallway to the foyer. I greeted what I guessed was a family of four: middle-aged parents, teenaged daughter, small son. The daughter had long blonde hair and wore a crop top and tight jeans. But I was taken aback by the beat up, soiled clothes they all wore, including the daughter's.

The father, in a crumpled tweed jacket two sizes too small, smiled pleasantly. "We would like to see—uh—him."

"Mr. Birx? This way."

I led them to the reposing room, then continued down the hallway back to the office. As I munched more burger, the daughter wandered into the office. I introduced myself and asked how I could help.

"Well, Amaro," she said in a voice slightly above whisper, "my father is, well, difficult to be with. Can I wait in here with you?"

"Ah, I'm sorry for your loss. The death of a loved one can be difficult."

She pointed to my burger. "I caught you during dinner."

"Sorry, I don't have another—"

"No, no, it's late. You must be hungry. Please eat."

She sat on a chair across the room from me. As I sat at the desk and took another bite, I felt her eyes drilling into my mouth.

After a minute, I heard a commotion from the hall, and I stood.

The girl came close and sat on the edge of the desk. She ran her fingers over my knuckles. "Don't bother with them. You're very cute. Are you in school? Are you in sports?" She squeezed my forearm.

She was quite beautiful, and her stare held my attention. Then the commotion increased, now very loud.

"Coyotes!" I blurted. "Your family!"

Without thinking, I grabbed the baseball bat from the closet and ran into the hall.

"Stay here!" the girl yelled, following me. "Please!"

I froze in the reposing room doorway, speechless, every hair on my body erect, a bolt of electricity traversing my back as if my spine were a lightning rod.

The dad's face was buried in Birx's stomach, the mom was sucking the deceased's eye socket, the boy was sitting on the divan,

159

chewing on what appeared to be a string of gut. The dad looked at me, intestines falling from his mouth. The mom looked at me, brain matter spilling from hers. Their faces had morphed from human to green globs, rutted with furrows and crevices like some kind of squash. Their fingers were green with stiletto fingernails.

"I told you to keep him busy!" the dad yelled.

The girl was now tugging my elbow from behind. "Come away, Amaro!"

I came to my senses, shook my arm loose from the girl, and lunged at the dad. The dad whipped me with the back of his hand, cracking the bat in two and flinging me across the reposing room. The girl lunged at him, and he struck her. She landed near me, her face now a green mass of rivulets and pocks. With no time to contemplate, I jumped up and rammed the man, aiming my shoulder low at his knees. He fell against the casket and onto the floor. I sunk my fist into his green face, my knuckles coming away with green ooze. The small boy had run from the divan and started slapping me with the gut. When I tried to shoo the boy away, the dad ran his fingernails across my chest, ripping my jacket and tearing my skin. Then I saw his fist come at me in a roundhouse punch.

I woke up on the floor of the kitchenette. The girl was applying a wet washcloth to my forehead. "Sorry for what we have done," she said.

I got up and tried the door.

"My father wedged a chair against the door," she said. "We're locked in."

"What are you?"

"There is more evil in the world than you know, Amaro."

I sat back down, wincing at my headache and the cut on my chest. The girl pulled my shirt away and started cleaning the wound with fresh water. She continued: "My father lost his job. At the unemployment office, he met a man who promised thousands a month if he'd telemarket fake scooters to old people. That led to making fake phone calls requesting SSNs and bank account numbers. That led to going to people's homes as FBI and threatening them with tax fraud. Finally, he was ordered to make ransom calls to parents whose children were actually abducted."

"He went along with all this."

She nodded. "He was making huge money. The evil man promised my dad would never be caught, and my dad believed him. Then last year my dad was arrested in a sting and thrown in jail. But that night he suddenly appeared in our house, said, 'We're leaving,' and we were turned into ghouls. We were cursed."

I watched her eyes tearing, her mouth quivering. Her hand rested on my shoulder to steady herself.

"You eat raw ..." I started.

"Flesh. We're not killers. We're compelled to eat raw, dead meat. We raid funeral homes, cemeteries, morgues, slaughterhouses. It's part of the curse."

"You broke in earlier."

She nodded.

"You're zombies."

"That's what people think. Zombies are dead and eat living flesh. Ghouls are living and eat dead flesh."

"You can look human."

"We can change form for a while. We stole clothes from the donation bin in your parking lot so we could finish the corpse. The bodies that aren't embalmed, like your Mr. Birx, are especially good."

"You could leave your father. You could get help."

"It doesn't work that way. There are others like us. Live in sewers and abandoned buildings. No one sees us unless we're careless. The ones that turn themselves in melt into a puddle of chemicals, losing all identity and protecting the anonymity of the underworld."

"My God."

She leaned into me, her hair falling on my chest, and licked the blood from my wound. Then she gave the wound a final wipe with the cloth. Her doctoring felt strangely pleasant.

"What's your name?" I asked.

"Juliet." She set her forehead in her hand. She looked exhausted, emaciated.

"Your father is angry with you," I said. "You're starved." I went to the refrigerator, brought out the remaining raw burger, and set it on the counter. "Salt? Tabasco?"

Juliet's eyes widened at the sight of the meat. She ravenously unwrapped it, sprinkled on tabasco, and began consuming, turning away as if embarrassed.

Though her body was green and the skin on her face gnarled, she had the shape of any human girl. Her bare midriff was trim. Her hair was still blonde, falling down her back in a straight line. Her face was wrinkled, her eyes sunken as if having been gouged in, her nose and cheekbones sharp like a skull's. But her beauty penetrated me.

She ate half the burger and put the rest back in the fridge. She rinsed her mouth in the sink. "Thank you, Amaro."

I went to her, cupped her face in my hands, and we kissed, my heart pounding furiously.

Just then the kitchenette door flew open, and Juliet's father was standing tall, a human leg slung over his shoulder like a fishing pole. His face was glistening with slime. The mother and son stood behind him, the son sucking on a tapered, shriveled bit of flesh I took to be an appendix from pictures in my Physiology AP text.

"We go!" the dad commanded.

The family trooped through the office and out the side door. Juliet looked back at me with a hint of smile, her face bearing human form, then quickly resuming a ghoul's, and they were gone.

I went to the reposing room. Mr. Birx was a mess, his torso flayed, many organs and a leg gone.

"COYOTES!" I texted my manager.

I'd been chewed out by coaches, by my parents, by others' parents, by the lady who ran the liquor store where I'd stolen Tootsie Rolls when I was five, but I'd never been chewed out like I was that night by Nash. Even if I could prove I'd been attacked by ghouls, he'd still be pissed that I'd used the hibachi to cook dinner.

"You're lucky you're alive! Look at you! I should fire your ass, but I need you to help me reassemble Birx. The family wants an open casket for service tomorrow."

He felt around Birx's hip where the leg had been filched and shook his head.

The doorbell buzzed. We exchanged panicked looks.

"Shoo them away!" Nash said, pushing me out the reposing room and closing the door.

162

I went to the foyer. "Juliet!"

The beautiful ghoul stood slumping in the foyer, Birx's leg now slung over her shoulder. "We were ambushed by ghoul hunters. I got away, but my parents and brother melted." She started crying.

"I'm sorry. Stay in here until … no, come with me!"

I took the leg from her, and we went to Birx's reposing room.

"I said not to let anyone in!" Nash snapped.

"This is Juliet. She can help us. Her family had Birx for dinner—but Juliet's a good ghoul."

Nash squinted.

"She brought back the leg." I pulled out the leg from behind my back and held it up.

Nash's jaw dropped. "My God!"

Juliet showed her ghoul appearance.

"My God!" Nash sat on the divan, eyes ballooning.

"Her family has been killed by hunters," I said. "She needs our help, and we need hers."

Nash looked around the room. "I've heard of zombies but didn't believe it. They eat—"

"No," Juliet said. "Zombies are dead and eat living flesh. Ghouls are living—"

"We can explain that later," I said. "Let's fix Birx."

With Nash stealing looks at Juliet, we inserted Birx's leg back into his hip. The leg snapped in like a Lego piece but didn't sit right, so we broke the foot to make it look correct. We inserted a plastic ball from a Guinness beer can into Birx's hollow eye socket and sewed the lid shut. Nash closed up Birx's abdomen as best he could, but Birx was elderly and his skin ripped when stretched too far, having already been repaired once today, so we left a bit of it open. Then we slit a fresh shirt and coat up the back with scissors and laid the garments over Birx. I can't say Birx looked as fresh as a daisy, but he looked good.

Juliet restrained herself from snacking as we worked, and when we finished, it was time for a pitch. I gave her a glance, and she took on human form.

"Mr. Nash," I said, "we've been wanting a presence on the property at night. Let's let Juliet stay in the apartment. We don't have to tell the handyman."

163

Nash looked at her and sighed. "This job doesn't include all you can eat."

"I'll bring her food," I said.

Nash nodded. "Okay, Juliet you can stay until it's safe for you to leave."

It would never be safe for her to leave, I thought. Over the next few weeks, she and I shared poke bowls, sushi, lightly hibachi'd steak, and we became very, very close. But she said she wanted to find a cure, and soon after I left for college, Nash told me she left the funeral home.

I never saw Juliet again. As the years pass, I reflect over her affliction—was it evil, demonic, bacterial, viral? How screwed up can our world be? I completed an MBA, got married, divorced, and am now assistant manager of a shoe store in a mall, a job even more boring than a mortuary night attendant. They say you never forget your first kiss. Juliet, where are you?

James Fitzsimmons' fiction appears in *Bards and Sages Quarterly*, the *Cast of Wonders* podcast, and the *Six-Guns Straight from Hell 3* anthology. James works in IT and says that writing a computer program is much like writing a horror story, especially when users scream. James lives in Long Beach, CA with his family and pet rabbit, Alice Cooper.

Love and Animal Control

By Gary Battershell

My mother grew up in a house full of cats. She woke up with cats on her bed, breakfasted with cats walking across the table, and went to school with cat hairs on her clothes and in her book satchel (yes, kids carried satchels in those days, not backpacks—I think Mom told me that hers was plaid). When she got home in the afternoon there were cats on the porch, and the front door opened to the sight and smell of, yes, that's right, more cats. Gramps and Gram never had less than twenty, Mom said, and she hated every mewling, hissing, shedding one. That's why Mom hated cats.

The other thing Mom hated was my sister-in-law. My brother brought her back from Korea at the end of his hitch in the Air Force. It was a pretty common story, I guess: serviceman, a long way from home, falls in love with an exotic girl and can't bring himself to leave her behind.

Jae-Min was really nice, and she was beautiful in a willowy sort of way. I was only eleven, but Jae-Min pretty much activated every dormant hormone in my prepubescent body.

But even better than her looks were Jae-Min's personality and disposition. She was the sweetest person I'd ever met and the first adult who really paid attention to me. We became such good friends that I thought I ought to get her something for her birthday, so I spent allowance money I'd saved on a cheesy little silver-plated pendant. It was shaped like a seashell and had a fake diamond in the center. I even had it inscribed: From Jackie to Jae-Min/ Happy

Birthday, 1974. She wore it all the time.

Jae-Min's English was good, and I loved our long conversations about everything from movies and TV to politics and religion, and I especially loved how Jae-Min never interrupted while I was talking, like what I said was important.

But even more than listening to myself, I loved listening to her. Jae-Min told me all about what it was like growing up on a farm in Korea and living in an exotic city like Seoul. She had done both.

She'd lived on her parents' farm until she was sixteen, and then got into some kind of trouble—she was vague on what kind—and had to move in with relatives in Seoul where she'd gotten a job working at a bank.

Looking back, I can't say how genuine Jae-Min's apparent pleasure in my company was, but at the time it never occurred to me that she might be faking—any more, I'm sure, than my brother ever wondered if she was faking with him at night. Their room was next to mine, and from all the moaning and thrashing I heard coming from there, only two conclusions were possible, either Chuck was the world's greatest lover or Jae-Min was the world's greatest actress.

One morning, about three months after Chuck and Jae-Min moved in, I was eating Cheerios in the breakfast nook when Mom came in from outside. I could see she was in a bad mood, and I wasn't surprised. She'd been like that pretty much all the time since Dad died, six months before.

He had gotten up early one morning and gone out to get the newspaper. It was a cold snowy January and, walking back up the driveway, Dad had slipped on a patch of ice. By the time we found him, he was frozen stiff with a pool of blood spread out from where his head had hit the pavement.

When Mom noticed cat prints in the new snow all around him, she swore that the neighborhood cats were responsible. "Ran under his feet, that's what. Same as murder! They killed him because they hate me."

The truth is that the cats had a right to hate Mom. She kept a BB gun by the door, and every time she saw a cat in the yard or even in the street in front of the house, she'd go out on the porch and let him have it.

166

Once Old Lady Marvin, who lived three houses down and had six cats, called Mom and complained about having to take her Sweetie to the vet to have a BB removed from his scrotum. Mom told Mrs. Marvin that there was a law against cats roaming free and that she was only sorry that there was also a law about discharging real guns, otherwise Sweetie would have lost both balls and everything in front of them.

Anyway, that morning in early July, Mom came in mumbling to herself and swearing under her breath. I wished that I had already left for school, because whenever Mom got like that, she wanted an audience for her venting.

"Goddamn disgusting pests," Mom hissed. "Those furry bastards are digging up my irises again. Two of them were sitting on the Dennison lawn when I went out for the paper, watching me and laughing."

The "Dennison" lawn shouldn't technically have been called that since the family had moved out of the house months ago, leaving the place deserted. I wondered if Mom's reputation as the weird cat-hating widow up the street had anything to do with the fact that it hadn't sold yet.

"Why don't you call the cops?" I suggested, "There's a city ordinance against free-roaming pets."

"Won't do any damn good," Mom said, and went to the coffee pot to pour herself a slug, which she tossed off like whiskey. "I've complained till I'm blue in the face. The cops are as useless as the Pope's dick."

I hated it when Mom talked like that. It wasn't dignified, and she usually didn't do it, but the cats made her crazy. Sometimes at night she'd get out of bed and just sit by her bedroom window with that BB gun's muzzle stuck out over the sill. And if you tried to talk to her about it, all she'd say was "They're out there. I can smell 'em."

Chuck got a job as assistant manager at the BurgerRama. He had worked there when he was in high school, and he and Mr. Parks, the owner, had always gotten along. Maybe that's because they were both weird. Mr. Parks was a kind of hermit. Nobody ever saw him anyplace except his front porch, where he liked to sit and read the paper on spring and summer evenings, and down at the BurgerRama on his weekly visits.

Chuck said that Mr. Parks came in once a week like clockwork. Every Wednesday night at eight p.m., he'd spend an hour or so looking over the books, inspecting the place for cleanliness, and just generally making sure everything was in good order. And if it wasn't, the manager "got holy heck," as Chuck liked to put it.

That was as close to swearing as my brother ever got. Chuck was one of those people that was born with a strong moral sense; he never smoked, or drank, or had any fun at all, as far as I could tell.

I guess that's what Old Mr. Parks liked about him. Chuck worked for him for three solid years, and he was never once late, or insolent to a customer, or otherwise deficient.

Of course all these traits which so endeared him to Mr. Parks and Mr. "Shitface" Sherman Soames, the Greendale High School principal, didn't exactly earn Chuck the reputation of being cool. In fact, he was probably the biggest dork in school. Even so, he didn't get picked on much. That was because he was as big and as strong as an Angus bull, and, just as his strong sense of morality wouldn't allow him to lie or cheat, it also wouldn't allow other kids to get away with bullying. Chuck would take on boys twice his size, and, as far as I know, he never lost or quit anything he started.

Chuck never did very well with girls. He didn't date much in school, and he never had a steady. I'm pretty sure Chuck was still a virgin when he left for basic training at the end of his senior year. But Jae-Min must have seen something in him. A girl with her looks must have had a lot of options.

A few days after Chuck started at the BurgerRama, I was home watching TV. Jae-Min had walked downtown to see a movie at the Greendale Twin Cinema, and Mom was sitting by the window with her BB gun leaned up against the wall in easy reach.

*M*A*S*H* came on and I settled back for my weekly dose of "secular humanist liberalist propaganda" as our pastor liked to say about shows like that. Actually, I thought that Hawkeye was a lot like Chuck, morality-wise, but with more of an edge and better comebacks.

The show had hardly started when a cat started to yowl. Mom swore and reached for her Daisy.

"Come on, you bastard, come out under the streetlight and

168

I'll blast your furry ass."

I looked at Mom, wondering for the ten thousandth time if we should be getting her some professional help, and I didn't mean professional cat catchers. Through the window I could see the lamppost across the street, and movement at the edge of the light.

Mom leveled her BB gun and swore as a cat streaked through the pool of light too fast for her to get a shot.

"Damnit! Nearly had the sumbitch."

Mom lowered the gun and looked away in disgust. But I was still looking when something as big as a German Shepherd slunk into the light.

Its snout was long and narrow, and its open jaws were full of spiny fangs as long as my fingers. It looked toward the house through eyes like shiny black baseballs, and far too large for its skinny face. It sat back on its haunches and raised front paws that looked like hands, but with claws, then it stood up on its back legs for a second before falling back to all-fours. Silky brown fur covered its gaunt, hellhound body, and it rippled when the thing wheeled and ran off into the dark.

I tried to talk but couldn't. I tried again and managed to croak out, "Mom, look!"

Mom looked at me quizzically and then looked out the window.

"Look at what?"

"It's gone now. A big animal. I don't know what it was."

"Another damn cat," she said. "They're everywhere."

"No. It was way too big for a cat."

"Stray dog?"

"It wasn't a dog."

Mom shrugged.

Jae-Min came home before *M*A*S*H* was over.

"I thought you were going to a movie," Mom said to her.

"I decided I didn't feel like it," Jae-Min said. "I just took a walk."

"If you're bored, you could get a job, you know. You worked in Korea, right?"

"Yes," Jae-Min said.

"Don't you get tired of sitting around here with me and

169

Jackie?"

"It's 'Jack,' Mom," I corrected, "just 'Jack.'"

"You shut up, 'Just Jack,' or I'll put you out on cat patrol. Maybe if I had somebody out in the yard at night, those little fuckers wouldn't always be digging up my irises and shitting in my grass."

"Oh, for Christ's sake, Mom."

"Don't you take the Lord's name in vain, Jackie."

"You say 'goddamn' all the time," I protested.

"Please," Jae-Min said, "don't argue."

"We'll argue if we want to, Missy," Mom snapped. "Just because you took advantage of a lonesome boy in a heathen place don't mean you can come to the U. S. of A. and tell us Americans how to act."

"I'm sorry," Jae-Min said, "I am your guest. It's not my place to criticize."

"Damn right, it's not!" Mom turned and looked out the window as though to say the audience was over.

The next morning as I came downstairs for breakfast, I overheard Chuck and Mom going at it in the kitchen.

"You hurt her feelings, Mom, that's what's wrong."

"I didn't ask for her. I thought you'd come back and marry a nice hometown girl. I wanted American grandchildren."

"If you remember, Mom, I wasn't exactly the most popular guy in high school, and what do you mean, American grandchildren? What other kind would we have?"

"The kind with the slanty eyes and funny little noses."

"I never knew you felt this way about Asians."

"How could you? The only experience Greendale ever had with them was from watching Charlie Chan on the late show. It never occurred to me that you'd go to slanty-eyed land and bring one back to live with me."

"All right. If you feel like that, I'll get a place for Jae-Min and me. We'll get out as soon as I can make arrangements."

Hearing that made me pretty sad. I'd sure miss Jae-Min, and I guessed I'd even miss Chuck. We'd never really been close, but he was family.

I heartened as the days and then the weeks went by and there was no change in the status quo. Mom and Jae-Min tried to avoid

170

each other as much as possible, which wasn't too hard. During the day Mom was always outside working in her flower garden or doing the marketing or visiting neighbors—the ones that didn't have cats, and at night Jae-Min was usually out.

Chuck worked from three until midnight most nights, and during that time Jae-Min made herself scarce. I don't know where she went, but since she didn't have a car, I knew it couldn't have been far. I supposed that she went to the movies or maybe just took long walks.

I was a little concerned for Jae-Min's safety on the streets by herself after seeing that thing under the streetlight. I mentioned it to her once, and she seemed bothered, but she said she could take care of herself. After discussing it, we both agreed that it had probably been a stray dog. After all, I'd only seen the thing for a moment and at a distance of close to thirty yards.

Mom suggested something more sinister about Jae-Min's nighttime absences. I heard her tell Chuck that she thought Jae-Min 'had something going on the side,' but Chuck just shrugged it off.

"Jae-Min grew up in the country," Chuck told her. "She spent a lot of time outside. Here in town, she probably feels cooped up and takes walks to unwind. That's how I met her in Seoul. I had something to think about, so I took a stroll through a park one night, and I met her doing the same thing."

"So, she liked to walk the streets at night? You sure she worked in a bank like she told you? Lazy as she is, it wouldn't surprise me if she found a job where she could lie down a lot."

I could tell from Mom's tone that she was trying to be more funny than bitchy, and from Chuck's response, he must have known that too or else he'd have been a lot madder.

"Mom, if you knew what Jae-Min's had to overcome in her life, I don't think you'd be so judgmental. The fact is, she was forced to leave her village and go to the city to live with relatives."

"Got herself in trouble, did she?" Mom asked smugly.

"No. Some trouble happened. I never learned exactly what kind, but I'm sure it wasn't her fault. She's a good girl, Mom, and if you'd give her half a chance, she'd be a loving and helpful daughter-in-law to you."

"Have you found a place to move to?"

171

"I think so," Chuck said. "We could be out in a couple of weeks, but I'm afraid that once we go, that'll be the end of this family for me. I don't want it to be just me and Jae-Min. I want you and Jackie in our lives too."

Mom seemed not to have heard. "Excuse me, I got to go and see if the damn cats dug in my irises last night."

Mom didn't find any evidence of cat damage that day, or any day after that, and the yowls of prowling cats came less and less often at night. Mom's mood improved with every catless day that passed. I began to seriously wonder if she was distributing arsenic-laden catnip around the neighborhood.

The last night that Chuck and Jae-Min were to spend with us was moist and warm. After dinner, Mom talked on the phone to a friend from around the block, another widow, whose name was Ora Simmons.

"The cats are just not a problem now, Ora. I hear one yowling once in a while, but they've stopped digging in my flowers and soiling my yard. It's wonderful. I feel like I've been freed of a burden."

After she hung up the phone, Mom went out and sat down on the patio. When the ten o'clock news started, I went out and joined her. I wished that I could have spent some time with Jae-Min tonight, but she'd gone out again.

"What time is it?" Mom asked. The night was bright, lit by a full moon, but a passing cloud intervened and made it suddenly dark.

I started to answer, but was stopped by the scream of an enraged or agonized feline. It came again.

"Sounds like it's coming from behind the Dennison house," I said to Mom. "Maybe a cat got its collar caught on something." When she didn't answer, I turned to her, but saw that her chair was empty.

The sound came again, louder and more frenzied. My mother hated cats, but I didn't, and this sounded like a cat in serious distress. I hurried across the backyard and down the street.

As I rounded the corner of the Dennison house, I saw movement through the chain link fence around the back yard. I leaned over it and saw nothing at first. Then the moon came out from behind the obscuring cloud, and I could see all too well. My throat

172

clenched and I couldn't move.

The thing I had seen under the streetlight, crouched on all fours and swaying back and forth, had backed a large cat into a corner of the yard. The cat let out another of those horrific screams and pressed itself tighter against the fence while the thing, swaying with a hypnotic rhythm, crept toward it.

At a distance of about six feet from the cat, the creature stopped dead still, as though it was waiting for something to happen. Something did. The cat, seemingly freed of its trance, turned and leapt for the top of the fence. As it did, the creature rose to two feet, shot out its paws that were more like hands, and caught the cat, which it proceeded to rip in half. Blood flew in all directions. The thing bolted the cat's lower half and then tossed in the rest; I could hear the skull crunch as it chewed and a gulping sound as it swallowed.

Then, still standing upright, it turned toward me. The moonlight was bright, and it glinted off a silvery, seashell-shaped pendant hanging around the creature's neck. I sensed a strange intelligence behind those alien eyes in the moment before it hopped easily over the four-foot fence and merged with the night.

I stood frozen until a touch on my shoulder broke the spell. It was Mom standing behind me. I must have looked pretty shaken up.

"It's all right, Jackie."

I wondered if she'd seen the pendant, and recognized it, but I didn't ask.

"Thought I might need this?" Mom said, hefting her air rifle. "But it seems as though I wasn't needed at all. Everything was taken care of."

Mom and I went home and turned on *The Tonight Show*. Jae-Min came home at eleven. She seemed kind of sheepish, and was obviously surprised to the point of shock when Mom gave her a sudden unexpected hug and a kiss on the cheek.

Chuck came in just as Johnny was saying goodnight. He looked like the bearer of bad news, and that look proved accurate.

"Guess you'll have to put up with me and Jae-Min a little longer," he told Mom. "I was going to rent an apartment from Mr. Parks, but he told me tonight that his deadbeat son had lost his job and he was going to have to let him have the place."

173

"Oh, don't worry about it," Mom said. "I don't know what was wrong with me before. I haven't been the same since your father died. Just forget all the stupid things I said. I want you and Jae-Min to live here. I'd be devastated if you moved out. There's even enough room for … additions."

"'Additions?'" Chuck looked perplexed. "Oh 'additions.' I get it. You mean you wouldn't mind grandkids with slanty eyes and funny noses?"

"Well, Jackie's funny looking, and I love him."

"Hey!" I protested, but I smiled as I said it.

"O.K., Mom," Chuck said. "I don't know what brought this change of heart, but I'm glad. Maybe if we give you some grandbabies to watch over, you'll stop obsessing about the neighborhood cats."

"I'm sure that they won't be a problem anymore, dear," Mom said. "Now why don't you bring Jae-Min down for some ice cream?"

"Mom, it's after midnight."

"Oh, that's all right. I doubt she's asleep yet, and she's earned a treat."

Gary Battershell is a recently retired college history instructor living in the Arkansas Ozarks with his wife, Emily, two cats, a dog, and a chinchilla. He writes speculative fiction, much of it humorous, and hopes to finish a fantasy novel in 2022. As of this writing, his work can be found in recent issues of *The Fifth Di…* and *SciFi Lampoon,* and in upcoming issues of *The Fifth Di…, The Society of Misfit Stories*, and *4-StarStories*.

Life of a Lesser Demon

By R. Gene Turchin

At least it wasn't raining. That was one good thing, even if it was cold enough to freeze the tits off a boar. Billy Lee Ray Bob Snyder was prone to colloquialisms though he would have choked on the word itself. Nothing could dampen Billy Lee's spirits because it was the first day of bow season. He'd packed his compound bow, a thermos of coffee, sandwiches, a package of extra filling Oreos, a fifth of Four Roses Whiskey, and his three best porn magazines. He wore insulated coveralls and a hat with ear flaps; he was all set for a day in the tree stand. The weather guy said it would warm up to thirty degrees by noon.

At ten degrees, the bitch truck was like a frozen dead dog in the road. It growled and whined for three minutes, then sputtered a few times before it got rolling. The overalls were too warm and bulky inside the truck. Billy Lee Bob became the Abominable Snow Man in dirty brown and blaze orange.

He pulled off the road a hundred yards from the tree, slid the bow from behind the seat. The rucksack wouldn't fit over the coverall's sleeves so carried it instead. Sweat trickled down his back and around his crotch as he slogged toward his tree stand. He should have waited till he got to the stand to put on the cold weather gear.

Life turned crappy after Darla Jean moved in five months ago. He regretted not saying no when she proposed the idea. She had big bazoombas so it couldn't be all that bad, right? Billy Lee wasn't prepared to commit to any one woman, so he considered the arrangement temporary. He'd laid down the rules early on, but lately she'd been chipping away at some of his pillars, making off-hand remarks about not spending time with her. The other night she said maybe he liked guys a little too much. He let it slide but should have slapped her to show who wears the pants. He didn't like guys that way. His buddies were just easier to hang out with.

The trees were still rich with fall leaves, so that he was well hidden in the tree stand. The location had a clear view of the valley and the deer trail.

It had been a great night with John Knots, Aaron Spitznogle, a case of Bud and some weed, but became one of those nights Darla Jean complained about. Their little patch was just wide enough to park a truck pulled off Route 19, but hidden enough so guys could do what they wanted without being harassed by the law. He'd stumbled on the ideal location for a tree stand when too many beers pressed on his bladder and he'd walked off to relieve himself.

Billy Lee Ray Bob was averse to spending time alone with his thoughts. He either dozed off or got a headache. Sometimes he made up fantasies about Darla Jean, other times it was those babes in the magazines. In the tree stand, it only took an hour before his thoughts were adrift like soft clouds.

He discovered the idea on the Internet. They called it erotic asphyxiation. You tied something around your neck and leaned over so it choked you a little. Not a lot. It was supposed to heighten the buzz from an orgasm. Alone in a tree stand was an ideal place to try. He opened the magazine to the centerfold, tied Darla Jean's pantyhose to a branch above, and unzipped his coveralls. His eyes blurred, his numb fingers released from the brace bar of the stand, and he slipped. He gasped, 'Oh shit,' before the lights went out.

Gressil stood with his partner, Jake, below where Billy Lee Ray Bob hung suspended by the pantyhose around his neck. His coveralls were undone to the waist, and it was obvious he'd been engaged in pleasuring himself when he fell from the tree stand.

Gressil sighed. "Why do we get the losers? This guy didn't have the brains of an amoeba. And now we're required to find 'rightful employment' for him."

176

Jake nodded. "We're pretty full-up now. Can't we just turn him over to eternal damnation? Let his ass roast for a few millennia?"

"I wish. Paperwork. If we make an exception for this dipshit, it's a slippery slope and our streets are paved with good intentions and all that. We gotta use him."

The demons had been together for several thousand years. Gressil was a short squatty sort with overlarge brown eyes. Those cow eyes were what drew Jake to him.

Gressil rubbed his pointed chin. "We do have some discretion in the field. The work order requires we use him."

"It also said 'subject' had great potential. I don't think HR did due diligence on this one."

"Where are we short on personnel?"

Jake consulted his tablet. "Torture, demonic appearances, possessions, signs and omens, messengers."

"Messenger might fit."

"I don't know. It requires exemplary social skills. All categories do, except torture."

"Two things can happen. He flowers way past his potential, or he screws up and is remanded to damnation." Gressil smiled.

"He's just a dumbshit screwup. His life doesn't reach the damnation bar."

"So we fudge the paperwork a little." They exchanged meaningful glances.

"That's why I love you," Jake stroked Gressil's arm. "You are so creative."

"Executive decision. Hit the button."

Jake pulled up the app on his tablet and punched REANIMATE.

Billy Lee Ray Bob woke up hanging ten feet above the ground. He wasn't choking but something was off. He felt nothing. He was as light as feather in the air. Below, two ugly-ass demons stared up at him. Somehow he knew their names too, and was now seriously freaking out.

The short one made a motion with its arm.

"Come down here. Now!" it said.

He reached up and pulled Darla Jean's pantyhose from his neck. It wasn't tight and he floated out of the noose.

"Today!" the demon said, a note of irritation in its voice.

Billy Lee Bob shoved his hands skyward and drifted toward the ground like a leaf. WTF?

He touched down in front of the demons. The smell roiling around them brought up choking coughs.

"You'll get used to it after a while," the taller one said. "We're not offended. Being immortal demons has its perks, but our body odor isn't one of them." He paused. "I am Gressil, and you fall under my purview because of the impurity thing." He gestured toward the smaller character next to him. "This is Jake, my assistant." Billy Lee saw Jake's eyes shoot flames at Gressil. Real flames.

Gressil coughed, "I'm sorry ... ahhhh, Jake is my partner. We've been together for quite a long time." A grotesque smile played across the feature that should have been a face.

"If I may," Jake said. "Let's get the hard part over—you fell out of that contraption in the tree. Your neck snapped and you died."

"That can't be ..."

Jake held up a distorted claw with sharp talons. Bits of flesh clung to the yellowed nails.

"May I finish, please?" He absently licked at the offal between the joints. "I have to say this officially. Like Miranda rights, so listen close. I will not repeat myself."

Billy Lee nodded.

"You are condemned to the neither regions for a period heretofore known as eternity or for time encompassing the end of the known universe. Your punishment for sins and crimes is perpetual suffering in the fiery pits of the location referred to as hell. Do you understand this judgment?"

Billy Lee shook his head and then nodded, confused. His life began to scroll before him, projected inside his eyes. "I guess. Maybe. I don't know."

"You must acknowledge with an affirmative. Say or spell, YES,"

"I can't go to hell." Billy Lee wanted to run. Where was his rifle? He'd shoot these dudes.

178

The demons exchanged another glance.

"Perhaps we can work something out, though rules must be followed. Your sins require eternal suffering; however, exceptions can be made." The one called Gressil cocked his head toward Billy. "Are you interested?" He held his hands palms up.

"Eternal suffering," he moved his left hand up and down. "Or swear allegiance to our boss and perform some tasks for us and life," he snorted. "or death, gets better. Trust me: quality ain't too shabby. And forget the rifle. We are impervious to your weapons."

"What kind of work?" Maybe he could bargain with them.

"This is a yes or no situation." The demon shrugged. "We don't like this anymore than you do."

Billy Lee nodded. Jake let loose an exasperated sigh. The scent of sulfur filled the air.

"Say yes or no," he said.

"Don't forget the blood," Gressil added.

Jake looked up toward Billy Lee's body swinging lightly in the winter breeze. A crow perched on its shoulder, picking at the Billy Lee's face. "I'll need to cut off a piece of flesh and a smear of blood to make it legal." The crow landed in his hand with a piece of Billy Lee's cheek in its beak.

Billy Lee coughed.

"Dip your finger," he said and pushed the chunk of flesh forward. "Then press here." He held the tablet within reach. Billy's face turned fungus green. "Hey! Don't you even think of spewing on me," Jake said.

His eyes opened wide.

"Yeah, the disembodied can spew and it is not pretty, so get hold of it, okay?"

"I got it," Billy answered and pushed his bloody finger onto the flame icon on the tablet.

"You're one of us now. Welcome to the family." Jake stuck out his hand/claw.

Billy Lee Ray Bob stared at the amorphous blob of protoplasm in front of the classroom. An annoying nasal voice emanated from the thing. Jake said he only had to attend this one seminar on presenting yourself to humans. He was glad, because school was not something that held his interest. Most of this gig would be OJT. The little demon had been a bit mean, saying, "You are a demon from Hell. How bad can you screw this up? Appear in a cloud of smoke and stink. Scare the crap out of the human, deliver the message, fill out the paperwork along with the billable hours form, and move on to the next assignment."

Jake's office was impressive. Dark wood paneling, a fireplace, massive desk, bookshelves, a couch, and a well-stocked bar.

"Have a seat," Jake said, ushering him toward a chair opposite the desk. "So, you've finished your training? Are you ready to go out there and inflict demonic terror on the human world?"

Billy Lee was conflicted or, if he were alive, constipated. The demon forced him to make too many decisions and made demeaning remarks.

Jake sighed and shoved a paper across the desk. "This is your initial assignment. You're going to appear to a guy named William Bruno Yates in Pittsburgh. He's been diddlin' the family babysitter and needs to have the warning of eternal damnation put before him."

"I thought we were the bad guys. Stealing souls and all. Why are we trying to scare him into being good?"

Jake sighed again. "Why do you humans always think it's black and white? Billy, it's not simple because we have a contractual agreement with upstairs. Good and evil. We work together to make things happen. Otherwise," he threw up his arms. "Chaos reigns and none of us want that. Right?"

Billy nodded. "I guess." Jake noted that he didn't appear convinced.

"It is complicated. But, since this is your first, it's all set up for you. Bruno will be taking out the garbage at 9:10 this evening, and you'll appear before him in all your awesome decayed and rotting flesh and say these words. Of course there will be the requisite clap of thunder, stench of brimstone, and a cold chill. You need only put on your mean face and read the words."

Billy stared at the single printed page in Gothic 16-point font.

"What does 'carnal relations' mean?"

Jake raised his eyes heavenward. Please. Please. Don't allow him to screw this up. I am really looking forward to retirement.

"One other thing: you have a new name. Henceforth, you are the demon Blurb. Catchy, eh?"

Billy looked blankly at Jake.

"It's an acronym for your full name."

Billy's face was a blank white canvas.

"Short for your initials?" Jake paused, counted to twenty. "Let's rehearse it. Read it for me.

'Woe to ye who behold the visage of 'insert name,' demon of the nether worlds. Wait for subject to react. Gauge reactions. Choose response according to reaction:

(a) Client is stunned and scared.

(b) Client is adversarial.

(c) Client is numb and dumb.

If (a), continue with message. Invoke demon voice app. If (b), toss flame balls at client's feet. Invoke demon voice app. If (c), disappear in flash of smoke and resort to dream appearance.'"

Billy read through it a second time.

"What does it mean to 'Gauge reactions?'" he asked.

Bruno dragged the two garbage bags down the back steps, letting them bounce on the stairs before he remembered the last time the bags had torn open and spread crap all over the sidewalk. Martha should buy better bags.

He had pried the lid off the can when a puff of smoke and sudden stench of rotten eggs came from the street. A guy with his neck twisted to one side stood beyond the cans. He looked dead, and pieces dripped off his face like a cheap candle. The guy squinted at a card he clutched in his hands.

"Woe to you. No. Woe to ye who be ... hold the vis, the visage of the demon BLURB, demon of the nether worlds. Ye have en ... engaged," the figure shook its head. "Shit. Look. You screwed up boffin' everything coming down the road and you gotta pay the price with your soul."

"Screw you," Bruno spat. "And get the hell off my street, pervert!"

Bruno watched the demon falter. Bruno was as wide as he was tall, and lifted with the iron men at Salvatore's Gym. He could push his way through a block wall, and he feared nothing. "If I have

181

to come over there, you're going to be wearing this garbage bag up your keister."

BLRB looked around as if he hoped a cop would come by, and then disappeared in a puff, a smoke, and thunderclap that had all the presence of a three-year-old stomping on the floor.

Bruno shrugged and went back to the kitchen. Maybe he shouldn't have chased that sinus pill with a beer.

Jake knocked quietly at Gressil's office and then opened the door the width of a demon finger.

His lover sat at his desk slumped forward, holding his head in his hands.

"I heard the knock. Come on in, Jake. I know what happened." He gestured to a stack of paper strewn across his normally neat desk.

"He screwed it up, Babe," Jake said. He tried to assess his partner's mood. At times it was better to let Gressil wallow in his misery, but he had the worst case of brown puppy-dog eyes he'd seen in two hundred years. He stepped behind the desk and began to massage his lover's shoulders.

"It's going to be all right." It sounded lame and Gressil let out a shuddering sob.

"Perhaps we can smooth this one down a bit, but if it happens again, we're both screwed blue. The chief is not happy."

"It wasn't that bad, was it? I mean, he blew the encounter, but we can send him back."

"Oh, you didn't get the follow up. We sent avenging demons to make this Bruno fellow crap his pants and he flipped them off. Even worse, he roughed one up before stuffing his ass in a trash can. Chief says it sets a precedent. If one guy gets away with giving the finger to demons, then our entire organization crumbles." He sobbed again until he coughed to catch his breath.

"They'll separate us if the department collapses. I don't know how I'd go on without you."

"It was his first assignment," Jake said. "There's got to be room for some mistakes."

"It's not so much him as the Bruno character. The boardroom says it is a culmination of lack of respect and they want to make an

182

example for others. They're upping performance criteria and making consequences. Hell to pay, they say."

"We've worked too hard to let this moron ruin our lives." Jake responded. He hated to see his lover this way.

"You have something in mind?" His voice held a note of hope. A sixteenth note.

"The Cockroach Protocol."

Gressil's eyes widened.

"I get it. Return him to life as a lesser being but something that has an element of punishment and, importantly, a plan that will provide ample time for reflection. It's the only way the boss is going to buy it. And we'll look good for thinking of it. It will show we're on board with the new direction, but it has to be a dramatic implementation. Bruno gets a pass for now."

"Oh, it will be," Jake answered.

Billy Lee Ray Bob could only remember the bad dream. He'd choked when he fell out of the tree. It got weird after that. Horrible ugly demons. Where was he now? The room was tiny. His closet in the trailer was bigger.

"Sister Billy, you sleepy head. It's time for morning prayers."

Billy pulled himself out of the small bed and staggered over to a tall mirror mounted to the bathroom door. A petite nun in a simple white habit stared back at him. He began to scream.

R. Gene Turchin writes short stories in sci-fi, horror and toe dipping in other genres along with occasional poems. He is currently attempting to finish two science fiction novels and comic book scripts. Recent published works can be found in *Oyster River Pages*, *The Sirens Call, Sunshine Superhighway Anthology, Cosmic Horror Monthly* and *99 Tiny Terrors Anthology*.
Website: https://rgeneturchin.com

Elias' Visitors

By Luke Foster

At ninety-five, Elias Krugman had few joys he could experience without difficulty. He had no idea that seeing ghosts would be so much fun.

Every morning, Elias' grandson, Dan, wheeled the family patriarch out to the patio, where he would bask in the warm glow of the sun and prepared for his daily callers.

"Looking good, Elias," his grand-niece, Alyssa, said.

"Nice to see you getting some color," his second cousin, Doug, added.

"You'll outlive all of us, believe me," said ... actually, Elias had no idea who that guy was, but he was too ugly to be a blood relative.

Like *any* of his relatives wanted him to outlive them. Not when he had a fortune somewhere in the six- or seven-figure range they couldn't touch until he croaked. Their kiss-ass routine was tedious, patronizing, and all too transparent, so one hot, July morning, Elias decided to screw with them.

"Mavis?" he asked, staring into the space between his two current visitors. "Mavis, honey, is that you?"

Dan and his sister, Melanie, turned as one and looked behind them. They were alone. Not that they could have expected to see their grandmother, mostly because she had been dead for almost twenty years. Still, he may have seen someone vaguely similar to his late wife, with her light gray curls and thin figure, and just couldn't tell the difference. He was, everyone assumed, as blind as a bat.

"Where were you, Mavis?" Elias asked as he reached toward the woman who wasn't there. "I thought you'd be home hours ago."

"Um, Grandpa …" Dan said. Melanie put a hand on his arm and shook her head.

"I'm just gonna take a little nap, now, honey," Elias said to his nonexistent wife. "I'll talk to you in a bit."

Elias let his chin drop to his chest and closed his eyes. His grandchildren whispered urgently, and he felt Melanie's hot breath on his cheek as she checked to make sure his own breath was still coming. Elias repressed a grimace. His granddaughter's breath smelled so bad, she might as well be the one dying. The rise and fall of his chest must have been enough to satisfy her, because after another whispered conference the pair slipped away.

Elias could barely repress a laugh. Was he ever going to have fun.

Mavis wasn't the only visitor to Elias' sun-drenched patio.

"Billy? Oh, Billy, I'm so sorry. I always knew who ran you over. But how do you accuse the mayor of murder?"

"Fido? Oh, Fido, you good boy! You good boy! Aunt Phyllis *did* poison you, didn't she?"

"Ginger, please, my wife will be home any minute. And I don't want your husband to shoot you again!"

Most of the scandals he made up to get his relatives whispering. Except for Ginger. She was real, and Elias knew learning about her would wind up Ann, his prude of a niece.

Naturally, his relatives—the living ones, of course—came around more frequently. His great-grandchildren were morbidly hopeful they might see a ghost or two, but he always thought children were stupid and would believe anything. The adults, on the other hand, hoped to hear more scandals they could then pretend they were horrified to hear. More than that, though, they knew— believed—hoped—that Elias' time had finally come. He even threw in some coughs, just to get them really hot and bothered. But the old man hung on, partially out of spite and partially because he was having too much fun with his "visitations." Imaginary ghosts were much more entertaining to him than his real relatives ever were.

186

Elias, slowly waking from a nap one August afternoon, blinked his eyes a few times and confirmed that, yes, someone was at the edge of his patio, and no, it wasn't one of his freeloading family members.

"Elias Krugman?" the man asked. He looked to be in his thirties. His piercing blue eyes stood out sharply against his pale skin, light blond hair, and white shirt and pants. Curiously, the man wasn't wearing shoes.

"Who are you?" Elias demanded.

"You can call me Michael," the man said. "And you're Elias."

It wasn't a question that time, but Elias confirmed it anyway.

"Good," Michael said. "I'm in the right place."

"Why the hell are you here at all?" Elias asked.

"It's my time to be here," Michael said.

Something about Michael's calm, even voice unsettled Elias. His eyes flicked nervously toward the house, but for the first time in thirty years, not a single one of the human vultures was watching him. He couldn't hear them, either. He couldn't hear much of anything. Even the birds seemed to stop chirping.

And then he knew why Michael was there.

"It's time, eh?" Elias said. "Funny, you're not what I was expecting."

"What *were* you expecting?" Michael asked. Elias opened his mouth to respond, but all that came out was a hacking cough. A real one. It had been two weeks since he needed to pretend.

Michael stepped back when Elias' fit started, and he remained where he was as the old man caught his breath.

"It doesn't matter," the nonagenarian said, waving his hand at the strange, barefoot visitor. "Funny, I never expected one of you to actually be real."

Elias didn't hear Michael's reply, the man's words drowned out by another coughing attack. This time, Elias couldn't stop it, and he wasn't sure he wanted to.

When the coughs finally ceased, Elias was standing next to his own body, which Michael stared at, wide-eyed.

"Okay, Michael," Elias said. "I'm ready."

Michael didn't reply.

"Michael? Michael!" Elias said, snapping his fingers at the man in white.

"Elias?" Michael said. "Eli ... oh, God. Daaaaaaaaan!"

The old man—the dead man—watched with confusion as his grandson came running.

"Dude, Mike, what are you doing? I said to come around the front! If my granddad wakes up, he's gonna ..."

Realization dawned on Dan's face as Michael somehow grew even paler.

"*Finally*," Dan said. "I genuinely thought I'd croak before him."

"I ... Oh, God ... I killed an old man!" Michael gasped.

"He was, like, a hundred and fifty years old," Dan said. "I'm not sure how he was still moving."

"Cocky young bastard," Elias said to ears that couldn't hear him.

"Should ... should I ..." Michael made awkward gestures towards the road.

"Nah," Dan said. "You came all the way out here; you might as well see the furniture. We'll just have to work out a deal sooner than we expected." They walked towards the house. "And for Heaven's sake, hippie, will you put on some shoes? What is that even about?"

Elias watched his grandson and the very mortal Michael walk away. The dead man's jaw hung open in disbelief. He didn't want to think that he let himself die because he confused a beatnik for someone who mattered. He continued staring as the pair of living men entered his house. Actually, it was his great-granddaughter Kelsey's house now. It would drive his family nuts to know a two-year-old owned his mansion and most of his earthly possessions, but he did promise himself he'd leave his fortune to whoever bugged him the least.

Still, his other relatives would have plenty to remind them of old Elias Krugman. They had visited him plenty while he was alive. He would be happy to return the favor.

Luke Foster is a writer from Charlotte, NC. A graduate of the

188

University of Connecticut, Luke has been a newspaper reporter, professional blogger, and advertisement copywriter. He has written short stories in every genre from comedy to horror for online and print publications in the United States, Canada, UK, and Australia. He also curated, edited, and published the Western short story anthology *Eight Gunshots: Stories of the Wild West*. He can be found online at www.ImLukeFoster.com.

... And You Will Know Us by the Trail of Dead. That, and T-Shirt Sales.

By Robert Bagnall

Death sat in reception, comparing the shine on his penny loafers, wondering whether the left had been buffed just a touch more than the right. The only magazine was a minimalist masterpiece, sized to be as inconvenient as possible to hold, each page either a block of color or a single word in bold typeface. *Specifiers. Accept. Datatrunk.* Death remained baffled.

"Saatchi, Saatchi and Watercress," the moon-faced receptionist intoned, a finger up to her earpiece, followed a moment later by, "Putting you through."

It had been like this for the last ten minutes. *Saatchi, Saatchi and Watercress.* Pause. *Putting you through.* Every thirty seconds. Rinse and repeat.

Half-heartedly, Death tried the magazine again. An entire page of glossy burgundy and, opposite it, the word *Arbitrage.* What did it mean?

Something made him look up. The pause had gone on too long. Moon-face's smile had become a confused frown. And she didn't even have *Obtuse Quarterly* in front of her.

"I don't know. It could be a legal practice ..."

"It's a public relations agency," Death called over.

She brightened. "It's a public relations agency, apparently," she informed her caller.

"Talent management, marketing. That sort of thing," Death

elaborated.

The receptionist passed on these nuggets and put the caller through, smiling her thanks at the austere but immaculately dressed elderly gentleman sitting across from her. "Are you here to see Mister Watercress?" she asked blankly.

I told you ten minutes ago, thought Death but, instead, suggested, "Why don't I go in?"

"Why don't you go in?" she offered.

Death rose, wondering how long he would have remained waiting otherwise. As he passed her, he muttered, "These are not the droids you're looking for," with a gnomic wave of his hand.

She blinked twice, reminding him of a goldfish, leaving him appalled at the cultural illiteracy of the young, which he defined as anyone who hadn't yet died. *My favorite movie,* he thought. *Over two billion deaths, and the MPA rated it PG...*

Pulling at his trouser creases, he sat down in front of Watercress who, shirt-sleeved and harassed, had one phone up to his ear, and was reaching for another. "Get me Saatchi," he barked into the fresh receiver. "I don't know, either."

Covering the mouthpiece he glanced over to Death, sharing his pain, "I can't believe we have to go through reception to talk to a colleague in the same building. Phone system from the Stone Age. And that receptionist..."

"If you want me to do something about her," Death offered.

"Death's too good for her," Watercress declared unthinkingly, before returning to his call, barking out contractual arrangements that meant nothing to Death.

Putting the phone down, Watercress explained he was negotiating a new series for Kimono Sullenly—"Eight years old, just completed a third season of *Work It Out with a Pencil*"—for a new show on the human digestive process.

"Know what it's gonna be called?" Watercress leant menacingly across the desk, all beetle brows and unruly locks. "*From Bunhole to Bumhole*. That's mine, that title," he boasted, stabbing himself in the chest with a thick index finger. "Mine. That's how we add value. Now, how can I help you, Mister..."

"Death. Just Death. No 'Mister'." And, with that, Death related how the world had been a very different place until relatively

192

recently, how life had been nasty, brutish and short, but he felt he had been performing a valuable public service. "I focused minds. Without me, there would have been no Renaissance, no Age of Enlightenment. Light only has meaning if Darkness is there to give it contrast. But, at some point, Mankind stopped trying to make the best of what they had and turned to belittling and sidelining me."

"And you want your place in the Pantheon back?" Watercress mused.

"Exactly."

Watercress seemed to go into a fugue state, lost in thought. After this had gone on a minute or more, Death leaned in, studied his glazed eyes, waved a hand in front of his face. Nothing. *This wasn't one I meant to take*, Death mused, *at least not right now*, before Watercress jerked awake, shouting a single word.

"Pirates."

Pirates? Death wondered whether Watercress was merely dictating an article for *Obtuse Quarterly*. What shade for the accompanying illustration? Should he be making notes?

"We'll do for you what we did for pirates," Watercress explained. "Pirates still kill dozens of people a year, rape, torture, kidnap, steal. They're the scum of the earth. Maybe I mean scum of the seas," he considered, his eyes flitting uncertainly back and forth. "Anyway, they came to us with their image problem ..."

"Pirates? Came to you? En masse?" He looked about him. It was a small office.

"... yeah, they have a trade body, sort of. Anyway, they came to me, and now they're just another kids' meme alongside bears, dragons and dinosaurs." His face clouded. "Hey, they'll all rip your face off at the drop of a hat when you come to think about it."

Death wasn't at all convinced.

"We're doing a similar thing for the Nazis. We aim, by 2050, to have kids dressing up as the Waffen SS without anyone batting an eyelid. But I think we need something quicker for you." He let out an excited scream. "I remember now. There were four of you, weren't there?"

"War, Famine, and ..."

"Get the band back together," Watercress declared. "That's what you need to do."

"We weren't actually ..."

Watercress was already out of his seat, opening the door, ushering Death out. "Get the band back together, and we'll make you huge again."

The day lounge smelt of warm milk and cleaning products. On the television, a cooking show burbled away, the presenters' grins as cheesy as the pasta dish being demonstrated. A line of geriatrics sat mesmerized. In one corner, an old woman glared at a jigsaw as though staring down a cobra, a piece clasped in her hand. Nearby, another clacked knitting needles. In the opposite corner, three old men sat on horseback, the ceiling forcing them to slump forward uncomfortably. It was the putting them to bed the staff really objected to.

"There was another one," Pestilence said in a faraway voice to nobody in particular.

"Stop saying that," War complained. "Please, God, make him stop saying that."

"I don't think God owes us any favors," Famine chided. "I don't think we were ever on the same side."

"What the hell was his name?" Pestilence mused, oblivious.

"Over and over. Ad nauseum. For eternity," War muttered.

But, at least, today they could enjoy a break from their routine. Because, for the first time in a long time, they had a visitor.

A male orderly with a cue-ball head, as wide as he was tall, led Pestilence's horse into the visitors' lounge where a sofa had been moved back, making room for the three equines and their riders. The other two followed. The horses contemplated the bowl of potpourri on the coffee table, across from which sat Death. Between them hung an awkward silence.

It was War who cracked first. "We wondered when you'd show up again."

"I didn't," said Pestilence, who was then shushed by Famine.

"How are you all?" Death opened, attempting bonhomie despite the nagging thought he should have brought something.

"Never better," said Pestilence brightly, only to be shushed again.

"Why are you here?" growled War.

194

"You could have brought pastries. Cookies, cupcakes, Krispy Kremes, anything," complained Famine.

Death winced. "I've taken some advice," he said. "I don't think it's too late for us to stage a comeback."

"A comeback?" Famine wondered.

"Get the old team back together." Death gave a little air-punch to gee them up. Something gave in his shoulder.

"Why should we give a damn, old man?" War spat.

The smile fell away. Death was never one for playing roles. "You want to know why I left? I was bored waiting for you half-wits to deliver the end of the world. That was your job."

"That was a quiet century, the Twentieth …" Pestilence complained dreamily.

"Quiet?" War thundered. "Two total global conflicts, the first use of nuclear weapons…"

"Mass starvations," added Famine. "Quiet?"

"Now, the Middle Ages …" Pestilence trailed off with a smile, mentally elsewhere.

"Exactly," Death said. "So many means of dying at scale and Mankind sends the world population past six, seven, eight billion. They teetered on the brink of Armageddon, and you failed to tip them over the edge. And you wonder why I went my own way."

"Maybe *we* left *you*," challenged Famine.

"Anyway, whoever made you leader?" said War belligerently.

"Of course I was the leader," said Death. "My job was to carry the bodies away; your jobs were to create the bodies to be carried away. I was the end, you were just the means to the end. You all needed me, but I didn't need you; there are plenty of other ways to die. How could I be anything other than the leader?"

"Other ways to die?" wondered Pestilence, childlike.

"And I'll give you another reason why I was leader," Death wagged a finger. "I'm not attached to my horse."

The three care home residents didn't reply, but the narrowed eyes and stony expressions told Death he'd touched a nerve. The degree of oneness with their mounts had always been a cause of friction, and Death tried not to make a point of it. In fact, he couldn't recall ever mentioning it before, let alone weaponizing it. He sat back, adjusted his tie, let his blood cool.

But maybe that had not been the cause of offence. "You said there were *other* ways to die," said Famine.

"I've been riding with Stupidity, Suicide, and Faulty Workmanship, but ... but it's just not the same. I want the old gang back."

"There was another one ... What the hell was his name?" Pestilence said, at which War shook his head disbelievingly.

"Look at you. An old people's home. Talk about low-hanging fruit. But they're all out there with their sudokus and large print James Patterson and the Cooking Channel. They should be coughing up blood, not doing cross-stitch. But together we can be great again," Death said, even considering another air-punch before remembering what happened last time.

Famine nodded. "*Make the Four Horsemen of the Apocalypse Great Again.* That'd look good on a hat."

War's horse banged a hoof on the coffee table, making the potpourri bowl bounce. "No," its rider declared with finality. "It's not going to happen. Not with me."

Famine shrugged. "It's all or nothing. We're a team."

"You're three-quarters of a team," Death corrected.

A stony silence descended again. War was adamant, Famine was adamant that a majority decision wasn't good enough, and as for Pestilence ...

"I remember now," Pestilence brightened. "*Deaf.* The other one's name was *Deaf.*"

Death sat at the head of the mahogany conference table. Through the floor-to-ceiling glazing he could look down at the city, thirty floors below. Industrial Accidents had brought pastries. It would have made more sense had it been Cardiovascular Disease. Comestibles always seemed less popular when it was Diarrheal Diseases' turn, he noted. Odd that.

His mind wasn't on the presentation Cancer was making. It should have been. It was the business plan for the next five years, all objectives, targets, key performance indicators, timelines, budgets. He gazed around at the eager faces lapping it up. *How had he gotten here?* In the old days, the four of them just used to ride out and get

196

the job done. And now … they were all so *young*. HIV/AIDS was little more than a baby. And they all took things so seriously, with their career coaches and hydration regimes …

"Stop," he said, rubbing a hand over his forehead, as if he could massage interest and engagement back into his face. "I have no idea where these numbers have come from," he said, waving a hand at Cancer's upward-pointing graphs and city-skyline histograms, "but what I do know is we have failed to make significant strides forward for centuries."

"We're playing a long game," chipped in Climate Change. "We have a strategy."

"Because our last strategy was so good, wasn't it?" Death challenged.

Everybody looked sheepish. Mutually Assured Nuclear Destruction, so bullish at first, was now rarely mentioned.

Death glanced over to Smallpox's black-lined portrait on the boardroom wall. "We'd be called a zombie organization if that didn't suggest we're doing something right."

Opiate Overdoses casually mentioned COVID, although COVID herself, still relatively new, remained shyly silent, and the mood changed. Death felt the room turn against him.

"The Plague of Justinian killed two fifths of Rome and a quarter of those living in the Eastern Mediterranean. That was a proper pandemic," he retorted to the barracking.

The others looked blankly at him.

"Five forty AD. *Not that long ago*, people." He rolled his eyes in disbelief. "Meeting adjourned until you can bring me some proposals for action. Real here and now action." And then, to cut off the question Misjudged Selfie was formulating, "*Without* a risk assessment."

He watched them gather their papers and troop out, Cancer last out, folding his laptop, switching off the ceiling-mounted projector. Before he left, he turned to Death and told him he put himself under too much pressure, that he needed a break.

What had he been doing for the last however many centuries other than taking a break? He needed more than a break. He massaged his temples again and said out loud, "Dear God, if you're out there, give me a sign."

The black screen of his tablet glimmered and an image of an elderly, overweight man with rock star hair appeared. Mirrors behind him, R&B blaring, he was on a treadmill. Death wasn't convinced about either the cerise vest or the matching sweatband lifting his leonine locks. It all smacked of dressing too young, trying too hard.

"Death," God crowed, "howyadoing?"

"God. You're looking good." That came out more sexually predatory than he intended, so he pressed on, outlining his current ennui.

"If you want to look this good," God advised, bouncing and weaving as he ran, "set yourself targets."

Targets, Death thought. *Like the demise of every living thing. Yes, I've tried that.* "The issue's not so much setting targets as hitting them. Things used to be so much easier. Do you ever want to go back?"

"Back?" said God. "To the beginning? Creation? Are you joking? So much to achieve, so few contingencies in the project plan."

"But how we did it was entirely up to us."

God raised an eyebrow. "Is this about the new team? You know, you've got to adapt to meet their ways of working as much as they have to adapt to you."

"They talk a lot about governance, and health and safety, and corporate social responsibility. They want to keep audit trails. I'm not even sure what 'antitrust' is."

God looked shocked. "I didn't realize it was that bad. Did you speak to ..."

"Watercress? Yes."

"He was an enormous help to me. Repositioning the brand from all that swift to anger, slow to praise stuff into something a bit more kumbaya touchy-feely."

"He seemed to think I used to be in a band."

"Well," God brightened, his finger already reaching towards the screen, "why ask for advice and then not take it? Got to dash—another call..."

The screen went blank.

There was a different smell in the care home. Different but

198

similar. Death guessed at fish pie and rice pudding. He'd brought a tray of doughnuts this time. They sat invitingly on the coffee table between them.

Famine glanced down at the peace offering. "We've just eaten, thanks."

"Maybe a smackerel," said Pestilence, his fingers reaching for the box only to be batted back by Famine.

"Two visits in, what two weeks," said War. "Has somebody died?"

"God spoke to me," Death began.

"Here we go," said Famine. War muttered something about Death *always being too close to that one,* crossed his arms, rolled his eyes and turned pointedly to gaze out of the window.

As Pestilence looked longingly at doughnuts and Famine warned Pestilence off with a glare, Death sighed and carried on regardless. "God told me how he'd repositioned his brand from all that fire and brimstone stuff to something more about well-being and mindfulness. He also said I shouldn't just expect people to adapt to me, that I need to change as well. All valid points, and it got me reflecting on how Cancer and Brain Hemorrhage feel putting a mission statement and corporate values in bullet-points on a little card you can keep inside your wallet are important. And about you guys, and what happened to us, between us …"

"Where's this going?" Famine asked.

War warily reached for a doughnut, coated in pink icing. Pestilence went for one with multi-colored sugar sprinkles. Death took it as a conciliatory sign and began his spiel. He'd been working on the basis his was the *baddest ass on the block* (a phrase he spoke as though picking it with tongs). But that wasn't so. A casual comment of Watercress' had played on his mind, composing a merry tune that refused to leave. *Death's too good for her.* And he was right. Death isn't the baddest ass. There are fates worse than death. Sometimes death is simply too good for them. He'd been shown how to move the business up to the next level, if only he could be bothered to see it. And for this he needed the old team again. Death was too easy. What they needed to be aiming for was *misery*. Inflicting misery …

"The issue is not quantity of death, but quality of life," he

199

said.

War nodded. "Kill a soldier on the battlefield and you remove one combatant. Wound a soldier and you take three: him, and the two others moving him to safety."

"I'm still not sure what it is you're proposing," Famine said, crumbs on his chin.

Pestilence was in raptures, having found jelly at the center of his.

"Exactly what Watercress suggested," Death said, smiling. "We've stalked the land for millennia. Are you honestly telling me you didn't learn an instrument in that time?"

Death looked out at the sea of heads before him, stretched out across the amphitheater, rising into the distance. The sun was setting, an explosion of pinks and yellows behind Red Rocks' famous sandstone buttresses. The crowd were in jubilant, expectant mood, cheering, clapping, whooping. Watercress had done a good job as promoter and organizer.

The microphone reacted to Death's touch with a wall of wailing feedback. The crowd went wild for it, feeling themselves close to lift-off. What was it they wanted? What was it they found so addictive? What kept them coming back for more?

Perhaps it was the atonal frequencies of War's lead guitar that resonated within the brain, *literally resonated*, causing synapses to dislocate and reconnect. Reports of fans returning from a Four Horsemen gig with altered personalities, an inability to grasp concepts such as time or space, or a childlike acceptance of social media or Fox News were legion.

Perhaps it was the rhythm of Pestilence's heartbeat drumming, backed by sixteen hammering hooves and Famine's bass that permanently recalibrated the ventricles, causing a lifetime of dizziness and blackouts, cold sweats and tunnel vision.

Perhaps, it was Death's strutting frontmanship, part Jagger, part Jim Morrison, part napalm jelly at a children's party, honed over the months since he put the band back together.

Or, perhaps it was the band's lyrics, weaving curses and hexes of ancient mages and wizards, that would bring forth a chronic dissatisfaction with material possessions, treatable only by acquiring

200

more material possessions, nagging ennui, and an impossible-to-satisfy all-encompassing FOMO to all who heard them.

But perhaps not, Death mused. Despite being blessed with intelligence, imagination and wisdom, human traits already included dissatisfaction with any gain unless accompanied by another's loss, seeking status through overwork whilst knowing full well that deathbed regrets would revolve around time not spent with family, and embracing small comforts today even if they came at the cost of the death of the planet later. What were they adding?

But isn't that the point? Death thought to himself, smiling. *Nobody ever simply lived and died. There's always been a whole load of misery and fear getting from one to the other. We've been playing these tunes since Adam and Eve ate that apple...*

"We've suffered for our art," he boomed into the microphone, his words reverberating through the speaker stacks, setting off a peal of fireworks, lining himself up for the payoff that would cue the howling guitar intro of the opening number ... *"Now it's your turn."*

Robert Bagnall is a writer of short and not-so-short fiction, working primarily in the genres of science fiction and new weird with a smattering of fantasy and horror. He was born in Bedford, England, when the Royal Navy still issued a rum ration and the nation had yet to accept everyone else's definition of a nautical mile, and now enjoys a life of quiet desperation on the English Riviera. He is the author of the novel *2084*, and the short story anthology *24 0s & a 2*, which collects two dozen of his thirty-plus published stories from the 2010s. He can be contacted via his blog at meschera.blogspot.com.

Made in the USA
Middletown, DE
25 November 2022

15996181R00116